ALL BUT WHAT'S LEFT

CARRIE MUMFORD

carrie@carriemumford.com
CarrieMumford.com

ISBN-13: 978-1-7753182-0-0 (Paperback edition)
IBSN-13: 978-1-7753182-1-7 (eBook edition)
ISBN-13: 978-1-7753182-2-4 (Large Print Paperback edition)

Cover design by JD Smith Design
Edited by Rachel Small
Proofread by Maya Berger

To Mom and Dad,
for always encouraging my tall tales.

uly 1981

"GET THE GUN," Daddy says.

The grizzly paces back and forth in front of the henhouse—a great mama bear, her fur hanging in clumps on her back. The air smells how the dogs smell after they go out in the rain.

I run from the porch and through the living room to the gun cabinet in the hall. My bare feet slap on the floor. Daddy always says I can't touch the gun cabinet until I turn ten, and I am only six.

"What one?" I call back towards the porch.

"The big one!"

I stand on tiptoe to push up the cabinet latch and pull open the glass door. The big gun's barrel is cold in my hand as I take it from the rack. It's heavy and the bottom part hits the floor but I carry it. I make my feet move fast.

"Walk careful, for God's sake!" Daddy hisses. I slow down but my heart keeps running. I hand him the gun.

Daddy opens it, snaps it shut again. He slides the bottom part forward until it clicks, and then he takes the gun and holds it up, close to his face. The grizzly stands on her back legs and slams her paws into the henhouse. I move closer to Daddy's leg. What if the bear turns around and sees me? My heart is running so loud Daddy might hear it. There is a ripping sound. The grizzly scrapes her claws along the henhouse door, leaving long scratches in the wood. This is the second time she's been here. She's trying to get the eggs. The last time she ran away when Daddy opened the barn door and yelled at her. Not this time.

Daddy squeezes one eye shut and points the gun at the bear. His nose holes flap in and out. Where's Momma? She'd want to see the bear again.

The bear snorts and the chickens inside the henhouse screech and beat their wings. From behind Daddy's leg, I see something in the henhouse window—a flash of skin or hair or feather. My tummy feels like it might throw up, so I wrap my arms around Daddy's leg and press my face into his blue jeans.

"Stay still, Hannah," Daddy whispers. I let go and stand like a statue beside him. The chickens stop squawking. The bear goes back to all four legs, facing Daddy. Her big head sways back and forth. She sniffs the air and looks right at us. Her bottom lip wiggles. Daddy's finger tightens on the trigger and the air feels the same as right before a big storm rolls in over the mountains. *Crack!* I clap my hands over my ears and step back. My back is against the house. *Crack!*

Daddy's mouth moves but I can only hear church bells in my ears. He points his finger at me. The bear twitches in the dirt. Blood is coming out of her mouth. Daddy jumps over the porch railing, still hanging onto the gun. I go down the steps and stand behind him. My ears won't work—they still only hear the ringing. Daddy takes the fat end of the gun and smashes it into the bear's face again and again. Warm splatters hit my face and arms and legs. Daddy's jeans are shiny from the blood. He drops the gun and picks up the bear's front feet. His face scrunches and he yells "Arggh!" and he tries a few times before he's able to pull her away so he can open the henhouse door.

My ears work again but there is a screaming. I've never heard a bear make a noise like this before. I've seen other bears at the edge of the woods. Where is Momma? She will know if bears scream.

Daddy's face is splattered with blood. The screaming has stopped. I take my hands off my ears. For a second it's so quiet, so so quiet. And then Daddy opens the door to the henhouse. There's a bullet hole the size of a quarter in the door. He yells Momma's name—"Elizabeth!" I look at my arms. They're red. Blood everywhere. I squat and push my face into my knees and cry.

une 1996

I SET the phone back in its cradle. For fun? What did "for fun" mean? I sank into a chair at the kitchen table and leaned my head back against the flowered wallpaper. A strip had pulled away from the wall by the ceiling above the stove. Another thing that needed fixing around here. One more to add to the list I'd have to deal with over the summer. I let out a long breath and rested my forehead in my hands, elbows on the table.

"What's going on, Chickadee?" Lily asked. She opened the fridge and took out leftovers from last night's dinner—fried potatoes, pork, green beans from the garden, apple sauce. A plastic clip in the shape of a rose held back her long black hair over her left ear. Her red polka-dotted shirt was tucked into her faded, too-tight jeans. If she was wearing jeans, she wasn't going to work.

I sat forward and drank the last of the glass of water in front of me. My hands were still dirty from brushing the horses. "Nothing."

Lily lifted a perfectly plucked eyebrow. "Doesn't seem like nothing." She pulled three plates out of the cupboard.

"I'm not hungry." I put my hands on my thighs and pushed myself to standing. The muscles in my legs ached. That new gelding would break me before I broke him.

"Was that R.W. on the phone?" she asked. She put the third plate back into the cupboard and scooped food onto the other two. "You told him about your dad?"

"He heard about it from his mom. He sends his best, hopes Dad gets better soon."

Lily smiled, but it didn't reach her eyes. The dark circles that had found their way under her eyes the night of Dad's heart attack were still there, even a week later. I wished I could think of a way to make her feel better, to bring her smile back, but I worried about Dad, too.

"When's R.W. back this summer?" she asked.

Oh yeah, and that. Not only was Radek—R.W. to everyone but me—dating a girl who wasn't me "for fun", he wasn't coming home for the first summer since he'd left Jessop on his football scholarship. The year before he'd come home for June and July to help out his brother Clarence with their ranch, and do whatever he could for Dad and me. We needed the help. It seemed lately that everywhere I turned I found another thing broken: the latch on the gate to the back field, the stall Red Gold had kicked apart during a spring hailstorm, the hole in the fence from Mr. Morton's escaped cow. I looked out the kitchen window, gauging how long I had before I had to go help Heather pack. At least three more hours. Time to go fix that hole in the fence.

"Earth to Hannah." Lily stood with her arms crossed, her back against the kitchen counter.

Right. "He's not coming home this year." I picked up my gloves from where I'd left them on the table. I'd ripped them off just in time to grab the phone. "He got a job at the gym, handing out towels or something. His coach wants him to stay and train. He promised him he'd be captain." Was I trying to convince her, or myself?

"Well that's too bad. We'll miss him around here." She picked up the plates and gave me a sympathetic smile. "He'll be home soon enough, sweetie." I watched as she walked out of the kitchen and went to find Dad in the living room. Was it only Dad's heart attack that had her looking so worn? He was fine—the doctors all said it had been minor, barely a heart attack at all, really. When I found him lying on the road by the mailbox, I had been sure he was dead. That he was gone just like Momma and I'd be the only Tatum left.

I rinsed the Tupperware containers and set them on the wooden dish rack to dry. With Dad's health and the lack of rain I had enough to worry about. I didn't need to be thinking about Radek and some girl. It was my own fault for going along with it when he suggested we take a break from our relationship while he was away at college.

"Not a break," he'd said. "Just time to sow our wild oats."

"I don't have any wild oats to sow," I'd told him. We'd been sitting on Blueberry Hill, the night before he left for training camp, almost two years ago. He'd tried to hold my hand, but I'd pulled it back and shoved it under my leg.

Radek had sighed and leaned back on his elbows. We'd gone up there to be alone, to drink a bottle of wine Lily had given to us, left over from the bar she worked at.

"Look, we're so young. Don't you want to know what it's like to . . . to be with other people? So we're sure?"

"I already am sure," I mumbled. We had a plan. We'd always had a plan. He would go away to the University of Texas—he'd be crazy to say no to a full scholarship—while I stayed here and took care of the ranch. Then he'd come back, we'd get married, take over Stillwater, and start our life together. I swallowed hard.

"Hannah! Stop. I can see your mind dissecting this whole thing." Radek knocked my shoulder with his, forcing me to pull my hand out from under me to keep myself from falling sideways. "I still mean everything I said. You, me, two-and-a-half kids." He nudged me with his elbow. "Or more if we act like tailless tenrecs."

I rolled my eyes. Our grade twelve biology teacher, Mr. Simpson, had told us that on average, human adults had two-and-a-half offspring, unlike tailless tenrecs—little mole-looking things from Madagascar—which had up to thirty-two. He was using biology to distract me because he knew I loved it. I sat forward and pulled my knees into my chest.

Radek held up his hand, little finger extended, just like when we were kids. "Pinky swear it," he said.

"Pinky swear what?"

"That you'll wait for me." He hooked his little finger around mine and squeezed and I smiled, despite the rock in my belly. He'd never broken a pinky swear before, not even once. Four years wasn't so long, right? I could wait four years. We'd been together so long already. So why was my chest so tight I could barely breathe?

I let out a puff of air and squeezed water from the dish cloth, hanging it from the kitchen sink faucet. Now, he was keeping the other part of the pinky swear. The part that made us have to make it in the first place. The "sowing wild oats" part.

"Hannah! Bring the milk, will you?" Dad called from the living room. I snapped back to reality. Radek had said he'd be back and he would.

I took the carton of milk from the fridge and padded into the living room in my wool socks. "Here."

Dad sat in his recliner, his feet propped up and the plate of leftovers on his blanket-covered lap. *Wheel of Fortune* played on the TV in front of him, on mute. He looked better—the colour was coming back to his face and lips. The pills the doctor gave him must be working.

"You talk to Bob about the hay?" Dad asked. He'd already asked me this twice that week, and I knew his memory was just fine.

"Yes. I told you, he can help. But we've got at least another three weeks, Dad. It's so dry out there. We'll be lucky if we get any hay at all." Things were always tight on the ranch, but they'd been even more so the past few years. One year with drought was bad enough, but we were going on two years now. Last year we'd sold a few more horses than I'd wanted to and used a portion of the money we'd saved to stay afloat, but there wasn't much more give left. We had to have a good year.

Dad set his plate aside and took the fresh glass of milk Lily handed him. "Good, good."

"You let Hannah worry about the hay," Lily said. She set the milk carton on the side table and leaned over to adjust the blanket on Dad's lap as he tried to nudge her away.

"Quit your fussing," he said. "You'd think I was being held hostage, kept away from my barn like this."

I stifled a snort of laughter. "You've been watching too many movies." A tower of VHS tapes threatened to topple near the VCR. *The Good, the Bad and the Ugly*, *The Magnificent Seven*, *True Grit*, and a bunch of other ones I didn't recognize. Lily had rented them the day she brought Dad home from the hospital, in the hopes it would keep him away from chores longer, but he'd already watched them all at least twice. I sat on the bench by the door to pull on my boots.

"Hannah, before you go . . ." Dad said.

Oh boy. What now? Yesterday it was the shingles that had come loose on the carbarn roof during the wind storm. The day before it was the level of oil in his old Ford farm truck. I wanted to get out of the house and into the field so I could figure out what the hell to do about Radek. I needed to convince him I was fun, that I was better than this girl—whoever she was. Heather would know what to do. I glanced up. Both Dad and Lily were staring at me, their faces pinched with concern.

"What? Is this about the truck again? I checked the oil . . ."

Lily looked at her hands, picking at her cuticles.

Dad cleared his throat. "I've decided to sell."

"Sell what?" We didn't have any horses ready yet, or hay.

"Stillwater. The ranch."

My face tingled as if it had been slapped.

"W-what?"

Dad grimaced. "It's hasn't been an easy decision."

I stood, one foot in a boot and one still without. "Why? You don't have to do this. I can take care of everything. I can fix everything." My blood pulsed through my limbs, pumping, pumping, pumping, trying to catch up. I needed the ranch. It was everything.

Dad shook his head. "It's not that, Hannah. I'm not getting any younger, and we need the money."

"I do the books! I know how the money is." I fought to keep myself under control. "What am I supposed to do?" I said, lowering my voice almost to a whisper.

Dad stared at me for a long moment before he replied. "Get a job in town, like Lily or your friends. Something, anything. Just not here."

I dropped onto the bench behind me. "Radek—we, we were planning to live here."

"I know you were." He pressed his lips together and jutted out his chin. "Look, Radek will be fine. Clarence wants to expand the cattle operation at the Baileys'. There'll be lots for him to do." *But what about me?*

"Let me try," I said. "Give me the summer to try. I'll train more horses, I'll make sure we get two hays in. I'll do whatever it takes." My voice turned whiney at the end, despite my best efforts to keep it steady. He couldn't do this. He could not. Lily met my eyes and gave me a look of apology, a small shrug of her shoulder.

"It's already decided," Dad said. He shifted his legs under the blanket, holding the plate steady. "It'll be a chance for you to start fresh." His eyes moved to the bay window behind me, and I knew he was looking at the henhouse in the yard.

"I don't want to start fresh! I want to be here." Tears streamed down my cheeks, hot and angry, stinging my dry skin. I wiped at them with my dirty hands. I hadn't cried in front of Dad since my accident.

"I have a new hand coming by tonight. He'll help us—you—get the property in order." Dad's voice was cold now, final. "We'll sell in the fall."

I bit my cheek hard to quell the tears. I wouldn't let it happen. I would figure this out. Radek and I needed this place. His brother was going to get his family's ranch. I had savings, but not nearly enough to buy us another property, let alone this one. Radek had to come home, but what would happen if he did and we had nowhere to go? Sure, he could work with Clarence, but how would I face the rest of my life without a place of my own? I took a deep breath. In, out. *Everything has an action and a reaction. Equal and opposite.* Basic science. I'd look at all the options, just like an experiment, and prove to Dad he didn't need to sell.

uly 1981

IT'S BEEN three days since Daddy shot the bear. I'm standing in the pantry. The walls have shelves that hold the jars—fat pickles in cloudy juice, purpley blueberry jam that stains my fingers and Momma can't get off, red beets I don't like to eat because they taste like dirt. The pantry light bulb flickers. Today I saw Momma lying in a coffin at the funeral home. She was wearing her blue dress with the ruffles. Someone tucked her in with the quilt with little birdies on it. I wished the birds would fly off the quilt and tell me where Momma is.

I know my momma was under the blanket, but it wasn't my *real* momma. She looked like my doll, Marianne.

I tried to listen for Momma while the priest man said words in his whispery voice and everyone sniffed and rubbed tissues on their faces and looked at Momma. But, nothing. Her mouth didn't move.

And now we're home and I don't know where Momma is.

"Oh, sweets," says Mrs. Bailey. She comes into the pantry and takes my hand. "What are you doing in here?" I don't tell her I came to see if Momma was playing hide and seek.

"Your momma's not with us anymore. Do you understand?" Mrs. Bailey is Radek's momma. She hasn't gone away.

I nod, letting my hair cover my eyes. "Yes, ma'am." I don't want anyone else to say Momma went away. I just want someone to tell me how to get her to come back.

Mrs. Bailey shakes her head and lets my hand drop so she can pull a tissue from the pocket of her apron. Except it's Momma's apron, the white-and-blue flower one with the big pockets. The apron hangs past Mrs. Bailey's knees. It's pulled tight around her big, squishy tummy. Mrs. Bailey dabs her eyes with the wrinkled tissue. "Poor Elizabeth."

Who will take care of the bear cubs left behind at the edge of the woods? I asked Daddy to let Radek and me go get them. He told me they'd have to fend for themselves. I pull one of my braids. Mrs. Bailey did my hair today and it's too tight. She brushed it and told me it was the colour of wheat before the harvest. It still hurts. She doesn't have any girls though, so maybe she doesn't know how to do hair like Momma does.

Mrs. Bailey blows her nose with a honk and puts the tissue back in the apron pocket. She bends in front of me and takes my hands. Hers are warm and soft, like dough after Momma leaves it on the counter to rise.

"We're saying goodbye," she says. "She's gone to live with God. Soon the priest will come and we'll take your momma to the cemetery, where she'll rest."

"Momma could rest in bed," I say. Momma and Daddy have a bedroom at the top of the stairs, right next to mine. The quilt covering her now used to be on the end of their big bed.

Mrs. Bailey makes a sound like her drink went down the

wrong tube. "Come on, honey, how about I get you a cookie? I just pulled a pan out of the oven and there's one with your name on it. Molasses." She turns my shoulders towards the kitchen and follows me. Even though my stomach growls when I sniff the warm, sugary cookies, I think I might be sick. Momma always makes chocolate chip cookies when I'm sad.

The kitchen is full of people, so I take the cookie and go to the cabinets in the corner near the sink. I press my back against them and slide down until I'm sitting on the floor. A few of the grown-ups watch me, shaking their heads. Why is everyone looking at me? Did I do something bad? Do they know about the candies? I focus on my cookie. When everyone turns back to the plates of triangle sandwiches on the counter, I count four pairs of jeans, two skirts, and one Mrs. Bailey in Momma's apron. She goes around pouring coffee into mugs and filling glasses with apple juice from the can. Everyone is dressed like they're going to church.

Light-brown pants stand in front of me. It's the RCMP man.

"Hi there, Hannah." He's drinking coffee from the mug with the green tractor on it. That's Daddy's. The RCMP man bends down. His bushy brown-and-grey moustache looks like a squirrel's tail. If I touched it would it be soft like kitty fur, or bristly, like the potato brush? I mumble hi and then take another bite of my cookie. Go away, RCMP man.

"Just the girl I'm looking to talk to," he says. He sets the mug on the counter and hikes up his pants to make room for his legs so he can sit on the floor.

Mrs. Bailey watches us. She makes an angry face, like when Radek and I wear our muddy boots into the house. "You remember she's a child, Harlon," Mrs. Bailey says. "She says she doesn't remember much." The two grown-ups she's standing with turn and look.

"I'm just doing my job, Mere."

Mrs. Bailey shakes her head and turns back to the grown-ups. Am I not supposed to talk to the RCMP man? Momma talked to him. I look around the room trying to find Daddy's legs, or even Radek's. Radek must be out in the yard. I wish I was out there with him. My tummy feels like I've eaten too many cookies, even though I only ate a half one so far.

The man looks right into my eyes and says, "If you don't mind, Hannah, I'm going to ask you a few questions about your momma. Would that be all right?"

I think of the long, skinny shape of Momma under the quilt. Where is the part of her that makes her move and talk and sing? Nodding, I put the last of the cookie into my mouth even though I don't want it and brush my hands along my church dress to get rid of the crumbs.

"Can you tell me about her?" The man's brown eyes have red around them and his lips don't smile. He lets air out of the side of his mouth and I smell the coffee on his breath. I play with a snap button on my dress and try to think of something that might make him think I'm a good girl or make him smile like he smiled at Momma on the lawn.

"She likes to paint," I say.

He writes on his notepad. "Good, good. What else?"

I shrug.

He crosses his big legs and hunches forward. "Can you tell me what your momma was doing two mornings ago, the day your daddy shot the bear? What did she usually do in the mornings?"

I snap the top button of my dress. *Click*. Momma told me this man was her friend, but now Momma is gone. He's using that voice grown-ups use when they want me to do something—a high, squeaky voice.

"I dunno," I say. *Click. Click.*

"Well, sure you do. Think hard. This is important."

Two mornings ago Momma woke me up, like almost every day. She kissed my cheek and said, "Good morning, sunshine," and then she showed me what to wear and took me downstairs to eat. "She made breakfast," I say.

"Yes, that's good." The RCMP man writes something else on his notepad. "Exactly what did she do to make breakfast?"

Click. "She got out the plates and the bread and the milk," I say. *Click.*

"Mmhmm. And what else?" The man pulls at the side of his moustache. Does he know about the candy?

"She went to get the eggs," I say.

The man's bushy eyebrows shoot up. He scribbles on the notepad with his pen. He doesn't ask me about Momma's purse. I push myself to my feet. There's Radek, by the porch door, his hands stuck in the pockets of his newest jeans. Good. I bet he'll go with me to catch the bear cubs. We could sneak back to the woods while Daddy is busy in the kitchen.

"Two days ago she did that?" The man's voice is low, his face right in front of mine.

Every day Momma did that.

Daddy steps in front of me, pulling me behind his legs by the shoulder of my dress.

"What the hell is going on here?" Daddy says. *Hell* is a word I'm not supposed to say or I'll get my mouth washed out with soap. One time I licked the soap bar in the bathtub to see if it was as bad as Momma said it would be. It was. I won't swear. Not ever. The rest of the people in the kitchen go quiet. Who will wash out Daddy's mouth since Momma's not here?

"Well, Luke, I'm just asking your daughter a few questions, is all." The RCMP man stands and brushes off his pants, even though the floor is clean.

"Any questions you have for her you can ask me," Daddy says, in his loud voice. I hug his leg. I don't want to answer questions anymore. "She's only a kid." Daddy scrunches his shoulders up close to his ears. His hands make balls at his sides. I peek out from behind his leg.

The RCMP man swings his arm out wide. "I don't need to remind you in front of all these people that this is still a criminal investigation." He holds up his notepad. "I'm trying to find out what happened so I can fill out my report."

"My daughter's here, and my wife—" Daddy's voice goes crackly. It sounds like he might cry, but daddies don't cry. "You need to leave. Now. You shouldn't even be here in the first place. Not after—"

Mrs. Bailey puts herself between Daddy and the RCMP man. "Now, now. This was a horrible accident, Harlon, nothing more. Don't make this harder than it already is. We're here to remember Elizabeth."

Daddy and the RCMP man stare at each other over Mrs. Bailey's head.

The RCMP man turns and takes long steps to the porch door, where Radek is. He takes his hat off the hook and holds it beside him. "I'll be going then, out of respect for Elizabeth." For a second his eyes look like they might cry too, but they don't. Radek moves so the man can open the screen door.

The four jeans and two skirts watch. A truck starts outside. Tires spin around in the rocks in the laneway.

After the RCMP man goes, Radek and I sit on the front lawn pulling up grass and tying it in rings. We decide not to go find the bears because Daddy's already mad.

"Was that RCMP man your momma's friend?" Radek asks.

"It's a secret." I stand and let the grass fall off my dress. "Momma said I'm not allowed to tell." I make the zipper sign across my lips like Momma did.

"Your momma's dead, just like my daddy," Radek says. He doesn't say it mean, he says it like it's a true thing, like how Momma told me if you cut a worm in two, only one half lives, even though both halves wiggle.

I lift my leg to kick him, but Radek's momma opens the door and comes to stand on the porch. I put my foot down and hold my hands together like I'm being good. "R.W.! Hannah! Dinner-time!" she says.

I follow Radek to the porch. All of the grown-ups have gone home, and Momma still isn't here. *My momma is dead*, I whisper, to see how it sounds. Even inside the house, everything is cold.

une 1996

I FOUND Heather in the trailer's back room, technically her mom's bedroom, stuffing clothes into a garbage bag. Her red hair clawed its way out of the scrunchie she'd tried to contain it with. It stuck to her flushed face.

"Is Barb going to be okay with you taking those?" I asked, plopping myself onto the small bed. Heather's mom had never been what you'd call a good mom. She'd been making Heather pay rent since she was old enough to bring in a paycheque, and Heather had spent her childhood enduring her mom's never-ending parade of boyfriends.

"I don't care. Not after Mr. Grabby." Heather mashed a jean shirt with tassels on the front pockets into the bag. Definitely not hers. We'd been best friends since grade four, when Heather fell off the monkey bars and lost her two front teeth—the adult ones. While the other kids gathered round to marvel at the blood spurting out of Heather's mouth, I ran my hands through the playground dirt until I found both of her teeth. I took them home and showed them to Lily, who put them in a plastic sandwich bag filled with milk. I brought them to school every day for a week, even after the milk had curdled. When Heather came back, we held a funeral for her teeth in the back corner of the playground. We dug a hole with sticks and then stomped dirt over it. Heather cried a bit, worried her mom wouldn't buy her fake teeth, but she did, a few years later.

I followed Heather as she dragged the almost-full garbage bag to the main room and started opening cupboards. "So does Barb feel bad? About Mr. Grabby, I mean." I sat at the booth table and flipped open one of the magazines scattered across it. *Make your man want you. Do you know this sex secret?* I rolled my eyes and let it fall shut.

Heather tied the bulging garbage bag and set it with the other bags and boxes crowding the space by the trailer door. "Well she's not yelling at me for taking all this stuff, so I guess she feels bad enough." Heather had decided to move out of her mom's place a few weeks earlier. Or, more accurately, her mom's latest boyfriend had made the decision for her, after he grabbed Heather's boob when Barb was in the bathroom.

"Anyway," Heather said, "let's not talk about Barb. I'm out of here tomorrow. Thanks to you."

She sat across from me at the table. I'd lent her first and last month's rent after she found the apartment listed in the *Jessop Mercury* newspaper. I'd been saving money in a Crown Royal bag in my dresser since high school. Dad paid me once a month, just like he would a ranch hand, but not as much because I wouldn't let him.

Heather stood and pulled a packet of strawberry wafer cookies from the cupboard over the table. "What's new at Stillwater?" she asked, stuffing a wafer into her mouth.

I took one from the packet and shook my head. "Oh, you

know, not much. Except Dad wants to sell," I said, sarcasm oozing from my voice.

"What?" Heather tilted her head and looked at me. "Like the house?"

"The whole thing."

"He can't do that!" Her eyes bulged.

I told her about his plan to have a ranch hand come and help us get everything ready for the fall. She sat back in the booth seat and folded her hands behind her head. She let out a long breath. "Well fuck. Hey, maybe it'll be for the best."

"How? How can it possibly be for the best?" I rammed a wafer into my mouth and chewed furiously, sprinkling crumbs across the tabletop. I corralled the crumbs into a small pile, and then brushed them off the edge of the table into my palm.

"Just drop them, you weirdo," Heather said, looking at my hand. I opened it and let the crumbs fall onto the floor. "Maybe you can go to university, take science or biology or whatever, like you always wanted."

I wrapped my hair around my index finger, pulling it tight and frowning. "That was just some little-kid pipe dream, not a real plan. It's not even remotely realistic." Every year since Dad brought Lily to come live with us at the ranch, Lily had me fill in a page in a memory book she'd bought at the gift shop in town. I had to write down what had happened that year, who my best friends were (always Heather, and then Chrissy too, after she moved to town in grade six), and what I wanted to be when I grew up—always a scientist. But by the time I'd finished high school, applying to university seemed pointless. Radek and I had a plan, and that plan didn't involve me getting a degree. Dad didn't want me paying for something he couldn't see any practical application for, and I had to admit he had a point. What kind of job could a scientist possibly get in Jessop, population 977? I certainly wasn't going to leave Jessop. So I'd left that dream in the back of the linen closet along with the memory book.

Heather stood and put the teapot on the propane stove. She hit the igniter a few times and swore before it caught. "Nothing in this piece-of-shit trailer works. I can't wait to get out of here."

"Where's Barb?"

Heather waved her hand dismissively. "Across the way at someone else's trailer, playing cards. Drinking." She leaned over the tiny sink and pushed the window curtain aside before turning back to face me. "So what are you going to do?"

I blew air out between my lips. "Make sure the ranch isn't ready to sell by the fall. And come up with a way to make more money. Maybe I can teach riding lessons or board a few horses for the winter after the barn's fixed up." I'd considered it before, the riding lessons. I'd just never done anything about it. We'd been getting by—barely, but still getting by—so there hadn't been any point. I'd preferred to spend my extra time reading the massive stack of *National Geographic* magazines I'd gotten for free from the library the summer before.

Heather turned back to the stove, lifting the lid of the kettle to check if the water was boiling. "Is he selling because he's too sick?" she asked, her back still turned.

Dad wasn't even that old. Why was everyone so worried about him? "I don't know. Maybe. I can take care of it on my own, though."

"Maybe he doesn't want that for you." She turned from the stove to look at me.

"How can he not want me to get married and build up the ranch he loves?" I said, my voice rising. I narrowed my eyes at her, daring her to disagree.

"Okay, okay, easy." She held up her palms as if I were holding her at gunpoint. "I'm just saying, maybe there are reasons other than money—reasons you don't know about. Maybe he's ready to start new, to get away from everything that happened there. Maybe he'll finally make an honest woman out of Lily." She grinned at me with her perfect, fake front teeth, and I couldn't help but smile back. Maybe she was right.

The kettle whistled and Heather took it off the stove and filled the two cups she'd set out with hot water. "Just figure out what's really going on before you do anything crazy. Not that you're one to do crazy things. Ever."

I pulled a face at her, half-smiling at the same time.

"Have you met the ranch hand yet? Is he anything like Old Spike?" She handed me a steaming cup of tea.

Old Spike had stayed with us the summer before for a few weeks. He'd helped out with the horses and harvest, but he and Dad had come to blows over a poker game paired with too much whiskey. I blew on the tea and took a sip. I loved Heather's tea. It was just plain old black tea, but she mixed in the perfect ratio of milk and sugar. It never tasted as good when I made it. "No. But he's coming for dinner tonight."

"How old?" Heather dipped a wafer into her tea. I grimaced. I hated soggy wafers.

"No clue. Why?"

"I might be in the market for a handsome cowboy." She gave me an exaggerated wink, scrunching up her face with the effort. Heather hadn't ever dated anyone seriously, unless you counted Avery, her mom's youngest boyfriend and the first guy she slept with, and that had ended in grade eleven. There'd been guys here and there, but none of them lasted more than a few months.

"Yeah right. Dad can only afford boring old guys. Especially now that money is so tight."

"Well, what a fucking waste that is. What does R.W. think?"

"He doesn't know yet."

Heather pressed her lips together until they went pale under her mauve lipstick. There was no way I was telling her about Radek and Fun Girl. Ever since he left and implemented our "sowing our wild oats" phase, Heather had been mad at him. And two years was a long time to be mad at someone.

"He used to be such a good guy," she'd said, when I first tried to explain it. "Now he's just like all the rest." We'd been sitting at the same table in her mom's trailer, a few days after Radek left for school, eating vanilla ice cream. Hers was covered in fudge sauce, mine plain.

"He's still a good guy," I'd told her. "He's thinking about our future." Which was exactly what I'd told Lily when she asked. It didn't convince her either. I didn't even bother to try to explain it to Dad.

Heather had snorted and then choked on her mouthful of ice cream. After a coughing fit and a good deal of nose blowing, she said, "He's off screwing cheerleaders while you're here doing all the work, keeping your future ranch afloat. Please."

"That's not how it is!" I let my spoon drop in my bowl with a clang that reverberated through the small space.

Heather shrugged. "We'll see about that. You better sow your own oats or whatever you're calling it while he's gone. There's no rule about that now, is there?"

"No," I said slowly. We hadn't discussed that specifically.

Heather pointed her spoon at me, her eyes meeting mine. "You promise me right now, Hannah Tatum. Promise me you will sow at least one wild oat."

Under normal circumstances I would have laughed, but I could see in her eyes she was entirely serious.

"Promise me!"

I ate another spoonful of ice cream. "What counts as a 'wild oat'?"

"At least a kiss, preferably more. Before Radek gets back from school for good. Shake on it." She reached her hand across the table. I stared at her blue nails, the polish chipped from working at the diner. I stood and gripped her hand.

"Fine. One wild oat."

I hadn't yet fulfilled my promise, and I knew Heather hadn't forgotten.

The light outside the trailer's small window was fading. I stood and pulled on my windbreaker, leaving most of my tea in my cup. "I've gotta go. Dinner will be ready soon. I need to stay in Dad's good books." Heather followed me outside.

"You're coming on Thursday, right?" she asked as I got into the truck.

"I guess so." Heather and Chrissy liked going to the Red Lion on Thursdays—cheap drinks night. I needed time to come up with a plan, but I could spare one night.

As I DROVE BACK to the ranch, I rolled down the driver-side window and let the warm evening air rush past my face. What was Radek doing? Was he with that girl? Were they doing something *fun*? The clock on the dashboard glowed in the failing light. I took a deep breath. Step one: I'd make sure Dad didn't want to sell the ranch by the time fall came. Step two: I'd figure out what to do about Radek.

I didn't see a flash or eyes or lightness at the edge of the road, nor in the headlights. I only heard the *THUMP!* as it smashed into the windshield.

5

*S*eptember 1991

I LEANED against the truck and kicked at the gravel in the high school's parking lot with the toe of my boot. Radek was late. We'd been sharing the thirty-minute drive to school from our neighbouring ranches since I got my licence in January, the day after my sixteenth birthday. Stillwater and the Baileys' ranch—Radek's mom Mere's place—were only a few kilometres apart, so we'd been catching buses and rides to school together forever. My stomach growled in protest. I looked at the Timex Lily and Dad had given me for Christmas. Best friend or not, five more minutes and I'd leave without him.

I looked for him in the trickle of people coming out the back doors, by the Athletic Hall. On Fridays he didn't have football practice, so where was he? Finally the blue metal door swung open and Radek walked out with Olivia Murphy. Current Jessop Rodeo Princess. Olivia had long, wispy pale hair that fell almost to her waist, and she stood just over five feet tall. She was tiny but she could ride, I'd give her that. I'd seen her compete in the junior barrel racing at the rodeo the summer before. She was supremely, irritatingly, perfect.

Olivia stood on her tiptoes and kissed Radek right on the mouth before walking off towards the apartments near the school. My stomach twisted. I'd never seen Radek kiss another girl, or any girl—unless our awkward attempt at kissing behind the tractor barn when we were eleven counted. Olivia had been spending more and more time in front of Radek's locker before class.

I forced myself to grin as Radek walked across the parking lot to the truck.

"What's that all about?" I punched him in the arm, harder than I'd intended. "A rodeo princess and a quarterback? Isn't that a cliché?"

Radek rubbed his arm and gave me a small smile. He reached in through the window to open the creaky passenger-side door as I walked around to the driver's side. The door handle had fallen off a few weeks after I started driving the truck and I hadn't bothered to replace it. Dad had gotten the old Chevy running for me to give Radek and I a way to get to school that didn't include riding the loser cruiser, otherwise known as the school bus.

Radek's short, dark hair was ruffled, standing on end in several places. Usually he kept it neatly combed. *Did Olivia run her hands through it? Ew.*

The truck started with a rumble, and I pressed the gas pedal a few times. Radek and I had kissed because he'd convinced me we should at least try with each other, so we'd be ready when we had to kiss other people. So far he was the only one who'd needed preparing. Guys were more interested in rodeo princesses and cheerleaders than scrawny ranch girls who liked to hang out on the picnic tables outside of school reading bio textbooks.

"So?" I asked.

"It's no big deal." Radek fastened his seat belt. "Mom's cooking lasagna. You should come."

"Don't change the subject."

Just as I eased the truck into Drive, there was a knock at Radek's window. He rolled it down. The window framed Olivia's perfect face, her pale skin flushed from running to catch us. She looked like one of the girls in those stupid teen magazines Lily kept buying me even though I told her they were for kids way younger than me. "They say 'teen'," she'd always say. "Last time I checked, that's what you are."

"Hey," Radek said, his voice way more casual than mine would have been if Olivia were a guy chasing after me.

Olivia grinned. Her teeth were as perfect as Heather's fake ones, but I guessed they were real. "I forgot to ask you. Do you want to hang out, like, after the game next week?" Her voice was high and pixie-like. Was that what guys liked? I didn't stand a chance. I'd been the tallest girl in our class since grade six. With too much arm and leg, I was a bumbling beast compared to small, compact girls like Olivia. Plus, she had boobs. I glanced down at my almost-flat chest—barely enough to need a bra.

I gazed out my window, across the dusty parking lot, trying to pretend I couldn't hear them. I hoped they wouldn't kiss again.

"Oh, yeah, sure. I think everyone is going to Chucker's place." Radek's voice sounded hesitant, not confident like usual. She didn't seem to notice.

"Fun! See you later, R.W.! Bye, Hannah!" Olivia practically bounced away.

Why did she annoy me so much? She seemed like a nice enough girl. I pulled the truck out of the parking lot and onto Main Street.

"'R.W.'?" I asked, glancing sideways at Radek.

"Yeah, apparently that caught on." He shifted in his seat. Only his mother called him R.W. Radek Walter. "Radek" was his Polish grandfather's name and "Walter" was his dad's name. I'd always figured Mrs. Bailey liked to call him R.W. to remind herself of her husband, who had died right before Radek was born. I gripped the steering wheel and stared straight ahead. My shoulders tensed towards my ears.

"You coming to the game?" he asked, rolling up his window as I turned onto the dirt road that would take us out of town and back home.

"I guess so."

"It's my first game as starting quarterback."

He waited for me to respond. Radek had always been athletic, but Coach Baxter was even more interested in him these days, with his new height and increasing bulk. I hadn't made new friends at the high school, even though we'd been there two years. Chrissy went to dance classes a few nights a week, and Heather worked all the shifts she could get at the diner, so I didn't see them as much either. Everyone was moving on without me.

Radek cleared his throat. "Clarence and Mom are coming to the game, but I'd rather drive with you." He kept his eyes straight ahead, on the road.

Before I could stop myself, I asked, "Am I going to have to watch you make out with Olivia all night?"

"Jealous?"

"Pft. Not a chance." I glanced at him out of the corner of my eye. "*R.W.*," I added, in a mocking tone.

"You sure sound jealous." Radek grinned.

"Yeah, well, you sound dumb." I took my eyes from the road long enough to stick out my tongue at him.

He laughed and said what we always said: "You sound dumber."

I thought about being at Chucker's place after the game, watching Radek and Olivia kiss, but pushed the image away. This was Radek, my best and oldest friend—we'd practically been raised together. I'd always known we'd start hanging out with other people of the opposite sex sooner or later. That's how it was supposed to work. I just wished I was the one doing it first.

"Okay," I said. "I'll come."

6

une 1996

I SLAMMED on the brakes and swerved to the side of the road. Luckily there was no one around—I was a few kilometres from the ranch, where the roads weren't busy. The windshield had a long, red smear across it.

I gripped the steering wheel, trying to get control of my breath. I strained to catch any sounds outside the open truck window. Total silence. I continued holding the wheel and breathing, waiting for my heart to slow to a normal pace. The crickets slowly resumed their dusk song. Mentally I checked myself over, scanning my body and then loosening my grip on the wheel. It wasn't like last time. I wasn't in the ditch. Radek wasn't here.

I slid out of the truck and approached the deer where she lay at the side of the road. I squinted to see if she was breathing, but couldn't tell in the dim light. I didn't have a gun—after Momma died Dad swore up and down he'd never teach me how to shoot one, even though we lived out in the middle of nowhere and chances were pretty good I might need to one day. Radek had secretly taught me though.

As I got closer to her, I could see her eyes were open, her nostrils flaring in and out. *Shit.* I couldn't leave her to die alone, bleeding out on the road. Then again, there wasn't much blood, aside from the streak on the windshield. I squatted a few feet from her face and tried to make out any injuries. Her legs looked fine. Her brown, furry body looked almost relaxed, half on the tarmac and half off.

"I'm so sorry," I said.

She snorted.

"I can't help you." I wanted to tell her about why I didn't have a gun in my truck, unlike everybody else around here. Did she have babies somewhere out in the field? Who was she leaving behind? Her fur looked so soft I had to keep myself from reaching out to touch it. She was probably full of ticks. What a waste. An ignoble death. Killed by a stupid truck and a stupid girl wondering what her not-boyfriend-boyfriend was doing without her. I glanced back at my truck. The front fender had been crushed and the windshield cracked, but I'd still be able to drive it. Clarence would come shoot her if I went to the Baileys' to get him. At least then she'd be out of pain and put to use.

"Holy shit!" The sound of my own voice surprised me. The deer had cycled her legs and flipped herself over so fast I almost missed it. She stood in the road, her legs askew, her chestnut brown eyes locking onto mine as if she were trying to memorize my face. I froze. "It's okay," I told her. "You're going to be okay."

She blinked at me a few times and then shook her head, turned, and walked off into the field.

I DROPPED my keys on the hall table and sat on the bench to work my boots off my swollen feet.

"You get Heather all packed up?" Dad sat at the dining room table with a guy I didn't recognize. The guy had shaggy brown-blond hair that brushed the tops of his shoulders. His eyes met mine and heat flooded through my chest. I frowned. Who was he?

"Not much to pack," I said. "But yeah." I didn't want to tell Dad about the deer. I'd have to live with the truck all messed up, or use more of my savings to take it into town to get it fixed. Or swallow my pride and ask Dad if he would do it.

Two half-empty coffee mugs sat on the table in front of Dad and the guy. Lily banged pots around in the kitchen. We didn't have any horses ready to sell, and there wasn't anyone in Jessop I didn't know. Was this the ranch hand? He was too young. Dad picked up his cup and drained it. Lily came to stand behind him and squeezed his shoulder, holding the coffee pot in her other hand.

"Dinner's almost ready," she said, refilling the mugs. "Hey, hon." She smiled at me. I wanted to ask about the guy. He kept looking at me, his electric blue eyes boring into mine. Usually I had no trouble speaking up, but something about the way he looked at me made me stay quiet.

"I'm going to clean up before dinner," I said. I'd tell Dad about the truck tomorrow. Or later, if Lily let him have any whiskey. I walked towards the stairs.

"Before you go—this is Will Ludlow, the new ranch hand," Dad said. "Will, this is my daughter. Hannah here is as good as engaged to a football star. A running back for Texas U."

"Dad, I told you, we're not engaged," I said through clenched teeth, embarrassed. My face flushed as the guy—Will—rose from his chair and crossed the living room to where I stood, on the bottom step of the staircase. Even though I was standing on the step, Will was still taller than me. His nose looked as if it had been broken at least once. His shoulders were square and strong under his plaid button-up shirt. I could see why Dad thought he'd make a good ranch hand. Up close, he looked to be twenty-nine or thirty. How had Dad hired him? Usually guys this young worked at the bigger ranches, like the Baileys', for more money and more excitement.

Will extended his hand and I wiped mine on my pants before taking it. He shook it firmly, no sign of the limp-fish handshake some men gave, as though they were afraid they'd break my "dainty" fingers. Could he feel my calluses?

"Nice to meet you, future wife of a college man." Will grinned at me and waited a beat before letting my hand drop.

I stole a glance at Dad. He rocked back in the dining room chair, leaning it on two legs. "Looks like you found me a good one this time," Dad said to Lily, grabbing her hand and holding it to keep her from going back into the kitchen. "Will here is a rodeo man. A bronc rider."

What the hell was a rodeo guy doing working at Stillwater? I raised an eyebrow at Will. He was still staring at me. I lifted the Texas U ball cap Radek had sent me and swiped at my forehead with the back of my hand. Did I have something on my face?

"Well whoop-de-do," Lily said. Will turned to face her. "Who isn't a rodeo man around here?" She winked at him. "I figured I'd run into a half-decent catch at the Lion eventually. The only hard thing most of my customers ride is a bottle of Jack Daniel's on their way to the bar floor." Lily laughed at her own joke. She'd been working at the Red Lion, the only bar in Jessop, since a few weeks after she moved to the ranch.

Great. Just f'ing great. Instead of some old guy who barely got around, I had this guy to deal with. Lily used to say Old Spike was slower than molasses running uphill in January—you really had to light a fire under him to get him to do much of anything. Will looked like he would finish half the chores on the ranch before breakfast. Why had he chosen Stillwater anyway?

I cleared my throat. "Rodeo man or not, we can use the help," I said to Will, pulling myself up straight. "We need to get the hay in, and there's no lack of things to fix around here." Dad and I used to drive barrels of water out to the back field together, before his heart attack. I'd been doing it alone since. There was a real possibility the crops we'd planted would fail. Maybe I could convince Dad the horse boarding and lessons would work. If I got enough people out here, Dad wouldn't need to work at all, so even if it was his heart he was worried about, he wouldn't need to sell. I'd just have to tide us over another two years, until Radek came back, and then we could even consider getting a few sheep, like Radek's mom had at her ranch. We both knew everything about sheep thanks to the time we put in at the Baileys', and the carbarn would work as a second place for livestock . . .

"Glad to help out," Will said, the grin still on his face. There was something almost smug about it, but not quite. Overly confident, perhaps? Something. Something irritating. I turned to make my way up the stairs and Lily called after me.

"Dinner will be on the table in ten!" I heard her walk back into the kitchen and open the pantry door. I knew every sound the farmhouse made. I'd lived in it my whole life. Dad was so proud of it. "Third-biggest house in the county when it was built," he used to tell me. He'd bought it from an old rancher who was selling off his land in parcels after his wife died. Little did Dad know he'd become a widower here, too.

AFTER A DINNER OF ROAST CHICKEN, mashed potatoes, and carrots from the garden, Lily, Dad, Will, and I sat on the front porch. Will had been quiet throughout the meal, and thanked Lily profusely when she dropped the last chicken drumstick onto his plate. The sun had gone down, but the air was still thick with its warmth. Dad smoked his daily cigarette and used his toe to rock the swing he shared with Lily. I sat on the porch railing across from them, kicking my feet back and forth. Across the yard, my truck sat beside the new guy's, its broken-up front facing the road. Had the deer found her way back to her family?

"Where's home for you, Will?" Dad asked. He took a long, slow drag.

"Nevada, near Reno." Will sat in the chair at the far end of the porch, furthest from the door. "Born and raised." He'd declined a cigarette when Dad offered one.

"You got family left in Nevada?" Dad asked.

Will looked at his hands. "I'm up here on my own, sir. Fell off a bronc, a real arm-jerker, and broke my collarbone last year. It's working fine now, but not fine enough to take another tumble just yet." He placed his right hand on his collarbone and wind-milled his arm. I glanced at Dad. Did he know this when he hired him? Maybe Will wouldn't be as much trouble as I'd thought. Dad took a long draw on his cigarette and turned his head to the side to blow the smoke away from Lily.

"I think it's about time for you to get to bed," Lily said to Dad.

"I'm not a child, woman," he said, but he smiled at her as she stood and pulled him to his feet. His stubbed his cigarette out in the sand-filled flowerpot he used as an ashtray and followed Lily to the back door, limping slightly. I held my breath. They'd said he would be okay. He was getting better, right?

"Hannah, show Will to the cabin, would you?"

Ranch hands stayed in the old log cabin by the creek. It had been on the property when Dad bought the ranch, long before I was born. Dad had added a woodstove and a few pieces of furniture, but other than that, nothing had changed since the seventies. Radek and I used to play house there, pretending to sip whiskey from chipped coffee mugs and making fake snacks in the open kitchen. I jumped off the railing with a sigh. This guy wasn't leaving. At least not tonight. "Sure."

"I'll get my stuff." Will walked across the yard to where his truck sat beside mine. I watched as he pulled a duffle bag from the truck's bed and sauntered back towards the porch, as comfortable as if he'd been on the ranch for months. I bit the inside of my cheek and narrowed my eyes at him. Fine—if he was staying, I'd have to work this into my plan.

WE WALKED SIDE BY SIDE, not speaking, as my eyes adjusted to the darkness. I hadn't bothered to bring a light; I had walked that path a million times. A dog howled at one of the neighbouring ranches, and Mickey Two called back from the porch, where I'd told him to stay. My mind whirled, trying to logic my way out of the mess I was in. Fact one: Dad wanted to sell the ranch. Fact two: Will was here to help him. I could try to stop Will from helping, or I could use Will to help me with my plans. I rubbed a hand across my face. Then it hit me. How had I not seen this right away? If Will worked on fixing up the ranch, I'd have time to get things ready for the riding lessons. I smiled to myself in the dark. Once we were a decent distance from the house, Will spoke.

"I can help you fix that bumper if you want." Ugh. He must have seen it when he went to get his bag from his truck. The last thing I needed was this guy meddling.

"No thanks." I kept my voice cold, hoping he wouldn't press. His shoulders moved up and then dropped. For this plan to work, I needed space, time to get things set up before Dad figured out what I was up to. Not a nosey ranch hand poking about in my business.

"Suit yourself," he said. "What happened?"

"None of your business." If I was short with him, he'd leave me alone, right? Nothing appealing about a bitchy rancher's daughter. I inhaled deeply and let breath out through my nose. It didn't help that he was so . . . difficult to ignore. Even in the dim light I could see the square line of his jaw, the slope of his strong shoulders, his jeans, tight across his thighs as he walked beside me. His eyes met mine and I looked away quickly, my face flushing.

"Just trying to make conversation," he said. He swivelled his head to look around the field. "How far is this cabin anyway?"

I ignored his question and kept walking, wishing my legs were even longer—at least long enough to make him have to struggle to keep up.

Assuming Dad wasn't ready to go out to the barn yet, I would start cleaning the stalls we weren't using the next day, get that disaster zone sorted, and convince him to board at least two horses. Then I'd need to paint the paddock fence and start advertising for lessons. The further along with the plan I was before Dad found out, the better. My mind whizzed, calculating how much more we would bring in each month.

"So what do you like to do?" Will said, interrupting my thoughts.

"What?" Why wouldn't this guy leave me alone to think?

"You know, for fun? Or don't you like fun?"

I clenched my teeth. That word again.

"Lots of things."

"Like?"

I sighed. The cabin was still almost ten minutes away. "I read."

"Sounds exciting," he said sarcastically.

"Whatever." I stepped around a rock in the middle of the path, not bothering to warn him about it. He tripped but caught himself. "I ride horses, work, hang out with my friends. What normal people do."

He made a grunt of acknowledgement that sounded like "huh."

"Why? What do you do that's so *exciting*?"

"Ride wild horses."

This guy was killing me. I stopped short in the middle of the path, my hands on my hips. If it weren't for him, my original plan might have worked. A broken-down ranch was not one you can sell—not for a good price anyway. "Why are you here? You could have gotten a better job somewhere else. Unless your shoulder is in worse shape than you're letting on."

He stood a few feet from me and let the duffle bag drop on the ground beside him. "Oh my shoulder's working just fine," he said.

I glared back at him.

"Fine. I need the money," he said, his voice serious.

"If you need money so bad, why didn't you go to a bigger ranch? I can put in a good word for you at the Baileys', across the way." I gestured across the field, towards Radek's.

Will was quiet for a moment, as if he were considering the offer. His chest rose and fell as his eyes scanned my face. I was suddenly aware of how close he was. How my heart hammered hard inside my chest. I let my arms drop from my waist and shifted, trying to avoid his unnerving gaze. His mouth curled into a half smile. He picked up his bag, flung it over his shoulder, and started walking again, forcing me to jog a few steps to catch up.

"Nah, I'm good here," he said, as I came in line with his shoulder.

I wanted to scream. "Fine," I said, feigning indifference. "Just stay out of my way." His arm brushed against mine and I stepped aside quickly, but not quickly enough to stop a flush of red to my cheeks. *Pull it together, Hannah.*

"Anyway, isn't it my job to help you?" he asked.

The cabin was visible now, a dark shape beside a grove of tall aspens, near the edge of the creek. I handed him the bag of linens Lily had left on the porch. "Your job," I said, "is to stay as far away from me as possible."

He raised his eyebrows and took the bag from me, his fingers brushing mine.

"Yes, boss," he said with a grin.

"Argh!" I turned and stomped back to the house.

uly 1981

THREE DAYS after Momma's funeral, Daddy drops me off at Radek's house. He has to go into town. It's a Sunday, so that means we go to church. Radek sits next to me on the grass. He tucks his shirt—the one with lassos on it—into his Wranglers. His momma is always telling him to tuck in his shirt, but it's always popping out.

"Ma says you're coming to live with us now," Radek says, hoisting up his jeans by his belt.

Why would Daddy and me go live with Mrs. Bailey? What about the horses and the hens and Mickey?

"Your daddy's going on a trip." Radek takes a stick from the lawn and starts digging a hole.

Daddy wouldn't leave me. "You're a liar." I pull up a handful of grass and throw it at Radek. It falls on his shoulders like green rain. I stomp into the house.

Mrs. Bailey is wrapping the squares for church. She winks and passes me a brownie with red sparkles. I push it into my mouth all at once. Daddy forgot to give me breakfast today and I couldn't find my stool to reach the cereal.

"Mrs. Bailey?" I'm going to ask her about Daddy going away.

"Yes?" she says. She turns and smiles at me. What will happen if Daddy doesn't come back? I don't want to know. At breakfast Mrs. Bailey said we can visit Momma today, behind the church. But it's not really Momma, it's her grave where her body is.

"Can I have another square?" I ask.

WHEN DADDY PICKS me up after dinner there are grocery bags in the back of his truck. It looks like a lot of food. Did he get Cap'n Crunch or Dracula cereal? "Can I open the groceries?" I ask. Daddy looks out the window as he drives along the short bit of road between Radek's house and ours. He doesn't say anything. He pulls his truck into the yard and stops by the horse barn. The lawn is wet from the rain and it sneaks around my church sandals and tickles my toes. Mickey is coming across the field, her tail wagging above the grass. Maybe she found a mouse.

Daddy leaves the groceries in the truck and squats so he is looking right at my face. Daddy almost never does this, but lots of other grown-ups do.

"I'm going away for a little while," he says. So Radek was right.

"Where?" I ask. My stomach gets all squeezy, like it does when I think about Momma or the bear cubs.

Daddy looks behind him at his truck and shrugs. "I'll bring you back a present, something special."

I hope he'll bring me the Barbie dancer horse, or a new doll to be friends with Marianne. Mickey comes and sticks her nose in my face and wiggles all around. No mouse.

Daddy stands and knocks the dust off his knees. "You'll have fun at Mrs. Bailey's. Radek will take good care of you." He walks to the house, but Mickey and I stay by the barn. I look over at the henhouse without the door. I count in my head. Momma has been gone for seven days.

I say: "How long until you come back?" I want to count. Daddy is already at the porch and I think he didn't hear me. He stands by the door. Is he counting days in his head too? He opens the door and goes inside without saying anything.

8

June 1996

I STEPPED onto the porch to call Mickey Two over from the barn and found Will sitting on the porch swing, a thin cigarette pinched between his index and middle finger. So he did smoke. He rocked back and forth and squinted as he looked out over the fields to the mountain range. Mickey Two raised his head from his spot beside Will's boot and then lowered it again with a contented sigh. Will bent to scratch behind the dog's ear with his free hand. Mickey Two rolled onto his side, exposing his brown-and-white speckled belly.

"Mornin'," Will said. He took a drag and blew smoke into the already warm air. His cowboy hat sat on the swing beside him. He wore clean jeans and beat-up cowboy boots.

I leaned against the door behind me and rubbed my eyes. I'd hardly slept the night before—after hours of tossing and turning, I'd drifted off only to wake up with a jolt from a filmy dream involving disembodied deer eyes and an auctioneer slamming a gavel on our kitchen table. "Sold!" he yelled, while Dad and Lily waltzed around the living room.

"What's the mutt's name?" Will asked.

"Mickey Two," I said, before I remembered I was mad at him for existing. "He's a stray that stuck around after the first Mickey died."

The dog's back leg kicked reflexively in response to Will's scratches. Will smiled up at me. The man was either completely oblivious or didn't give an F. "Mickey Two's one happy dog. A bit of Aussie sheepdog in him?"

I nodded.

"What happened to Mickey One?"

"She ran onto the road," I said, and looked towards the barn for Dad. The smell of frying bacon and grits drifted through the screen door behind me.

"You smoke?" Will held out his cigarette.

I shook my head. "No. Not ladylike, according to Lily." I tilted my head towards the kitchen.

"Your ma's quite a character. She practically runs that bar."

People always thought Lily was my mother, even though I called her Lily and not Mom, and even though she had brown skin and black hair, while I'd inherited Momma's pale, freckled English complexion and Dad's mousy-brown hair. "Lily's my dad's girlfriend. And you're lucky you didn't say that to her. She'd be pissed at you for thinking she was old enough to be my mother."

Will sat forward and leaned his elbows on his knees. I followed his gaze to the yard. Although small by ranch standards, the yard held the henhouse, with its mismatched door, and two barns—a big one for the horses and a smaller one for Dad's trucks and tractors. *Soon to be a sheep barn.* During my tossing and turning the night before, I'd decided to forgo painting the paddock and only offer trail rides. I just needed a way to advertise and get a few customers before Dad could say no.

Dad opened the man door on the horse barn and made his way towards his truck with his uneven gait. *Shit shit shit.* He'd see my truck. I wasn't ready to explain that yet.

Will smushed his cigarette into the flowerpot then stood and stretched his arms above his head. As his T-shirt pulled up over his taut stomach I caught a peek of the soft blond hair there. I looked away and reached down to pat Mickey Two, who sniffed around my legs, looking for breakfast. Maybe Dad wouldn't see the bumper . . . or the windshield.

"Hannah! What the hell happened to your truck?" Dad strode across the lawn, looking more spritely than I'd seen him since before his heart attack. Why had Lily let him out of the house anyway? I glanced at Will and shrugged as Dad steamed his way to the porch steps.

"Hit a deer," I said. I straightened my back and raised myself to my full height, a hair taller than Dad.

Dad's face was bright red as he came to stand in front of me. Out of the corner of my eye I saw Will sit back on the swing, his arms crossed over his chest. *I bet he's enjoying this, watching me get scolded like this.*

"I told you to pay attention. How many times have I told you to pay attention!" A bubble of spit sat on Dad's lip. I took a deep breath to steady myself. I knew this wasn't only about the truck. He was scared because of the other accident. The big accident.

"I'm sorry. It came out of nowhere." He didn't ask about the deer.

"We can't afford this," Dad said, moving away from me to the porch railing. His eyes scanned the property. I imagined him seeing all of the imperfections, the things that needed fixing. The money we'd need to pour into the place to sell it like he wanted to. It had never seemed like much of an issue before; we'd get to things when we got to them. But nothing was the same now.

"I can pay for it myself," I mumbled, thinking of the partially emptied Crown Royal bag in my sock drawer. "I'll take it to Marv's in town."

Dad spun to face me. "No you won't. Not a chance. He would just love that." When Dad wasn't ranching he was fixing anything with four wheels in his shed. Marv Grisholm ran the garage in town and Dad loathed taking vehicles there. "Overcharging old fart," Dad called him.

"I'll pay for the bumper then. Leave the windshield—the crack is low enough."

Dad closed his eyes and pinched the arch of his nose. Then he took a deep breath and glanced at Will, as if just realizing he was there. Will stood and shifted from foot to foot.

"You'll need the money," Dad said, his voice softer this time.

Bile rose from my empty stomach. I didn't care if Will was there. "What exactly do you think I'm going to do if you sell this ranch, Dad?"

"When, Hannah. When I sell the ranch."

Will edged his way past Dad and around me to open the back door. "I'll go see if Lily—"

"No!" Dad and I said in unison. Will paused with the door open. Dad cleared his throat.

"You're fine, Will," Dad said. His shoulders slumped.

"I still don't understand why you're doing this. I can take care of the ranch on my own. I can fix all of this." I swung my arm out to the yard, the fields stretching beyond it, all the way to the mountains. "I can do it myself, Dad," I said, my voice almost a whisper. I didn't dare mention his heart, or his age, or any other reason why he couldn't work the ranch anymore. Especially not in front of Will.

Dad's eyes met mine. The anger had drained from his face. Now all I saw was sadness. "I know you can. But I can't."

Lily appeared in the screen door behind Will. "Breakfast's ready," she said, her eyes darting between Dad and me.

. . .

LILY HAD COOKED Dad's favourite breakfast: bacon, grits, and scrambled cheese 'n' eggs. We all passed dishes around the dining room table and filled our plates. Lily poured piping hot coffee into our mugs. Will piled his plate high with eggs and bacon but barely touched the grits. I noticed he'd put the paper towel Lily had set out as a napkin on his lap. I was used to ranch hands with dirty clothes and nonexistent table manners. Most of them came from poor families and had been hopping ranch to ranch since they were young. They typically ate as much as they could as fast as they could. Will looked up and caught my gaze. I flushed and pretended to focus on smearing butter onto my toast.

Will pushed his hair behind his ears and jutted his chin towards my plate. "You don't like eggs?"

"Hannah-bean hates eggs," Lily said. "She gives hers to that mangy dog out there."

I smiled at Lily and took a bite out of one of the strips of bacon from my plate.

Dad echoed in a teasing tone. *"Hannah-bean* hardly eats enough to keep a small cat alive. Until wham—" He clapped his hands loudly. We all jumped. "You'll find her in the pantry raiding the pickle jar and anything else she can get her hands on. Has an appetite like her mother." Dad stopped talking and looked at his plate. Lily and I exchanged glances. Dad almost never talked about my mother. He sighed and picked up his fork. At least he wasn't talking about my truck.

I furrowed my brow, trying to remember the date. Dad only talked about Momma close to the anniversary of her death. She'd died in July, fifteen years ago. The time after Momma's death had been horrible for me and for Dad. Everyone thought he'd done it on purpose, which I never understood. I knew Dad and Momma had fought—I'd seen it enough myself. But Mrs. Bailey had explained their marriage was a passionate one. One of those relationships where you fought hard and loved harder. Maybe that's why I liked Radek so much: we almost never fought.

I glanced over at Lily. She never seemed to mind when Dad talked about Momma. She'd come along a few months after Momma died, and she was the one person who would talk to me about her death. Not that I did much anymore. Lily was also the one person in Jessop who couldn't tell me anything about Momma's death, other than what she'd read in the newspapers or heard through gossip at the Red Lion. But Momma had been dead a long time. I tried not to think about it too much.

Will looked from Dad to me, and back to Dad again. To his credit, he didn't ask any questions.

Dad chewed his last bite of eggs and then smacked his lips, as if clearing the air. He looked at Will. "We'll run the water barrels out to the back field this mornin'."

"Yes, sir," Will said, taking a sip of his coffee. I hoped he wouldn't let Dad do too much with the barrels.

"And *Hannah-bean*"—the name grated at my ears—"can go to the Baileys' and help Mere with her baking."

"What?" I stood quickly, my chair screeching on the wood floor. "Why? I was going to work with that gelding. I have stuff to do—" Like make a sign that advertises trail riding at Stillwater ranch.

Dad shook his head. "Will can take care of it."

Will at least had the decency to grimace at me apologetically from across the table. I glared back. Baking? I wasn't even good at baking. Besides, Mere was pretty much the last person on earth I wanted to see right now. I knew this was penance for the truck though, so I said, "Okay," with resignation, and walked my plate into the kitchen.

"That lawn needs mowing, too, when you get back," Dad called after me.

I glanced out the kitchen window at the brown thatch covering the massive front lawn. It hadn't rained in weeks. There was more dirt out there than grass. I clenched my jaw and scraped the leftover eggs from the casserole dish into Mickey Two's metal bowl on the counter.

"Here." Will came up behind me and dropped the few grits he'd put on his plate into the bowl. He stood so close I could feel the heat of his chest through the back of my T-shirt. He smelled like fresh soap and something spicy, maybe cedar.

"You don't like grits?" My voice came out in a whisper.

"Nah." He paused there a moment before walking away. I heard the porch door slap shut behind him. I took the bowl to the porch, where Mickey Two whined and danced in circles. I set his double breakfast in front of him, my hand trembling slightly. "Lucky dog."

$\mathcal{S}$eptember 1991

THE DAY after I had to watch Radek and Olivia suck face outside school, Dad sent me over to the Baileys' to help Mere with her church baking. He rarely sent me over anymore, now that he needed my help with the horses, but Mere had called and asked him. And Dad never said no to Mere. Rather than ride or take the truck, I walked across the field. I liked walking the ranch, being on the ground, being close to the actual land. I played a game with myself, trying to name as many plants as I could, letting their scientific names roll off my tongue: *Chrysopsis villosa* (golden aster), *Linum rigidum* Pursh (flax), *Asclepias speciosa* Torr (milkweed, not in flower). I'd started the game before a biology test in grade nine and it had stuck.

As I approached the house, Clarence, Radek's older brother, came out of the sheep barn. He raised his hand high and gave a curt wave. People always said you could tell the Bailey boys had a good mother because they were well behaved and polite.

Clarence was a man of few words, but you could tell he was good by the way he took care of his mom, and by how he treated the sheep. Once I'd seen him try to breathe for a stillborn lamb. He covered her mouth with his. It didn't work; the lamb still died. I never forgot the sadness on his face.

I stepped onto the back porch, opened the door to the mudroom, and kicked off my boots. "Mere, I'm here!"

After her fiftieth birthday, Mrs. Bailey insisted I call her by her first name, Meredith—Mere for short. She said hearing a sixteen-year-old call her "Mrs. Bailey" made her feel older than she looked.

"In the kitchen!" I heard running water, and an old country song on the radio. She was alone in the kitchen and the rest of the house was quiet. *Radek must be in the barn.* A stab of disappointment shot through my chest.

Weird.

Mere was what I imagined every mom should be like, always bustling around, cooking things and making sure everyone was taken care of. Had my momma been like that? I liked to imagine she had been more like Mere than Heather's mom, or even like Chrissy's mom, who always wanted to hear about our lives even though she tried to get us to wear turtlenecks and long pants. If Momma were still here, she might be in our kitchen at the ranch mixing batter for a chocolate cake, like Mere, but also asking me about what I wanted to do with my life, what my dreams were, what I wanted to do next. And painting. I imagined she'd still be painting.

"Hey, sweetie." Mere wiped her soapy hands on her apron and hugged me. When I pulled away, there were damp spots on my shoulders where her hands had landed. "I'm so glad you're here," Mere continued. "I promised Ruth Morton I'd cover for her tomorrow. It's her day for refreshments, but she's been down with the flu all week."

Any chance she had, Mere dragged Radek, Clarence, and me

to church on Sundays. Clarence never fought it, but Radek and I had become experts in making up excuses. If we wriggled our way out, we'd stay home and watch cartoons, eat bowls of the sugary cereal Mere complained about but still bought, and drink milk right out of the carton. We'd been doing it since the first time we missed church, when we were nine, because we both had chicken pox. Mere set us up in the basement for a week and would come down to dab calamine lotion on our spots with cotton balls and scold us for picking at our scabs.

"So how's school?" Mere asked, handing me a freshly washed glass measuring cup.

I took it from her and dipped the cup into the flour. "Ask me something else." I'd never been a big fan of school, and high school hadn't made things any better, even though everyone kept telling me it was supposed to be the best time of my life. Most of my classes were boring, except for biology and environmental science, and barely anyone talked to me in the halls. Everyone looked at me when I didn't want them to, and no one looked when it mattered. I wanted to fade into the walls, but I also wanted to be seen, to make friends, to be like those girls who walked the halls with their backpacks casually swung over their shoulders, smiling and saying hi to people, always so sure someone would say hi back.

"I thought you were enjoying your science class? Radek told me you got a perfect score on your last quiz."

"Well that part's not so bad," I said. I poured sugar into the bowl.

"How's your dad?" Mere never asked about Lily. I didn't know if it was because she and Lily were so different, or out of loyalty to Momma. Mere and Lily were polite to each other when they met at functions, but Mere never reached out to Lily to ask for a cup of sugar or invite her to her quilting group, like she did other neighbours.

"He's good, working on Mr. Morton's tractor again."

"Bob needs to buy a new tractor. Lord knows he's got the money."

Mere chatted away, telling me about neighbours and members of the church, about whose cows had run away, who had bought a new truck on credit, who had become a grandmother. While she talked, I mixed, rolled, and cut out the cookies. I left half an inch of space between the cookies as I placed them on the pan.

"So what can you tell me about this Olivia girl?" Mere asked.

Radek had told her? He didn't appreciate his mom's curiosity as much as I did. He usually only divulged enough to keep her happy.

"She was rodeo princess last summer," I said.

Mere nodded gravely. "Yes, yes, Clarence mentioned that. Wouldn't you know, R.W. didn't even say a word to me. Marcy told me they'd been seeing each other when she rang up my groceries yesterday. How embarrassing to be told by Marcy of all people that my son is dating."

I smiled. "You know how Radek is."

"I do."

Mere came to stand in front of me and took my hand. Her hand was soft where mine was rough and calloused. It always was, no matter how often I remembered to slather on the lotion Lily had given me.

"Sweetie, how do you feel about R.W. dating this Olivia? Are you—" Mere seemed uncharacteristically lost for words. "Are you okay?"

I wanted to grab my hand back but didn't because I knew it would hurt her feelings.

"Okay? Of course I'm okay. Why wouldn't I be?" I carefully extracted my hand from hers and turned to set the timer on the oven.

"I guess because we all always assumed you two would eventually get around to dating. Marcy's daughter is already engaged."

Marcy's daughter had finished high school three years before. "You're not babies anymore, or even kids," she continued. "In a few years you'll be done high school and all grown up."

People had teased Radek and me in grade school about being more than friends, but after we started high school it had stopped. Our families were a different matter.

"He's allowed to date," I said. "He asked her out. He didn't ask my permission." I mumbled the last few words and then regretted it when I saw Mere's eyebrows nearly shoot right off her forehead. She opened her mouth to say more when the mudroom door creaked open, and Clarence's and Radek's voices filled the hall.

AFTER DINNER we sat in the TV room in the basement watching *Night Court* reruns. Mere excused herself for bed first, and then Clarence selected one of his well-worn Zane Grey novels from the bookshelf and went to his room. Radek changed the channel to a movie, *The Goonies*. We'd seen it a million times before but I didn't care. He kicked his feet out across the couch, keeping his knees bent just enough that his toes didn't touch me at the other end.

We talked about school, the game the next weekend, how Coach Baxter had made them run extra laps at practice because Chucker kept dropping balls, how it was unfair to have a biology quiz so close to a test. He didn't mention Olivia so neither did I. While we talked I thought about how close Radek's feet were to my left thigh. Once or twice his toes brushed my leg—I kept my eyes on the TV screen, but it made my stomach flutter.

When we got to the part in the movie where the chunky kid gets kidnapped by the bad guys, Radek yawned and slid down on the couch until his feet were right on my lap. Normally, I would have pushed his feet off and told him to stop touching me with his stinky toes. But this time I let them stay; I pretended it hadn't happened. We stopped talking and looked straight at the screen. I left my hands at my sides, one on the arm of the sofa and one pinned under Radek's heavy legs. I didn't watch a second of the movie after that. All I could focus on was the warm weight of Radek's calves and feet on my lap. I wondered what he was thinking but was too scared to look over at his face. Should I touch his foot? Give him a sign I was okay with it? Was I okay with it?

My legs were restless and I wanted to stretch, but I worried he'd move if I did. When the credits rolled, I snuck a glance in his direction. His head had tipped to the side. He was asleep. Was it an accident his feet were on my lap? Did he even know? I gently moved his feet aside and slipped out. I stood in front of the couch, watching his chest move up and down, his dark brown hair falling across his face. Stubble had started to sprout on his cheeks. He must not have shaved that morning. Everything about him seemed different.

Mere was right. We were growing up.

I walked up the stairs to the second floor, avoiding the creaky steps. The bed in the guest room was made up perfectly, as usual. The lacy pink pillowcases and bedspread were always clean and ready for me whenever I decided to stay over. I pulled off my jeans and slipped under the blankets in my T-shirt and undies. I didn't want to walk back across the field this late, and Dad wouldn't worry—he'd know where to find me. Instead of falling right asleep, I found myself listening for Radek on the stairs. I stared at the ceiling, thinking about his feet on my lap. Had he done it on purpose? Had it meant anything, or was he only tired? What about Olivia? I didn't know her, but I guessed she wouldn't be too pleased about it. I finally rolled over and fell asleep after deciding I might not ever have answers to my questions.

1 0

une 1996

I STARTED out on the well-worn path through the field to the Baileys' but took a sharp right once I was out of sight of the house. No way was I going to spend the whole day with Mere, pretending everything was fine with Radek, listening to her chat about football stats or whose daughter had gotten engaged and whose was pregnant. Grasshoppers frantically jumped out of my way as I strode through the field, my pace too fast for someone trying to waste time. I'd tell Mere Lily needed my help. It wasn't like those two talked.

Without even thinking about it, I found myself walking towards the cabin. I paused in the aspen grove—*Populus tremuloides*—enjoying the respite from the sun. Trickles of sweat ran down my back and pooled above the waist of my jeans. It wasn't even close to noon yet. The sky was foggy blue above the leaves; no sign of precipitation. If it didn't rain soon we wouldn't get hay until August. I leaned against a tree and tried to make my brain stop swirling.

We were all worried about Dad's health, but if he was going back to work with Will, he definitely felt better. So what did he mean by "I can't," then? The tiniest of breezes came up, and I lifted my face to catch the fresh air. The leaves in the aspens above me shook, living up to their nickname: trembling aspen. I was as helpless as those leaves, getting shaken around wherever others wanted me to go. I needed to think of this logically, like a high school science experiment: observe, question, hypothesize, experiment, analyze, conclude. OQHEAC. Only Question Hairy Elephants Around Christmas—Radek and I made up the acronym to remember the scientific method. Mr. Simpson had told us hypotheses often come from the gut, from an instinctive feeling, that scientists were artists too, in their way. I shook my head and resumed my walk towards the cabin. Well, my gut told me Dad's selling the ranch had nothing to do with his health and everything to do with Momma. But why now, so many years after she'd died?

THE CREEK TRICKLED a few yards away from the cabin's porch. A coffee can sat on the railing—for Will's cigarettes, I guessed. At least he had the sense not to throw them into the grass. I used to come out to the cabin a lot, especially right after Radek left. I'd bring a bottle of wine, pilfered from Lily's stash from the Lion, and sit on the porch. Sometimes I'd read *Nat Geo*, and sometimes I'd daydream. Without Radek next door, I didn't have company as often. Heather and Chrissy didn't come out to the ranch much —when it came to the country, cars seemed to go only one way. In fairness to my friends, there wasn't much to do out here except drink and look at the mountain range, and work.

I stepped onto the porch and ran my hand along the railing. The paint had long ago peeled away, and the wood had grown smooth with wear. The coffee tin was filled with sandy loam from the edge of the creek and contained three cigarette butts. So he wasn't a serious smoker. Old Spike left so many butts around the cabin I had to bring a rake and grocery bag down to clean up. The screen door to the cabin was closed, but Will had left the wooden interior door open. I pressed my face against the screen, trying to see if he'd changed anything yet. His bag sat open on the tattered sofa. Everything else looked the same. Dad would be keeping Will busy with chores and I had time to burn. What was the harm in going in? It was my cabin, after all.

I nudged the screen door open and stepped in, breathing in the familiar mustiness, with Will's cedary scent mixed in. I walked around the small room, opening and closing the fridge (empty) and checking the cupboards (also empty). He'd rinsed the coffee pot and left it to dry in the sink. Another coffee tin sat on the counter. I peeked into the tiny bedroom. The bed was covered with the linens I'd given him the night before, but hadn't been made that morning. *You're being a total creep.* I was running out of ways to procrastinate. I should have snuck back to the barn after Dad and Will left and tried to find materials to make a sign for the trail rides. I paced back and forth in the small kitchen, my eyes landing on the pot in the sink. I could make a coffee, put everything right back where it had been and he'd never know. I pulled the coffee tin towards me and popped the plastic lid open and reeled back. What the heck was that smell? Not coffee, that's for sure. I held my breath and looked into the can, holding my face a few feet away, just in case.

It was filled with what looked like clumps of dried grass, and as soon as I saw it I recognized the scent, too. *Cannabis.* Weed, and a lot of it. I'd seen it at parties, passed discreetly in small baggies or film canisters, and rolled in joints people I didn't hang out with smoked outside. Heather went through a weed phase, but it hadn't stuck. The can was full—what was he doing with so much of it? And right out on the counter like that. Was he a drug dealer?

I fit the lid onto the can and put it back on the counter, hoping it was in the exact same place as before. I let the screen door slam behind me and went out onto the porch. I leaned on the railing, my heart pounding. Dad hired a drug dealer. If he found out, he'd fire him for sure; he barely tolerated ranch hands who liked to drink. But if he fired Will, he'd find someone else. And what if he found another young guy? Someone without a broken collarbone? What was it Lily said? Better to deal with the devil you do know than the one you don't? I took a deep breath, trying to get the skunky smell out of my nose. Clearly I had the wrong impression about Will.

By the time I got to the Baileys', Mere had put her baking in the oven and was cleaning the kitchen. I took over washing while she dried.

"So your Dad hired a new hand?" How did she know that already? As if in response to my raised eyebrows, she continued. "I saw Marv Grisholm at the grocery store this morning. He said he'd been in to buy a new bumper."

I groaned. "I hit a deer on the way home last night," I said. Mere took the glass baking pan I passed her.

"Your dad must have been so worried." The phone rang.

"Something like that," I mumbled, as she wiped her hands on the dish towel.

I scrubbed a batter-coated wooden spoon, rinsed it, and set it beside the rest of the dishes on the drying towel. Mere crooned into the phone behind me and my stomach clenched.

"Hi, sweetie . . . Yes, of course. Oh my! Well that's just wonderful." Mere held the receiver to her chest and mouthed "He got a job" at me.

I gave her a thumbs-up and ran the dish cloth around the glass mixing bowl. At least he wasn't telling her about his latest date with Fun Girl, not that I imagined he ever would. Mere didn't understand our "break" either—she treated me the same as before: like a member of their family.

"Handing out towels doesn't sound so bad!" Mere exclaimed into the phone.

She was proud of both of her sons, but especially of Radek, the town hero. I patted my hands dry on a dishtowel and leaned back against the counter and looked at my fingernails. At least they were clean—ish.

"She's right here," Mere said. She held the phone out to me while I backed away, holding my hands up.

"Oh no, it's okay. I can call him later . . ." I started, but Mere had already placed the phone in my hand and walked into the pantry.

"Hey," I said, holding the phone to my face.

"Hey," Radek said. "Thanks for helping Mom."

"Sure." I walked into the living room, pulling the phone cord to its maximum length, and sat on Turtle, the ancient leather footstool.

"You sound mad."

I put my elbow on my knee and propped my head up with my fist. I heard a guy talking in the background. A female voice answered. Radek lived off campus with one of his football team-mates, Bucky. There always seemed to be people around when we talked. In my head, I counted the number of months left until Radek graduated: twenty-three. Less than two years.

"Dad hired a new ranch hand. He's young." I bit my lip. Why did I mention that? I didn't want to admit it, but over the past few months, conversations with Radek had become awkward. We hadn't seen each other since Christmas. And even though we knew each other better than we knew anyone else, it seemed like we were running out of things to say. Plus, the giant "what the heck are we right now?" cloud looming over us was suffocating.

"That'll be good—give you more time with the horses." He didn't wait for me to respond. "Coach has me on a new weight-gain program. He says if I can bulk up this summer there's a good chance I'll make the All-State team. I've been eating so many hard-boiled eggs I might turn into one."

"Ha." I wished I sounded more interested. Since he'd gone to college Radek only wanted to talk football and his training regimes. He told me stories about this world I could only imagine based on TV shows or the odd novel I'd read. I tried my best to feign interest in things like the coach's boiled-egg plan, but it was getting harder and harder. I just wanted him to come home.

"Are you okay? I know it's been a while since we saw each other. I had to take this job to pay my rent for next year." Now Radek sounded annoyed.

How could I be okay when he was dating, or whatever he was doing with that girl? *Having fun.* I wanted to ask about her, but I was afraid of what he'd say, afraid I'd sound even angrier. I'd never imagined we would grow so far apart. When he left, things had been good between us, or at least okay. We'd been best friends. We'd had everything in common. Things had changed in our last year of high school, when people started paying so much attention to Radek-the-football-star, but we still had a plan. But since he'd been gone, his life had changed and mine had stayed exactly the same—until now. I'd always assumed things would get better when he got back, but now I wasn't so sure.

"Yeah, I'm fine." I leaned forward and glanced into the kitchen to see if Mere was listening, but she leaned over the sink, peeling potatoes and humming to the radio. I'd agreed to this crazy thing. I couldn't blame him for it. And maybe he'd go out with this girl a few times and realize he liked me more. Maybe that was the whole point. "I'm just tired," I said. I considered telling him about Dad putting the ranch up for sale, but decided not to. It would only make him feel bad, being so far away. And I had lots of time to figure it out before the fall. The girl in the background giggled again.

"Does Bucky have a friend over?" I asked. Radek's roommate had earned his nickname from his massive front teeth. I'd seen a photo of him in one of the newspaper clippings Mere stuck to the refrigerator door.

"Uh, yeah."

"What?" I said. "Why are you being weird?" I watched a truck speed by on the road out front through the living room bay window, kicking up dust.

On the other end of the line, a door shut and the background noise went quiet. Radek must have gone into his bedroom. In all the years he'd been gone, I'd never been to visit, so I was guessing. Radek had asked me to come a few times after he first left, but it never seemed like a good time—there was always something to do on the ranch, and he came home for holidays and the summer. After a year he stopped asking.

"Radek, is the girl there?" I squeezed my fist shut, digging my short nails into the meat of my palm.

"Look, it's no big deal. Bucky and I are taking some girls out tonight."

"*Some girls?*" My stomach dropped. What the hell did that mean? I took a deep breath, bit down on my lip. "Is it the same girl?" I asked, my voice quiet.

Radek breathed on the other end of the line. "Do you really want to know?" I heard bedsprings squeak as he sat. He always complained about the crapiness of the bed in his rental apartment.

So it was her. I pictured him lying back on the navy- and light-blue bedspread Mere had sent him back with at Christmas. Did he still make his bed now that his mother wasn't there to get after him if he didn't?

"Han . . ." He took a deep breath and let it out slowly. "This is harder than I thought it would be. Maybe we shouldn't tell each other about it, you know, if we do go on dates." He sounded like himself again, my best friend Radek, not football-star Radek.

If, I thought bitterly. Total transparency had been part of the agreement. Best friends first. After all of these years apart, all of these years where he hadn't even talked about other girls, I'd thought we were done with it, that we were both thinking about what would happen when he got home, how we'd start our grown-up lives together.

"You there?" he said, his mouth close to the receiver. I imagined I was there, sitting beside him on his bed. Instead of taking this girl out tonight with Bucky, he would take me. We'd go to the campus bar, I'd meet everyone he talked about, and he'd introduce me as his girlfriend, his high school sweetheart, his oldest and closet friend. But I was sitting at his house, on his dad's ancient footstool, trying to figure out how to hold our lives together while he dated another girl.

"I'm here," I said. I needed to keep him happy, go along with his plan until he got home, and everything would be better. He was still a good guy. Maybe he was right—maybe he needed this to be sure about us and forever. "Sure. If that's better for you, we don't have to talk about it." I bit into my knuckles, blinking the tears from my eyes.

I SAT in the living room after he hung up, long enough that the phone made that frantic beeping sound, alerting you to put it back on the cradle. While the tears dried on my face, I pressed the phone to my thigh and let the noise blend in with the familiar sounds of the house. The oven opening and closing. Another truck on the road. Clarence coming in and closing the back door. Had he kissed her? Of course he had. Aside from Olivia Murphy and Allison Grisholm (before she married one of our high school teachers), he hadn't kissed anyone but me. How serious was it?

That was another rule: we could date other people but it must never get serious. I didn't understand how people could casually date. How could you kiss a person you weren't in love with? Heather had tried to explain this so many times, but I still didn't get it.

I WALKED BACK into the kitchen and set the phone in its cradle when I thought my eyes wouldn't be red. Mere had set a pan of date squares on the counter. "Have one," she said, smiling at me.

I shook my head. Not what my stomach needed right now. "No thanks, I better not ruin dinner."

Clarence walked in from the mudroom and took two squares. "Hey, Hannah."

I nodded at Clarence, and smiled.

"Met that new ranch hand of your dad's just now," he said.

My mouth fell open. "What? Why?"

"He came over to say hi to the guys." Clarence shrugged and leaned over to kiss his mom on the cheek. "Gotta get cleaned up," he said. I watched as he walked up the stairs.

'Say hi to the guys,' I thought, anger boiling in my empty stomach. Say hi to the guys, or sell them weed? He wouldn't be that brazen, would he?

As I WALKED BACK to the house, carrying the basket of eggs Mere insisted I take home "for Dad"—not Lily—exhaustion took over. I hadn't worked hard that day, but I was spent. Radek was out with another girl right now, and there was nothing I could do about it. I was thousands of kilometres away. Dad was planning to sell the ranch, and I didn't know if there was anything I could do about that either, and I was right here. I opened the gate and paused to look at the broken latch. I needed to fix that too, before the horses figured out how to nudge it open. Will stood with Dad by my truck. The new fender glinted in the late afternoon sun. And Will. You know what? If Will wanted to sell weed, whatever. Let him get caught. At least I had nothing to do with him. Maybe he'd get caught too late for Dad to hire another hand and I'd have a hope in hell of keeping the ranch.

 ugust 1981

AT MRS. BAILEY'S HOUSE, I help Clarence feed the sheep every day at six o'clock in the morning. It's been twelve days since Daddy left. At the back door I pull on my rubber boots and then go meet Clarence at the big barn. Radek is in charge of getting the cow-milking started, so he goes to the other barn.

The paint on the big barn is red and flaky. I can see right inside the barn in a few places where the wood wasn't put in close together, or has pulled away. Clarence's nose is long, and his fuzzy eyebrows wiggle like two caterpillars when he talks. Clarence is a grown-up, but he isn't old or married.

In the mornings, the barn is quiet. The sun peeks through the cracks between the wallboards and lights up the dust floating in the air. Clarence pours the grain for the sheep and I get to use the hose to pour the water. The sheep wake up and make their crying sound.

I like the lambs best. They kick their legs and twist their

bodies as they jump. When I get close enough, I run my hands over the curly wool on their sides. I like to feel their warm skin and their little hearts beating. With the older sheep, I dig my hands into the thick, wiry-soft wool, imagining how fur like this became the sweater Mrs. Bailey made for me. When Clarence isn't looking, I rub my face into the wool of a ewe—that's what the ladies are called—while she eats. I breathe in her milky-hay smell. I used to sit in Momma's lap and rub my face in her hair.

Now Daddy is gone too—"run off." That's what Radek says, that Daddy ran off and left me, so now Radek will take care of me.

"I'm going to marry you and you can make quilts," he said. When Mrs. Bailey heard this she told me, "Your daddy will be back. He just needs time. Don't you worry."

I hope Daddy comes back more than anything. When I think about Daddy, my chest gets tight and my eyes burn and I have to think about something else. I have to be a good girl and not cry, like Daddy said.

After we finish feeding the sheep, Clarence opens the barn door, pulling the sunlight along behind it. The dust disappears and fresh air rushes in. The lambs and their mommas go out into the back pasture to eat the grass there.

I go back to the house with Clarence, and Mrs. Bailey makes us breakfast. Radek comes in and we eat pancakes and bacon and potatoes. Clarence and Mrs. Bailey drink coffee, but Radek and I have to drink milk.

MY FAVOURITE THING at Mrs. Bailey's house is when she tells me stories about Momma. Tonight she tells me about Momma's hair and how Momma would brush it one hundred times before bed to keep it shiny. I sit still for Mrs. Bailey so she can brush my hair so it's as nice as Momma's. And she tells me about how Momma helped her after Radek was born.

74

"R.W.'s daddy was killed right before he was born."

"Why did Radek's daddy die?" I ask Mrs. Bailey. Radek always says his daddy died from a truck, like how my momma died from a bear.

"He was hit by a man driving too fast. They both died." I don't know if she means both of the men or Radek's daddy and his truck, but I don't ask.

She brushes my hair slower.

Mrs. Bailey always says Momma and Radek's daddy are in Heaven together. Today I want to ask what they are doing up there, but she has turned away and is rubbing her eyes with a tissue again.

"Your momma came to help me after Walter—Mr. Bailey— died. R.W. was born only a few weeks after that, and your momma took care of me and the baby. I couldn't have done it without her." She helps me under the covers and pats my hair.

"And when was I alive?"

"You were alive already. Your momma brought you with her in a basket."

I smile when I think of myself in a basket, like a kitten.

Mrs. Bailey tucks the sheets in around me and says goodnight. I watch the shadows from the tree outside dancing on the ceiling and wonder if Daddy misses me.

une 1996

DAD PATTED the truck's hood. His face was red—I assumed from standing in the sun to fix the bumper—but he seemed to be in a better mood.

"All fixed up. And we got the lawn mower going again. Will knows his way around an engine."

Of course he did. Will seemed to know about everything. Engines. Rodeos. Drugs. We followed Dad as he made his way back to the house.

"How'd your baking go?" Will asked.

I glanced at him to gauge his expression—his face was neutral, no sign of mockery. I let my eyes linger a moment too long and he smiled at me. I flicked my eyes away, frowning.

"Fine," I said. *Or the exact opposite of fine.* How was I supposed to pretend everything was normal when at that very moment, Radek was most likely sucking face with a girl who was way more fun than me? I looked at the horse barn. As if reading my mind, Will answered.

"Fed, brushed, and run," he said. "I did that while your dad worked on a broken bridle."

"Oh, thanks." I felt silly, having been banished to a kitchen for the day. But at least I didn't have to do the chores now. All I wanted to do was sink into my bed, curl up, and make everything go away.

"You been working with that gelding long?" Will asked as we reached the porch. I kicked my dusty boots off on the mat outside the door.

"Whiskey? Only a few weeks. Not that it's getting anywhere." I'd trained more horses than I could count, but Whiskey was by far the hardest. We'd make progress; he'd let me lean on his back, even set a saddle pad on, but the next day it would take me an hour to get a halter on him.

Will nodded and pulled a pack of cigarettes from his chest pocket. He tapped the pack with his other hand, thinking. "I can help you with him."

I glared at him. And horses. Apparently he also knew everything about horses. "I told you I don't need your help." *I need you to leave me alone so I can sneak back out to the barn to make the trail ride sign.* I thought about the can of red paint, leftover from painting the barn years ago, stashed under the work bench in the tack room. Would it have dried up?

He shrugged and pulled a cigarette from the pack and stuck it between his lips. "Managed to keep your dad busy today," he said. He brought his lighter to the end of the cigarette and inhaled, creating bright embers.

"So what?" I put my hand on the screen door's latch.

"I know you don't want him to sell this place."

I let my hand drop and spun to face him. "And how do you think you're going to help with that?"

He blew smoke out the side of his mouth, lifting his eyebrows, but didn't speak.

Just great. Who the hell did this guy think he was? Old Spike would have been so much easier to deal with. He'd left me alone after the first day, when he offered to lift a bale of hay for me and I shot him daggers so sharp he stepped back, hands raised.

"Mind your own business," I said, and walked into the house, letting the door slam behind me.

LILY KNEELED on the carpet in the living room, bent over a shape on the floor.

"Dad?" I rushed to Lily's side, my eyes adjusting to the low light. Dad sat on the floor, looking confused. "What happened? Why didn't you call me?" Fear gripped my chest, sending shots of adrenaline down my arms. Not again. Dad's face was pale, but his eyes were open.

"I think he fainted," Lily said. Tears sprang to her eyes and she wiped them quickly. "He's breathing fine . . . Here, hold him up. I'm going to call Dr. Masterson."

"Don't call the doctor," Dad grumbled. He tried to push himself to standing but I held him where he was.

"Stay still!" I held my hand to his wrist, checking his pulse like they'd taught us in grade nine phys ed. It was there, but who was I kidding—I didn't know what it was supposed to feel like in the first place. "Does anything hurt? Did you fall?"

Dad tried to push me away. "I'm fine!" he said, louder this time. "I just got dizzy. I was out in the heat all day, fixing your—" He saw the expression on my face and stopped.

Lily was already in the kitchen on the phone with the doctor when Will stepped into the house, bowing his head to avoid banging it on the door frame. His eyes widened when he registered Dad and me on the carpet.

"Is everything okay here?" he asked, his face drawn with concern.

"We don't know," I said.

"Yes, it's fine." Dad escaped my grip and pulled himself into his recliner. "I could use a glass of water though. Only a bit light-headed." He tried to regain his dignity as he adjusted himself in the chair. "What I really need is a glass of whiskey, if that woman would let me," he said, loud enough to make sure Lily could hear in the other room.

I stood and started towards the kitchen, but Will put a hand on my shoulder. I looked at his hand there, firmly pressing into my T-shirt. The hard warmth of his hand penetrated my skin, reassuring. Our eyes met.

"I'll get it," he said. "Go sit with your dad." Did he feel guilty for keeping Dad busy all day? Was that why he'd collapsed?

I looked at Will a moment longer and then nodded, watching as he squeezed past Lily where she stood in the kitchen doorway, phone cord wrapped around her hand. "Yes, yes, he's breathing fine. Yes, he's sitting up now . . ." She gave me a weak smile and stepped back into the kitchen.

Will returned with the water—no whiskey—and sat beside me on the sofa. I slid over towards Dad to make sure our legs didn't touch.

"Quit staring at me," Dad said. "Turn on the boob tube or something for God's sake." He took a sip of the water and set it down.

Will stood and turned the TV on, flipping channels until he reached *Wheel of Fortune*.

"I don't understand how this woman never ages," Dad said, more to Will than me. "Is it that surgery they're doing now?"

My mind drifted as they talked. I stared at Momma's painting across the room, trying to count the number of greens she'd used for the blades of grass on Blueberry hill. What was the scientific name for grass again? Dad was not better. He might not ever be the same. What was I thinking, trying to run the ranch on my own? Dad needed to rest, to fully heal—as much as he could, now that he was older. I blinked my eyes fast to keep from crying. What if he died? What would Lily and I do? I glanced sideways at Will and was surprised to find him looking at me, his eyes scanning my face. Before I could say anything, Lily came up behind Dad's chair. She squeezed the headrest but didn't touch Dad.

"Dr. Masterson says you don't need to go to the hospital unless anything changes. You just need to rest. No work for at least another week, not until after you've seen him at your next appointment."

Dad blew air out through his lips. "There aren't enough movies in the world."

"You'll do what he says." Lily's voice was as hard as I'd ever heard it. "You stubborn old goat." She tapped him on the shoulder and he reached up and held her hand there, patting it before letting her go. She took a deep breath and stepped away from the chair, tucking her shirt into her jeans. She'd bedazzled the edges of the pockets with little fake diamonds. "Who wants dinner?"

LILY GOT Dad to go to bed shortly after we ate, so only Will and I headed to the porch after dinner. I watched as he smoked, my feet on the railing across from the swing. The cicadas buzzed a symphony in the warm night air. Will took a long drag and then pushed his cigarette into the flowerpot.

"I'm trying to quit," he said.

The weed? Had he figured out I'd found it? He held up the cigarette and I realized he meant smoking.

"Likely smart." I let my feet drop to the porch floor. *I should go to bed too.* But I didn't want to be alone, tossing and turning, letting my brain run in circles, trying to figure out what to do about everything.

"What did you have Dad do today?" I asked, trying to keep my voice neutral. I wanted to know what had caused Dad to collapse —if it was working on my truck or a different chore.

Will glanced at me. "Fix a bridle. That's it."

I nodded, scrunching my eyebrows together.

"He didn't work on your truck either," he said, resting his ankle on his knee and leaning back into the swing beside me.

I closed my eyes for a second and let my breath out slowly. It wasn't my fault.

Will shifted beside me. "I hope you don't mind me asking this, but what happened to your momma?"

No one had asked me that in a long time. Everyone in Jessop knew, or had decided they knew, what had happened to Momma. "She died in an accident."

Will nodded.

I ran my sock feet back and forth on the porch boards, stretching a toe out to scratch Mickey Two, who lay halfway between Will and me. The empty henhouse was a dark shadow across the yard. Clarence had replaced the door long ago, but we'd never had chickens again.

"She got shot," I said.

"I heard."

I swivelled my body to face Will. Who told him? Lily? In his eerie way, he answered my question before it left my lips.

"The guys at the Baileys'."

Ah—the ranch hands. I'd already forgotten he'd gone over there that afternoon. I stood and stretched my arms over my head. I knew how this conversation went now. Like a rock that had been smoothed by a river.

"It was an accident, like I said." Next, he would ask if I was sure it was an accident—how did he not know his wife was in the henhouse? Why didn't she make a noise to let him know? Had we kept the bear pelt?

I'd heard it all before.

Will nodded. "Didn't say it wasn't." He stood and faced me.

"But now I understand why you don't like eggs." He gave me a half smile and then walked down the porch steps. "See you tomorrow." He headed off in the direction of the cabin.

I ROLLED OVER, pulling the quilt to my chin. The glowing clock on my bedside table read 3:33. I sighed and twisted to turn my lamp on. I'd tried but failed to stop my mind from running around like a wild horse in a paddock for the first time. It was too early to get up, too late to keep lying here doing nothing. I pulled a sweatshirt over my flannel PJs and crept down the hall, avoiding the places where the floor creaked. I stopped outside Dad and Lily's room, listening. Dad's deep snores penetrated even the thick wooden door. My chest loosened, just a little bit.

The horses snorted and shifted in their stalls as I entered the barn through the man door. I flicked on the light in the tack room and dug around under the bench until I found the can of red paint—not dried up—and a half-decent brush. At the back of the barn I found a piece of scrap wood just big enough. I kneeled over the wood, carefully guiding the brush: "Stillwater Ranch. Trail Rides by the Hour." And then a fat arrow. I'd put this one on the main road, leading people down our sparsely populated side road. The shabby sign with the ranch name at the end of our lane might be enough to get them to stop. And then what? I leaned back on my heels, looking at my handiwork. Then they'd ask about the trail rides? And Dad would flip. I set the paintbrush across the top of the can and pressed my hands into my thighs to stand, shaking out my stiff legs. This was ridiculous. At best I'd be able to keep Dad from finding out about the sign for a few days. And if it worked? It was likely he'd be chasing some poor, would-be customer off the property with a shotgun. I looked at the red paint stains my hands had left on my flannel PJs. One bad idea after another. Who I was kidding? I couldn't stop Dad. I couldn't fix anything. I might as well start applying for jobs in town, the way things were going.

I opened Honcho's stall and stepped in. He shook his head and blew air through his lips in greeting. Honcho had been my first horse and was the oldest at the ranch. I'd learned to ride on him, when I was three, my stubby little legs sticking straight out from his sides. Now his hair was wiry and patchy in a few spots, and I didn't take him out for rides often. I rested my head against his neck, breathing in his musky scent. He nuzzled the pocket of my sweatshirt, searching for sugar cubes. I thought of Dad sitting in the chair, his face pale. Lily had restarted her hourly blood-pressure checks, using the cuff the doctor had given her. She recorded the results in a notebook. "Eight o'clock and all's well!" she'd called out, after her post-dinner check.

I clenched Honcho's mane in my hand and swung my leg over his back, pulling myself up. He shifted slightly and then settled back in. I let my hands and legs hang loose, let my body rest heavy on his warmth. I rubbed my cheek on his neck, like I used to do after a bad day at school.

The image of Dad's bluey-white skin kept coming back to me. Tears ran down my face and soaked into Honcho's thick brown hair, now flecked with grey. What if Dad died? That question kept circling. It made everything else seem so small, so menial. My chest convulsed. I slid off Honcho and pressed my back into a corner of the stall. My face in my knees, I let the tears that had been building up all day fall. Honcho sniffed at my heaving shoulders and then went back to his hay, somehow knowing I wanted to be left alone. Eventually I caught my breath, wiped my eyes, and stood, brushing straw from the back of my PJs. I rubbed Honcho behind his ears. "Thanks, buddy."

The barn door eased open and I caught my breath. Had Dad snuck out from under Lily's watchful gaze? I wiped at my eyes, hoping they weren't too red but knowing they were swollen to all heck.

Will stood in the shadow of the single bulb I'd turned on to light my way as I painted the sign. "What are you doing here?" I said, anger in my voice. I felt bad as soon as I said it. I was just trying to cover up for crying. I dipped my head so he couldn't see my face in the low light.

"Couldn't sleep, so I figured I'd come start the morning feed, make sure your dad stays inside the house, keep Lily from tanning his hide." He walked closer to the stall as I stepped out and closed the latch, giving the soft skin on Honcho's muzzle a final rub through the bars.

"Thanks," I said quietly, keeping my eyes on my boots.

Will looked at me a moment longer then turned and walked into the tack room. He came back with a bucket of feed. The sun was rising, hot and orange, through the window in the man door. If Will had noticed I'd been crying, he didn't say anything.

"You sleep at all?" he asked, filling Honcho's trough with feed. He was close enough I smelled that fresh, cedary scent again.

"Nope." I leaned against the stall and watched as he made his way down the aisle, bending as he scooped feed, his back muscles visible underneath his T-shirt. He was getting closer to the sign and the can of paint. I held my breath.

"Why don't you go do that. I'll keep your dad occupied until you get up." He straightened and smiled at me. My stomach tightened as our eyes met. Sun filtered into the barn, leaving a long trail of light on the floor between us. Will glanced at the sign, squinting to make out the letters.

"Trail rides?" he said.

I hurried past him and gathered the paint can and brush. "Uh, yeah. It's something Dad and I have been considering." I lied. I dabbed the paint with my finger to make sure it was dry and then pushed the sign to the back of the pile of spare wood that leaned against the wall of the barn.

Will rubbed his hand over his freshly shaven chin. "It's a good idea," he said. "I worked on a ranch in Montana that did that. Made good money at it too."

"Yeah well, we'll see." I walked past Will to the tack room. I wiped my hands on a rag after hiding the paint back under the work bench. I needed to get properly cleaned up before Dad or Lily saw me.

When I came out of the tack room, Will had opened the back door of the barn, letting the fresh morning air in. He leaned against the door frame, one ankle over the other, his arms crossed, like he'd been waiting for me to return. He pushed his hair behind his ear and smiled at me, sending spikes of warmth into my lower belly.

"Thank you . . . for helping," I said. "See you at breakfast."

13

*S*eptember 1991

THE DAY OF THE GAME, I raced to finish my chores before lunch. Dad and Lily were planning to drive into town to catch the second half, before Lily's shift at the Red Lion. I wanted to go early to meet Heather and Chrissy at Heather's new trailer. Heather's mom had traded their old one and her car for a bigger, newer trailer a few roads over on a lot at the edge of town.

Heather and her mom moved every few years, depending on whether or not Barb had a job. She'd stayed at the gas station for the last two years, so between that and the money Heather brought in from the diner, they'd been able to upgrade. The good thing about going to Heather's was Barb was hardly ever around. And when she was, she was usually with one of her boyfriends, drinking on the makeshift cement-pad porch or watching TV.

Football games were held in the stadium behind the high school—it was less a stadium and more a field with a few rickety old bleachers. Heather had told me townies liked to go there to hang out. Town kids grew up so differently from country kids. Radek and I spent our weekends doing chores and going to the odd barn dance, or watching movies and playing cards. The town kids met behind the school and drank whatever alcohol they'd been able to steal from their parents, or went to the diner to smoke.

After I finished checking the horses, I jogged from the barn to the house, taking the porch steps two at a time. Lily hadn't called us for lunch yet, but I could tell it was close by the way the sun sat high over the house. I'd promised to drive Radek to the game, and they had to be there hours before it started.

"Where's the fire?" Lily asked, as I speed-walked through the living room.

I glanced at the clock on the mantle. "I've got ten minutes to get cleaned up before I pick up Radek."

"Then it's a good thing I already chose an outfit for you," she said, leaning against the kitchen doorway.

"Noooo," I whined. I knew it would be too tight, too short, too sparkly, or a combination of all three.

"It's on your bed," she said, grinning.

I showered quickly and dragged a comb through my unruly hair. In my room, I glanced at the jeans and leopard print shirt that Lily had laid out, and then pulled on my favourite old Wranglers, a pink T-shirt, and a ball cap. No way I was wearing a shirt with leopard print, let alone to a football game. Lily had also hung my jean jacket on the bedroom doorknob. I shrugged and picked it up before I closed my door.

"WELL, that's not what I picked but it's not half bad," Lily said. "Especially since it looks like you shrunk that shirt in the wash." She sat at the dining room table sipping from a mug of coffee. "Who you trying to impress? Hmm?" Lily teased.

I avoided her eyes, thinking of Radek's solid legs against my thighs. "I'm late," I said.

"You have fun, Chickadee. See you in a few hours." Lily smiled at me in a way that made me wonder if she knew why I'd chosen to wear the pink T-shirt. I paused in the doorway for a moment as she hovered her pencil over her crossword. I opened my mouth to ask her about what had happened with Radek and me the other night, and then shut it just as quickly. It was nothing. He was asleep.

RADEK WAITED for me in front of his house, his shoulder pads and a bag with his cleats tied to it beside him.

We didn't talk on the way to the school. Radek was always quiet before games. He played the *Rocky* theme song over and over again on the truck's tape deck. Each time it finished he'd hit Rewind to start it all over again.

I pulled into the parking lot and cut the engine as Radek got out and took his gear from the bed of the truck. He came around to the driver-side window. Usually when I dropped him off at practice he waved and walked out to the field.

"Have a good game?" I said. Is that what he wanted to hear? Did he remember putting his feet on my lap? Something was different between us. I watched his lips as he smiled back at me. I noticed for the first time how full they were, how the lower lip was slightly bigger than the upper, almost like he was pouting.

"Thanks, Hannah." My eyebrows shot up at the sound of my name. He never called me Hannah. Han, or H, but never my whole name. He stood there for a few beats and then walked backwards towards the school doors, lifting his bag in a wave before turning and breaking into a jog.

HEATHER AND CHRISSY took turns running in and out of the tiny bathroom in Heather's mom's trailer, sharing lipsticks and eye shadows. They both wore button-up plaid shirts and jeans so tight I wasn't sure how they'd gotten them on. Chrissy's fuzzy blonde hair had been gelled into perfect curls, and her lips were plump with gloss.

Heather relinquished her spot at the bathroom mirror to Chrissy and strode into the kitchen. She opened a cupboard above the little stove and stood on her tippy toes, reaching for a six-pack of coolers her mom had tried to hide from us. "Help a girl out!" she said.

I reached over Heather, pulled out the case, and passed it to her.

"Why don't you play basketball or something?" Heather took the drinks from me, her face sulky.

"When would I have time for that?" I slid into the booth table. Heather popped the tops, poured two of the coolers into a juice jug, and added powdered Kool-Aid and stirred.

"You and your *responsibilities*," Heather said, rolling her eyes. "You're not going to drink any of this either, are you?"

It drove Chrissy and Heather crazy that I didn't drink much. I'd tried drinking with them when we were in grade eight, but I hated the floaty fuzzy feeling that came along with it. The lack of control. I shook my head. "I'm driving."

Heather sighed and poured the cooler mix into two glasses. That was another thing about living out in the country: someone always had to drive home. There were way too many stories about people going off the road after too many drinks.

Chrissy emerged from the bathroom, her hair pulled into a half ponytail. "Hey, Hannah. Guess what?" She slid onto the seat beside me, reaching for the chips. "I'm pretty sure Chucker winked at me when I walked by his locker before calculus."

She'd had a crush on Chucker since he maybe-sorta smiled at her on our first day of grade nine. Chucker was two years ahead of us, a giant linebacker with pale hair and massive butcher-block hands. He was taking what he called "an extra lap"—staying at school for another year to get enough credits to graduate because he had failed so many courses in grade twelve.

"That's good," I said. Sometimes it seemed like Chrissy's life was too easy. Heather had to deal with Barb and her revolving door of boyfriends, I'd lost Momma and had to help Dad keep the ranch going, but Chrissy's family was stable and oh-so-perfect. Her parents were still together, and she and all of her four siblings did well in school, were good-looking, and excelled at everything they tried. They lived in a huge house on the most expensive street in town; her dad was the bank manager. Chrissy always had the best clothes, the best car, the best makeup. I tried to think of a time I'd seen Chrissy want something she hadn't gotten, and could only come up with Chucker. I glanced at Heather. She frowned slightly, perhaps thinking the same thing. I guessed that's why Heather and I had always been closer. Our troubles were different, but more equal.

By THE TIME I pulled the truck back into the school's parking lot, it was almost full. I had to drive to the last row, furthest from the field, to find a spot. We'd be lucky to get a seat in the bleachers. I squinted, trying to make out Radek on the field as the team warmed up, but I couldn't find him in the sea of blue-and-white jerseys. Chrissy led us to a row where three girls who were friends with one of her older sisters sat. We squeezed onto the bench and Chrissy began chatting with the girls.

Heather elbowed me in the ribs. "Don't think I didn't notice your shirt. It looks like you might actually have boobs under there."

I punched her in the arm, laughing. I'd shrunk the pink T-shirt when I washed it the first time and had left it in my drawer ever since.

The cheer team warmed up in front of us, jumping up and down with their pompoms and doing elaborate stretches. Olivia was directly below us, her hair in a high, bouncing ponytail, her pompoms swinging energetically over her head.

"I should try out," Heather said. She'd been in gymnastics when we were younger but had to quit when her mom said it was getting too expensive. Heather used to do flips on the grass in the playground at the trailer park while I pretended to be an announcer at the Olympics. *And the crowd goes wild, as Heather McCarthy lands the jump perfectly.*

"Why don't you?"

She shrugged. "Same as you. No time. Mom's making me pay rent now, so I had to take extra shifts at the diner."

The loudspeaker squealed to life and the announcer began calling out the players' names as they ran onto the field. Radek jogged out and waved when everyone cheered. He looked relaxed, even though he was in front of pretty much the whole town. I glanced down at Olivia. She stood with the rest of the cheerleaders and stared straight at Radek, a wide smile on her face. Why did she have to be so nice? I wanted to hate her. The sun had dipped behind the arena across the field, and I shivered in my thin jacket. The cold metal of the bleachers permeated my jeans.

"Here." The older girl beside Chrissy leaned over and passed me a plastic Coke bottle. "A little something to keep you warm."

"Oh, no thanks, I'm good." I looked at the bottle of brown liquid.

"Just a sip," Heather said. "It's not gonna kill you." I looked at Olivia jumping up and down on the sidelines, trying to stay warm. I took the bottle and tipped it to my mouth, making sure I didn't touch the rim since so many other girls already had. That thing would be like a Petri dish from science class. I winced as the liquid hit the back of my throat. Rum? Maybe whiskey. The only thing I knew for sure was there wasn't much pop in it.

Just before halftime I caught sight of Dad and Lily setting up folding chairs to the left of the bleachers. Lily searched the crowd for me and waved wildly until I waved back. Each time our team scored, Olivia and the other cheerleaders leapt to the edge of the field and went crazy, thrusting their pompoms into the air and kicking their bare legs. I watched Radek and tried to keep up with what was happening in the game so I could talk to him about it later. I took another long swig from the Coke bottle when it came around again. The liquid was warmer now, but just as strong.

The crowd rose to its feet as a streak of blue-and-white sprinted down the field.

"That's R.W.!" Chrissy said, pulling me up beside her. She'd adopted his new nickname, too. "He's running the ball!" Chrissy's dad was obsessed with football, so she understood what was happening. Blood rushed to my face and I crossed my cold fingers at my side, willing Radek to run faster.

He slowed as he crossed into the end zone and turned to face the crowd. Then he pointed in my direction as he dropped the ball. I saw Olivia look up and behind her. Her eyes met mine. My face burned.

"Uhh, did he just point at you?" Heather said as we sat, her eyes wide.

I bit back my smile and shook my head, but excitement bubbled in my stomach.

une 1996

I SNUCK out of the house and into my truck without Lily seeing. I'd forgone the tight pink dress she'd laid out for me and opted for a much more reasonable outfit: jeans and a tank top. She wouldn't be happy when she saw me at the Lion, but at least I'd brushed my hair. We walked in a small pack, Chrissy, Heather, and I, a cloud of hair spray and Baby Soft perfume, Lily's signature scent—she bought it for the girls every Christmas—surrounding us. Our boots tapped on the sidewalk.

Chrissy tugged at her black spandex skirt, which barely covered her butt. "You sure this isn't too short?" She'd changed into it right before we left Heather's new apartment. Her conservative mother would not have approved.

Heather and I looked at each other. "It's fine," Heather said. I guessed she didn't want Chrissy to make us go back to the apartment so she could change.

When we got to the Red Lion, Lily came out from behind the bar to divvy out her epic hugs. She held Chrissy and Heather at arms' length and admired their outfits. My friends had always loved Lily. "Coolest mom ever," Chrissy had told me the first time she came to Stillwater, in grade six. "She's not my mom," I'd said. I figured Lily wouldn't find Chrissy's skirt too short, and I was right. Chrissy seemed relieved.

Lily shook her head when she saw what I was wearing. "It wouldn't hurt you to dress like a lady every once in a while," she said, pulling me into a hug.

"How was Dad after dinner?" I asked.

Lily frowned and moved back behind the bar. She wiped a cloth across it as Heather and Chrissy went to find a table. "The same I guess. I left him watching *True Grit* again." She sighed. "I don't know what I'm going to do with him." She looked like she might cry. I patted her hand, the cool lump of the large turquoise ring she always wore on her left middle finger pressing into my palm. Lily had been living with us for well over a decade. She'd never hidden her desire to have a big wedding and a baby. She used to bug Dad about it, leave wedding magazines all over the house. There were still a few piled on the side table in the living room, their edges curling with age. But lately it seemed as though she'd given up. She told me Dad refused to talk about it anymore. I didn't understand why he wouldn't let her have her wedding.

"It'll be okay," I said, squeezing her hand. At least I hoped it would.

Lily rolled her lips in and nodded.

"Do you know why he's so set on selling the ranch?"

I'd wanted to ask her for days but hadn't been alone with her for more than a few minutes.

"Money, honey," she said, giving me a sad smile.

I leaned against the bar and let out a long breath. "Is that it, though? Money's always been tight."

Lily looked at me, tilting her head to the side and drawing her eyebrows together. "Seems like you don't think it is," she said. A man waved at her from the other end of the bar and she waved back. "One sec, Herb!" she called out to him over the din.

"I dunno. I was thinking it had to do with Momma." I rubbed my hand across my face. I'd had too much Baby Duck at Heather's. "Any chance it's because you're getting married?" I thought back to what Heather had said the night I helped her pack. Maybe Dad wanted a fresh start of his own.

Lily let out a puff of air through her nose. "You know as well as I do there's little chance of that." She leaned in closer. "The only other thing he's mentioned is that there was a researcher guy asking around town about what happened to your momma."

"A what?"

"A graduate student, I think he said. Working on a paper about cases where men killed their wives."

I reeled back a few steps. "But Dad didn't—"

"Oh I know, honey. But this researcher got hold of the story from an old newspaper and was digging around. It got your dad thinking." The old man—Herb—waved at Lily again, and she stood up straight. "Don't go worrying about it. Go enjoy your night." She turned and pulled three beers from the fridge and popped the tops off. "Here—take these." Lily smiled at me before moving down the bar to deal with her customers.

THE RED LION was dark and smoke-filled. And loud. The exact opposite of where I wanted to be. I needed a quiet place and a clear head so I could figure out what was going on with this researcher. Why Dad? Why speck-on-the-map Jessop? What newspaper article? The centre of the room had been cleared for a dance floor, with tables and chairs set up around the perimeter. One woman swayed to the music by herself in the middle of the makeshift dance floor, her eyes closed. Didn't she care about people watching? Heather waved at me from a table near the back. I settled into the chair beside her and handed her and Chrissy each a beer.

"When's R.W. back next?" Chrissy asked. Her eyes scanned the room.

"I don't know—maybe he'll visit before school starts." I followed her eyes. She was looking for Chucker. Someone had told her he was back in town for the week. After high school, Chucker had become a long-haul trucker. He was away from town for months on end. Chrissy cited this as the main reason they'd never gotten together.

"You don't sound like absence is making your heart grow fonder," Heather said. She tipped beer into her mouth.

I shrugged. I still hadn't told her about Fun Girl. Hopefully I'd never have to.

"There he is!" Chrissy squealed.

Heather and I craned our necks to look.

"No! Don't look!" Chrissy said. "That's the worst thing you can do."

I laughed. "Says who?"

Chrissy gave me an exasperated look. "Says everyone. I just read in *Cosmo* that there was this study about how men are like lions, and they need to stalk their, er, prey, to really appreciate it."

I laughed again, almost choking on my drink. "Are you kidding me?"

Before Chrissy could answer, Lily arrived at our table.

"Hey there, girls." She balanced a round tray full of drinks on her hip. "What's shakin'?"

"Chucker is here," Chrissy said, a wide grin on her face.

"Ahhh," Lily said, setting down three shot glasses. "Well that makes sense. Because these are from those cowboys over there." She used her free hand to point at the table of guys where

Chucker sat. He raised a massive, plaid-covered arm and waved. Chrissy's face turned bright pink. "Tequila," Lily added, with a scrunch of her nose. She pushed a salt shaker and a bowl of limes our way.

"Wow." Heather waved to the guys on our behalf. She hated tequila, but she loved free drinks.

"To tonight!" Chrissy said, as we clanged the shot glasses together. The liquor burned my throat and bubbled into warmth in my stomach. I bit my lip and shook my head, trying to shake the taste from my mouth. I tried to remember how many drinks I'd had. The Baby Duck, the beer, the tequila. My stomach turned. There was no way I would feel good tomorrow. When Lily came back I'd ask her for a glass of water.

A few minutes later, Chucker rose from his seat and drained the glass in front of him. The band had started a decent rendition of "Come On Eileen." The Red Lion was packed; it would be a good tips night for Lily.

I nudged Chrissy. "He's coming over."

"Ohmygodohmygodohmygod." She fussed with her hair. "Do I—?"

I smiled at her. She always looked perfect.

"Hey there." Chucker stood at the end of our table, his huge body looming over Chrissy's tiny one.

Chrissy stared, apparently unable to speak.

"Hey, Chucker," Heather said. "Nice to see you back home."

He smiled, showing a mouthful of charmingly crooked teeth. "Just got back from a run down to Oklahoma." Chucker shifted from one foot to another. "Chrissy, I was wondering if you might want to dance?"

Chrissy pulled herself together and managed a smile. "Sure." She passed her shiny black patent purse across the table and followed Chucker onto the dance floor.

Heather and I chatted about the people around us until

Chrissy returned a few songs later, Chucker in tow, her cheeks flushed. "These guys are going to come sit with us," she announced. Had she stopped by the bar for another shot? She seemed a lot drunker now. Chucker waved his big hand in the air, motioning to his friends.

I moved Chrissy's purse to the floor below my seat to make room as Randy Redding sat beside me.

"I'm Randy." I'd known his name for at least seven years, but I pretended I was meeting him for the first time ever, a smile pasted on my face. Maybe I could get out of there, go home early, drink a ton of water, and not be a mess for chores the next morning.

Randy stuck out his left hand for me to shake, and I gripped it awkwardly. Everyone knew Randy Redding, partially because he'd been one of the most popular guys in high school, but also because he had only one arm. He'd lost his right arm just past the elbow in a bailer accident. Even though he'd been three grades ahead of me, I remembered the day he came back to school with the big bandage covering the place his arm used to be. "I'm Hannah," I said.

"Hannah Tatum?"

"Yeah."

"You're the girl whose dad shot her mom."

I gave him a hard smile. Still, even now, this was what people thought. Even though Dad had been cleared long ago. What had the researcher heard, talking to people around town?

"That's me," I said, bitterness seeping through my voice. Randy didn't seem to catch my irritation.

"I've always wondered—did your dad keep the bear pelt?"

Are you f'ing kidding me? I opened my mouth, but Heather jumped in.

"Randy! How's your mom's flower shop doing?"

Heather to the rescue. Randy smelled of Polo cologne and cigarettes. The sweet smoky smell made me feel sick to my stomach. I turned my head away and finished my beer in one go. Lily watched from the bar, her eyes on me as she served a guy with long grey hair and a red bandana.

Across the table, Chrissy had moved onto Chucker's lap, because, as she pointed out, there were no chairs available. Chucker pawed at her bare leg with one hand, his other holding his beer. Her mouth was peeled back into the biggest smile I'd seen in ages. Chrissy had always wanted to get married and start a family young, just like her mom had. She'd even chosen names for her first three children—Sienna, Mason, and McKenna, if they were girls, Colt, Jacob, and Marshall if they were boys. I caught her eye and smiled. She could do worse than Chucker.

"You know, I've got a new truck." Randy's breath came hot on my cheek. He'd moved his chair closer to mine.

"That's nice," I said. Usually, guys left me alone and focused on Heather and Chrissy when we were out. For one thing, most people knew Lily was my stepmom, or they knew who Dad was, or Radek.

The other bartender, Tina, a middle-aged woman with giant breasts, dropped off another round of drinks. At home, Lily called her Ta-Ta-Tina and made fun of the black socks and white sneakers she wore to work. "Doesn't even have the sense to put on a pair of cowboy boots," Lily always said.

Randy dropped a crumpled handful of bills on Tina's tray and said, "Keep 'em coming, doll." I cringed. I hadn't talked to him much, but I couldn't remember him being so off-putting.

Heather talked intently with an older guy I didn't recognize. Chrissy kissed Chucker. The drinks crept up on me. The room slanted and blurred and I shook my head to clear it. This was the part of drinking I didn't like. One of the parts.

Randy reached his arm around my back and rested his hand on my shoulder. I shrunk into myself, my shoulder blades involuntarily throwing themselves up to shield me from his touch.

"I like your tank top," Randy said. "Wanna dance?"

"No, thanks." I edged myself away from him. "I had a long day." I feigned a yawn. Heather and Chrissy would be mad if I broke up the party, especially given Chucker's sudden interest. They always complained I didn't understand how hard it was to meet guys in Jessop. "You have it easy. You met the man of your dreams before you hit puberty," Chrissy once said.

Cheers went up across the room. "Chug! Chug! Chug!"

Will stood on a chair a few tables away from us, drinking from a beer mug. Foam ran down the sides of his face and dripped onto his green T-shirt. I inhaled sharply. What was he doing here? My mouth felt dry. I took another sip of my drink, forcing myself not to smile as my stomach did back flips.

He hopped off the chair and slammed the empty mug on the table. A few of the other ranch guys clapped. Will said something I couldn't hear and pointed at Clarence. Clarence shook his head and laughed. I was surprised to see him out—he rarely came to the bar. I recognized two of the ranch hands from the Baileys' place. Had Will known I was coming here? Maybe Lily had told him.

"Who's that?" Heather asked, jutting her chin towards Will as he sat down at the table.

I shook my head, but she must have seen something in my expression. She stood and grabbed my hand, pulling me towards the washrooms.

Randy looked up at me. "Where you headed, sweetheart?"

I grimaced and followed Heather.

Heather cornered me against the back wall of the washroom. "Spill it," she hissed. A toilet flushed in a stall near us. My head spun.

"He's the new ranch hand." I tried to act calm, but my heart was racing. Why was he here? Ranch hands usually only came to the Red Lion on Saturday nights—there were generally fewer chores on Sundays. Many ranchers kept the traditional day of rest where they could.

"You didn't tell me he looked like that!"

I leaned my head back against the cool tile wall. "I didn't know I needed to." I rubbed my face with my hands. "What's the big deal?"

"He's fucking hot, that's what!" Two ladies rinsing their hands at the sinks giggled and looked at us. "Excuse my French, girls," Heather said. They waved as they left. "I saw your face," she said to me, when the door shut. "I saw the way you looked at him."

"I'm just surprised he's here."

"Bullshit." She rummaged around in her purse and pulled out a tube of lipstick. She turned to the mirror and opened her mouth to apply it. She pressed her lips together and pursed them, examining her reflection. "I've never seen your face look like that, not even with Radek." She put a hand on her hip.

"Yeah, well, Radek is dating someone," I said. I turned on the tap and stuck my head under, gulping cold water. I didn't care how many germs were incubating on that tap. I needed water.

"Come on!" Heather said, beside me. "Are you fucking kidding me?" Her eyes were wide with anger when I straightened up and wiped my mouth.

"He says it's 'for fun.'"

Heather capped her lipstick and dropped it into her purse. She put her hands on my shoulders and looked right into my eyes. "Well, fuck him."

My head spun again, sending the bathroom careening around me. I leaned into her palms and she straightened me.

"Seriously, fuck him. It's time for you to pony up on that promise you made me. I want my wild oat."

I gave her a pained look. Kiss another guy. Nothing about right now made me want to kiss another guy. Except possibly Will. Definitely not Randy Redding. I shook my head. *Don't think about Will like that, ever. Bad, bad, bad Hannah.*

. . .

WE WALKED BACK to the table together, Heather by my shoulder to steady me. "Let's talk about that stallion of a man who's hitting on me," she said, close to my ear.

"Stallion!" I laughed. "He's balding!"

"He's nice!"

15

September 1981

"YOUR DAD IS A MURDERER." Jimmy Bertram leans over the back of the bus seat in front of me. It's hot and I can smell the plastic seats. My feet are sticking to the floor where juice spilled. I look at Radek beside me, at the Velcro on my sneakers, at the granola bar wrapper under the seat. Anywhere but at Jimmy's face. I've heard kids say this before. Once I even heard Ms. Adams, the grade four teacher, talking to another teacher about it.

Jimmy is still leaning over the seat. His face is all scrunched and mean, like a cartoon bad guy, and his hair is sticking up. He had a Kool-Aid stain on his lip.

"He's not," I say. I open and close the clasps on my lunchbox in my lap and think about the bear. Daddy killed a bear. Only a bear. The thing happened to Momma by accident.

"My momma says he is for sure, and it's a crime the Mounties didn't get him."

My hands make fists over my lunchbox. I'll get in trouble if I am bad on the bus. The driver, Mr. Checkers, once kicked a grade five off the bus for saying a swear and throwing a sandwich at another kid. If I don't look at Jimmy, maybe he'll go away.

"Hannah's dad is a murrrrrderer!" he yells to the bus, turning to face the kids ahead of us. He twists back to watch my face. "Murrrrderer!" His spit hits me.

All of the other kids turn. My face is burning hot. My eyes sting. I press my hands together, trying hard not to cry. There is a noise like a smack, but hard. Radek is holding his hand and waving it around like it hurts, and Jimmy grabs his nose and starts yelling. His face is red and blood is running everywhere. Mr. Checkers yells: "What's going on back there?" And Radek says, "Nothing, Mr. Checkers." The kids go quiet. Jimmy doesn't look over the seat again.

AFTER DINNER I help Mrs. Bailey with the dishes. Mrs. Bailey hands me a dry plate and I carry it to the cupboard and put it on the stack.

"Mrs. Bailey?" I say.

"Mmm?" She is drying a bowl now.

"Is Daddy a murderer?"

She drops the bowl and it makes a splash in the sink that's filled for rinsing dishes. "Who told you that?" she says. Her voice sounds angry. She pulls the bowl out of the sink.

"Jimmy Bertram." I don't tell her Radek punched him.

Mrs. Bailey puts the bowl on the dish rack, wipes her hands, and comes to stand in front of me. Radek is downstairs watching TV. Mrs. Bailey said I could go with him, but I like helping her with the dishes. "Your daddy made a mistake—an accident," Mrs. Bailey says.

"But did he shoot Momma?" My shoulders relax when I say these words. I've wanted to ask for so long, since the day the bear came.

Mrs. Bailey kneels down and takes my hands. "He did, sweetie, but it was an accident. Don't you listen to any of those kids. Your daddy loved your momma more than anything."

Daddy and Momma used to yell at each other. Did Mrs. Bailey know about that? After Daddy left, I stopped counting the days since the bear came. I tried counting how many days Daddy had been gone for, but I gave up after thirty.

"Sometimes grown-ups fight," Mrs. Bailey says, like she can see what I'm thinking. "Your parents were in love but they were so different." She rubs the tops of my hands with her thumbs and then pushes on her knees to stand. "Besides," she says, turning back to the sink, "you can bet that if your dad did anything bad, that Mountie fellow—Harlon—he would have found out about it before he left for Billings. He sure seemed to like your momma."

"Where's Billings?" I asked.

"Far away, sweetie. Far away. Now go get washed up for bed."

 une 1996

WHEN I LOWERED myself back into the chair beside Randy my buzz had started to dissipate into exhaustion. The water had helped ease my head, but I ached for my bed, the warm quilt and cool sheets. I had to get up early the next day. Maybe if I stayed off the dance floor Will would leave without seeing me and I wouldn't have to face him. And I could escape Randy and his terrible cologne.

I turned to Randy and yelled over the music. "Where's Chrissy?" The band had turned up their amps—it had gone from a dull roar to obscenely loud during our bathroom visit.

"Out for a walk with Chucker." Randy pulled his lips back in what I guessed was a grin, but it looked more like a sneer.

Across the room, Will was deep in conversation with one of the other ranch hands at his table. Maybe he didn't even know I was here. Maybe he was trying to sell him weed.

Randy put his arm around my shoulders. I leaned forward to shake it off. Lily glanced over at me from the bar again and tilted her head before a man slammed a bill in front of her and she turned on her smile.

"I'm going to head home," I told Heather.

"No! Already?" She tapped her watch. "It's not even midnight!"

"Yeah! Stay!" Randy grabbed my hand under the table. His palm was hot and sweaty.

"I've got an early day tomorrow." I tried to pull my hand out of his grip and failed. "Tack cleaning day," I added lamely.

"You calling Georgio?" Heather asked. Georgio was an old guy who lived in town. He'd drive people home, even out to the country, for ten bucks, regardless of distance. He drove an ancient brown station wagon with wood panelling, the closest thing to a taxi Jessop had.

"He's out front," Will said. He stood beside Heather's chair. I'd been so intent on avoiding Randy's spidey hands, I hadn't noticed him approach. Heather twisted her neck to look at him. It was strange to see him in something other than work clothes. I felt light-headed, and this time I didn't think it was from the alcohol.

He nodded at the people around the table. "I'm Will."

Randy stood and shook Will's hand. Will didn't seem fazed by Randy's offering him his left hand.

"I'm heading home now if you want to split," Will said to me.

Yes, yes, yes. I wanted to be anywhere but there right then. But I couldn't leave with him. *You're not the kind of girl who gets rides home with random guys,* I told myself. Especially when they looked like Will. I wiped the palm of the hand Randy had held on my jeans and stood. "I'm fine. I might stay at Heather's," I lied. As if on cue, Heather turned to look at the semi-balding guy on her other side.

"You sure about that?" Will said. He nodded towards Heather and the guy, an amused look on his face.

"You're welcome to stay here, sweetheart," Randy said. He

moved closer, his damp hand finding mine once again. "I'd be happy to teach you a few dance moves." He grinded against my leg.

Before I reacted, Will shoved Randy, sending him flailing and struggling to catch himself before he fell over a chair. People turned to stare. Lily put her hand on a bouncer's chest, holding him back.

Randy scrambled up and faced Will, glaring. His friend, the bald guy, came to stand near Will but didn't make a move.

"We're going home now," Will said to Randy, his voice calm.

We? I glanced at Will, but his eyes were fixed on Randy's. He held his hands at his sides. Something about the way he stood made it clear this wasn't the first time he'd been in a bar fight.

Randy stared back, seemingly unsure of how to react. He straightened his shirt.

"Didn't know you had a boyfriend here," Randy said. Was I imagining it, or had he put emphasis on the word *here*?

I met Will's eyes. "He's not my—"

Heather cut me off, pulling me into a hug. "Call me tomorrow," she whispered in my ear, her hands clutching my neck a little too tightly in her drunkenness. She let go and pulled the balding guy onto the dance floor.

OUT FRONT, we found that Georgio had left with another passenger. "He'll be back in ten," said Frank, who sat on the curb. He was a skinny man, and he always wore a moth-eaten black trench coat. He'd lived in a small room beside the gas station forever. Rumour had it he'd fallen off a horse when he was in high school and was never quite right after that. "Have a cigarette?" he asked.

Will pulled out his pack and handed him three, swaying slightly. I'd seen him chug one beer, and I doubted that had been his first. He seemed less guarded, more open, even in the way he held his body; his arms hung loose at his sides and his eyes followed me.

I lowered myself onto the bench in front of the Red Lion and Will sat beside me. I didn't move when his thigh brushed against mine.

"Tell me about home," I said, brave from the alcohol.

Will leaned back and folded his hands together over his belt. "Dad runs a cattle ranch, Mom does the things moms do, and my brothers take care of the rest."

"How many brothers?"

"Seven."

"You're lying!"

"Yeah, I'm lying." He grinned. "Two brothers. Greg and Anders. They're older than me."

"So that's why you need to rodeo?" I rubbed my hands up and down my bare arms but couldn't get warm. I wished I'd brought my jacket. "You won't get the ranch?"

"Well, that, and I love the rodeo," he said, sitting forward and jiggling his leg up and down. "And . . ." He rubbed his chin. Stubble had formed there since I'd seen him in the barn that morning.

"And what?"

"And I'm not so good at staying in one place for very long."

"Huh," I said. The exact opposite of me.

"What?" He sat up straight and turned to face me, his thigh pressing harder against mine. He put his arm over the back of the bench, around my back. I didn't move away like I had with Randy. His warmth seeped into me, sending waves of heat through my body. We looked at each other for a long moment.

"Let me see your collarbone," I said, breaking the silence. I reached up and pulled his T-shirt aside so I could see the bone jutting out under the skin there. My hand left a trail of goose bumps across the small amount of his chest that was showing. I rubbed my thumb over the bone, Will's eyes on me.

The bar door opened behind us, releasing a cloud of smoke and music, and I let my hand drop. Randy and his friends tumbled out, pulling lighters and packs of smokes from their pockets. I slid lower on the bench, hoping they wouldn't notice us.

"Are you hiding?" Will asked, amused.

"Shh—no!" I hissed.

Randy spotted me as Georgio pulled to the curb.

"Does your boyfriend know you're going home with this guy?" Randy pointed at Will with the cigarette he was holding.

"I don't have a boyfriend," I mumbled.

Will let out a sound like air coming out of a tire and stepped to Georgio's window. "Got time to head out to County Road 7?" he asked.

Georgio leaned over to his open passenger-side window. He wore a newsboy cap and needed a shave. His white hair stuck out from under the hat. "Ten dollars," he said.

Randy moved closer. "Well if you don't have a boyfriend, why aren't you coming home with me?" He turned his head away and blew smoke out in big Os.

"That's enough, buddy." Will came to stand between Randy and me, forcing Randy to take a few steps back.

"So that's how it is," Randy said. He smirked. "I see."

Will took my arm and opened the car door for me. Randy watched from the sidewalk.

When Georgio pulled away from the curb, Randy gave us the finger. Will laughed. "I'm not sure about the company you keep, kid."

Kid? How old did he think I was? Anger coursed hot through my body. Just when I was starting to think he wasn't such a bad guy. I turned towards the window, conscious of how close we were in the back seat. Why did I even care what he thought?

We sped through town. Georgio drove fast—faster driving meant more money for him, and the cops seemed to give him a free pass. I think they were just glad he was sober. Once we left Main Street the car was dark and silent. Georgio never played music, even if you asked. The story was that Georgio drove people home because he'd lost his daughter in a drunk driving accident, but he never talked about it and no one could remember his daughter, so I wasn't sure if it was true.

Georgio glanced at Will and me in the rear-view mirror, raising a bushy white eyebrow. He pointed over his shoulder at the sign he'd duct-taped to the back of his headrest: *No funny business.*

"You see the sign?" he asked us. "Those are the rules."

"We'll do our best to behave," Will said, and winked at me.

My face turned red and I was grateful for the dark car. I pressed myself against the cool door and rested my head on the window.

17

*S*eptember 1991

AFTER THE GAME, Heather, Chrissy, and I waited in the parking lot by my truck. The girls wanted to go to Chucker's party. Lily and Dad pulled up, waving, and stopped to chat. "Don't be late," Dad said. Lily rolled her eyes at him.

Once the parking lot had cleared, Radek made his way over to us. His hair was wet. He wore a fresh blue shirt. Drops of water lined the collar.

"R.W.!" Heather said, too loudly, clapping Radek on the back. "Congrats on the game."

Radek shifted his bag on his shoulder. "Thanks."

"Nice run," I said. I moved my weight from one foot to the other, my feet like blocks of ice in my boots. Radek smiled his goofy smile.

"We'd practiced that play but I never thought we'd get to try it."

Sweat pricked itchy in my armpits despite my freezing limbs. Was that from the spiked Coke or because of Radek?

Chrissy grabbed Radek's arm. "Are we going to Chucker's place?"

"You girls can go if you want to. I'm beat."

Where was Olivia? Hadn't he promised he'd meet her there?

"What about you?" Radek looked at me. "You up for giving me a drive home, or do you want to go to Chucker's too?"

I raised an eyebrow. "Sure, I can take you." I didn't care about the party anyway. Before Chrissy could protest, Chucker sauntered over to the truck.

"R.W., good game, man." He clapped his hand into Radek's, shaking vigorously. "We've got high hopes for you this year. We might actually make playoffs. We need guys like you to carry the torch next year." Chucker was the size of a truck and had facial hair like a grown man. Chrissy, Heather, and I had spent our most recent sleepover at Chrissy's house talking about Chucker, and Chrissy had decided she'd marry him if he ever noticed she was alive. She stood beside me, her mouth wide in a grin, her frizzy blonde hair framing her face.

"Not going for grade fourteen?" Heather asked. Chrissy hit her arm, hard. Heather winced and rubbed the spot.

"Ha ha," Chucker said dryly. "You guys coming to my place?"

Heather and I waited a beat for Chrissy to speak, but she kept her mouth shut. Her eyes were wide, as if she were stunned by Chucker's mere presence.

"Uh, yeah," Heather said for her. "Can you give us a ride?"

Heather and Chrissy walked across the parking lot with Chucker. It was odd that Radek wanted to go home. He usually went to the after-game parties. For me, after-game parties meant hiding out in a corner, sipping from a can of pop, and waiting for Heather and Chrissy to be ready to leave. Radek threw his bag into the bed of the pickup and waited for me in the truck's cab. He rubbed the back of his neck as I got in.

"You could have gone if you wanted to," he said.

"No, that's okay." I pulled the truck out of the parking lot.

"Put your seat belt on," Radek said. I let out a groan, but clicked the clasp into the buckle at the next stop sign. The *click* was loud in the quiet truck. I wasn't used to being at a loss for words around Radek. Now I was thinking about whether my hair spray was still holding and if my jeans were tight enough. Maybe I should have worn the shirt Lily put out for me. Were guys into leopard print? Why had Radek pointed at me after he scored the touchdown? And why did it make me feel all jittery and weird? I tried to remember when I'd felt like this around him before, and a memory of us swimming in the canyon when we were twelve popped into my mind. I had a new bathing suit, and Radek had stopped and stared at me until I yelled at him to quit it. "You have boobs," he'd said, his mouth hanging open, like he was shocked I'd turned out to be a girl.

The cold turned to rain and then a sleety snow. The roads were slick. I thought about the Coke bottle with its warm sting and wondered how much was too much for driving. I had taken at least three sips, possibly more. The truck slid as I rounded the corner onto our road. Four ranches from home. I pushed the wipers into high speed to combat the snow and turned the heat up a notch, hoping to thaw my frozen feet.

Radek broke the uncomfortable silence. "I don't know how next year is gonna go with seniors like Chucker gone. We don't have many guys his size."

I slowed the truck as the sleet thickened. The wipers couldn't keep up. My head felt fuzzy in the hot truck.

Suddenly I was aware of how close we were sitting on the bench seat, of where he had his hands. Was he looking at me? I stole a glance at him across the cab. His damp hair was mussed up and sticking out in all directions, and I watched his mouth move as he talked about plans for next season. Maybe kissing him for real wouldn't be so bad. "Watch out!" Radek yelled.

The world went dark.

FLASH.

UPSIDE DOWN. Something warm tickling my face.

FLASH.

PAIN IN MY CHEST. Cold against my cheek.

FLASH.

RADEK YANKING on the truck door. His mouth moving, yelling.

FLASH.

QUIET SNOW FALLING.

June 1996

GEORGIO PULLED INTO THE LANE. The TV flickered blue in the living room. Will passed him a handful of bills and we stepped out of the car and stood in the laneway, watching the taillights disappear back down the road to town. I glanced over my shoulder to see if Dad was looking out of the window. Maybe he was asleep. He'd been more tired since he started taking the blood-pressure pills.

Will shifted and kicked at the gravel with the toe of his boot. I crossed my arms over my chest, more confused about who Will was than ever. I should thank him—for paying for the ride, for helping with Randy. I remembered his face, calm as he waited for Randy to stand. And then the way he'd said "kid" in the car. He was only looking out for me because Dad was his boss. Why did that bother me so much though? I stood straighter and forced my face into what I hoped was a neutral expression. Whatever the reason, I wasn't about to let him know.

"Well, have a good night then," I said curtly. "Wouldn't want to stay up past my *bedtime*." I turned on my heel and marched towards the house without looking back.

"Good night then," Will called after me. He sounded amused, which only made me angrier. By the time I'd gotten inside the house and closed the door behind me, my nostrils were flaring. I clenched and unclenched my hands. The living room was empty; Dad must have gone to bed. At least I wouldn't have to answer a barrage of questions about my night. I stood on the front mat, not sure what to do next. I wasn't tired—at least not in a way that would let me sleep yet. It seemed impossible, considering I'd barely slept the night before. I took a deep breath, inhaling the familiar scent of home: wood, Lily's perfume, and whatever leftovers Dad had heated up for dinner—pasta? And the not-so-familiar bar smoke in my hair and clothes. I leaned back against the door. *You are acting like a kid.* Will had been kind to help with Randy. Who knows how messy it would have gotten if I'd had to deal with that on my own. My head swam. What I needed was air. Fresh, cool air.

I pulled the door open and stepped onto the porch.

Will sat on the bottom step, as if he'd been waiting for me. *Dammit.* Why hadn't I looked out the window before I opened the door? Because I'd assumed he'd walk to the cabin, that's why.

"Not tired yet?" he asked. He looked over his shoulder at me. I was surprised he wasn't smoking.

"No . . . yes . . . What are you doing?" I snapped.

Will stood, turning to face me. He looked at me for a long moment. His eyes shone in the low light from the single bulb on the porch. "Let's go." I half expected him to add "kid." I didn't move.

"Where?"

He shoved his hands into the pockets of his jeans and looked at his boots. Was he smiling? Why was everything so freaking funny to him? "I'm not moving until you tell me." I folded my arms across my chest.

"Do you always need to know where you're going?"

"I don't see what's wrong with—"

He cut me off with a shrug. "Suit yourself." He took long steps towards the path to the cabin. "But now you'll never know."

I pushed an irritated puff of air between my lips and glanced behind me at the house. Dad's bedroom light was out. I didn't want to go to bed and stare at my clock, wondering what Radek was doing. Plus, the part of me that was still rational realized I needed to at least say thanks, no matter how much I didn't want to.

"Fine." I followed Will, stepping carefully to avoid rocks. The moon was half out so I could see a foot or so in front of me, enough to avoid bumping into him. Was he just bored?

"Do you like it here?" I blurted out before I could stop myself.

Will glanced back at me. "It's not so bad. It would be better if the rancher's daughter would stop being pissed at me all the time."

I let out a snort. "Who says I'm mad at you?" No way I was giving him the satisfaction of admitting I was in fact irritated with him most of the time. It wasn't all his fault, but since the day he'd shown up, nothing had been going right.

"Sure seems like it."

I ran my hands through my hair as I walked, trying to shake the smoke out of it. I tried to remember a time when someone had annoyed me the way Will did. This wasn't who I was—I was Hannah Tatum, nice girl, the girl no one noticed because she stayed out of everyone's way.

"I meant to say thank you for the Randy thing." I kept my eyes on my boots, pushing through the grass. "I don't have a lot of experience fending off men, for obvious reasons."

He slowed his pace until we walked side by side. "And what exactly does that mean?"

"It means I've only ever had one boyfriend. Well two, if you count Dennis Parker in grade six. We dated for two weeks and one day, long enough to hold hands at a barn dance. And long enough for him to dump me the first day back at school, after I refused to kiss him in front of a group of guys." Out of the corner of my eye, I saw Will smile. I uprooted a piece of long, dry grass and shredded it as we walked.

"What about your boyfriend? R.W. is it?"

I sighed and dropped the blade of grass. "That's complicated."

"Try me."

I did my best as we walked, telling him about Radek's plan for us to see other people, about how he'd only started doing that now, after two years. About how I didn't know what to do next.

"So you're taking a break," he said. We'd reached the cabin porch. I hugged myself to keep from shivering. The night air was cool, the sky above us almost entirely black. Clouds must have rolled in. For the second time that night, I wished I'd brought my jacket.

"I guess so. He definitely is."

Will waited, his piercing blue eyes on mine. I wanted to be able to explain this, to understand it myself.

"I guess—I guess I realized tonight it's real. He meant it. No matter what he calls it, when I break it all down and analyze it, I'm here by myself and he's with her." Images of Radek with a faceless girl flashed through my brain, like scenes from one of Dad's Western movies. Radek on a black-and-white screen, the picture faded and choppy. He's at the university pub, tipping a cowboy hat at a girl whose face is hidden behind her hair. Cut. He's in front of a movie theatre screen. His hand bumps the girl's as he reaches into her bag of popcorn. His head turns to the side and he smiles. Cut. He's running in slow motion, slamming down the football in the end zone and pointing into the stands at a girl who isn't me. Cut. He's leaning in to kiss a girl. Her hair covers her face; her long fingernails press into his neck.

I swallowed hard. And here I was, with a ranch hand who was hanging out with me because he felt sorry for me. "Anyway, this probably sounds stupid to you."

Will shook his head. "Why would it sound stupid?"

Because you think I'm a child. I pressed my lips together and shrugged.

Will put a foot on the bottom porch step and leaned against the rail. "Well if you want a guy's opinion, I think he's crazy."

My eyes widened. "What? You've never even met him."

"No, I haven't. But I know enough about you to know any guy who would take a chance at letting you slip away is out of his mind."

I had to stop my jaw from dropping open. I searched Will's face for evidence of humour, but there wasn't even a hint of a smile. His eyes were trained on mine, the most serious I'd ever seen him. I shifted to my other foot, not sure how to respond. "Is this where you were planning to take me?" I nodded my head towards the cabin. Why hadn't he just said that?

He smiled, walking backwards up the steps. "Not quite. Wait here."

I stood on the porch, watching the creek trickle by, my heart pounding in my chest. What had he meant by that? I'd never thought of it as Radek letting me get away; I'd only ever focused on the possibility he might meet someone else, the ever-present fear that he might not come home, that our plans might not work out.

Will was back in a few minutes, carrying a bottle of red wine. "Won this at a rodeo in Wyoming," he said. He set two chipped coffee cups on the railing beside me. I recognized them from when Radek and I used to play house. Will dug the cork out with his jackknife and poured the wine to the brim of each cup. He handed one to me and raised his. Wine spilled over my fingers as I lifted my cup to meet his.

"Should we cheers to something?"

"Hmm." He furrowed his brows. "How about narrowly avoiding bar fights with one-armed men?"

I let out a short laugh and tapped my cup against his. The wine tasted expensive, but I didn't know enough about wine to be sure. We stood at the railing and looked at the creek, neither of us talking as we sipped.

"What about you?" I said after several minutes. "You have a girlfriend? Or a wife or something?"

He swallowed the mouthful of wine he'd just taken. "No girlfriend." He held up the bottle. I nodded and he filled both of our cups again. "Come on." He set the bottle of wine and his cup on the rickety table and I followed him off the porch. He walked until he reached the aspen grove and paused, waiting for me to catch up.

"Can you hear that?"

We stood a few yards in from the edge of the wood. The tall, white-barked trees surrounded us. The air was even cooler here, fresh with the scent of grass and dirt and things that were real. Crickets sang around us and a light breeze swayed the leaves in the trees, but other than that: silence. "I don't hear anything," I said, frowning.

"Exactly." He tipped his head back and I followed his gaze. The night sky showed itself in pieces through the trees. "It's places like this that make me stop and wonder how I ended up here." He tilted his chin down and looked at me. "Do you ever think about that? How life is a series of choices? We choose to turn left and end up in one place, turn right and end up here." He swept his arm out and held it there for a moment before letting it drop to his side.

I looked around the grove. Had I made choices to end up here? It seemed less like choosing and more like fumbling along the path set out before me so many years ago. Being blown along like the leaves from the trembling aspens. I tried to remember the last time I'd done something unexpected, something out of the ordinary. This walk to the cabin was likely it. Maybe Radek was dating this girl because she *was* more fun than me. My eyes burned. I would not cry, not in front of Will again.

"You okay?" Will asked. He touched my bare arm. "Are you cold? We can go back."

My skin warmed under his fingers. I shook my head. "Did you know aspens have rhizomatic roots?" I asked.

Will scratched his temple. "No?"

"Mmhmm. It means they grow in colonies. The trees can live for, say, one hundred years, but the roots continue on, making more trees, long after the others have died. They continue on for thousands and thousands of years. They can get really big, but this colony hasn't because there usually isn't enough water." I looked towards the creek, my voice trailing off. Great. Now I was babbling about science.

"Never knew that," Will said. He looked at his feet, as if trying to see the roots below them, and then back up at me. Our eyes met. Neither of us moved.

Without letting myself think, I leaned forward and suddenly we were kissing, his hands running under the hem of my tank top, around my waist, igniting goose bumps wherever they touched. With an urgency I'd never felt before he kissed me harder. I fisted my hands in his shirt, pulling him closer. And then, just as suddenly, he stepped back, his hands still on my waist, holding me away from him, breathing hard.

We stood like that for a long time, breathing and looking at each other under the aspens, over the roots. I wanted to kiss him again. More than anything I wanted to do that again. I started to move forward and he stopped me with a shake of his head, firming his hands on my waist.

"What?" I said quietly. "You don't want to?"

He closed his eyes and shook his head. "Trust me, I want to." He took a deep breath and let his hands drop. My waist was cold where his fingers had been. "But not like this."

I wrapped my arms around myself. My voice sounded hoarse. "Like what?"

"I want it to be because you want to, not because you're trying to get back at your boyfriend—or whatever he is."

"You think that's what this was?" I stumbled backwards, away from him, and almost tripped over a fallen branch.

"Woah," he said, catching my hand. His voice was soft and deep, as though he were calming a spooked horse. I turned my face away so he couldn't see my eyes. "I know why I want to," he said, rubbing his rough thumb in circles on my palm. "I'm just not sure you do."

I grabbed my hand back and walked to the cabin, my face burning with humiliation. First, I'd acted like a child, then I'd tried to jump him in the woods. What kind of girl did he think I was? I could hear Will's footsteps, close behind me, not nearly as stompy or fast as mine.

I stopped by the porch and turned to face him, arms crossed once again. "It's late," I said. "I'd better go."

"Hannah—"

I held up my hand to stop him. Whatever he wanted to say to try to make me feel better, I didn't want to hear it.

"Fine. At least take this." He took the porch steps two at a time and was in and out of the cabin so fast I didn't have time to leave.

He came back down the steps and held out a faded green sweatshirt, its cuffs frayed, the words *John Deere* in bright yellow on the front. "You're freezing."

I took the sweater from him and walked into the field, forcing myself not to look back to see if he was watching. His words rang in my ears. *Not sure what I want?*

Well, he was right about that.

ay 1981

I SIT CROSS-LEGGED on the front porch. I'm drawing a tree, a barn, a Momma, and a Hannah on the biggest piece of paper I ever got. It's as big as my arms if I stretch them out. My paper flaps in the wind and I have to hold it down with one hand so I can draw with the other.

Momma stands on the lawn in her bare feet, her toes in the grass. She's talking to the man with a moustache who is dressed like the sheriff in my cowboys book. Momma tries to hold her hair back in the wind, but pieces are whipping around her face like a dark cloud. The man is tall—taller than Momma, and Momma is taller than Daddy. His big silver belt buckle is shiny in the sun. He has curly brown hair. He waves to me and then goes back to talking to Momma. I draw a tall policeman on the paper and add curly hair. Did he come to buy eggs? A horse? Daddy can't sell any horses today because he's in town at the garage.

The man steps closer to Momma and takes her arm in his

hand. The wind blows and I jump to catch my paper before it flies away. When I look back up, Momma has a big smile.

After the man leaves, Momma comes to see my drawing.

"Very good," she says, leaning in close. I smell her face cream, flowery and sweet.

"How come the policeman came?"

"He's my friend." Momma looks down the road, where the man drove away. "He's in the RCMP—they stop bad guys and keep us safe. Some of them even ride horses. Wasn't it nice that he brought you a sketchbook?"

I switch to a red crayon and fill in the barn. "Did he want eggs?"

Momma looks at me. Her eyebrows squeeze together, and she says, "Would you like a tea? Seems to me we missed teatime today."

Teatime means crackers, and juice in a special cup for me and warm milky tea for Momma. Sometimes she lets me have a sip.

"Teatime!" I say, trying to sound like Momma. Daddy says she has an accent, like the Queen, but to me she just sounds like Momma. I jump up and take my drawing into the kitchen. Momma tapes it to the fridge. Then she makes the tea and gets out the fancy cups.

"Tea for two." Momma holds her cup and lifts her little finger and wiggles it at me. I laugh and wiggle mine back.

Before dinner, I want to show Daddy my drawing but it's gone. "Blown away by the wind," Momma says, and smiles at me. She makes a zipper across her lips. Our secret.

2 0

 une 1996

THE SMELL of bacon and potatoes filled the house. My stomach growled. "Morning, sunshine." Lily smirked at me as I padded into the kitchen.

I rubbed my aching forehead and took the mug of coffee she handed me. Her car had been in the laneway when I crept into the house after leaving the cabin. Had she heard me on the stairs?

"Late night?" She turned towards the stove.

Lily had always been supportive of my relationship with Radek, although she was disappointed I hadn't dated more guys in high school. Unlike my friends' mothers, who wanted them married off by the end of high school and pregnant shortly after, Lily had always warned me not to settle too young. "You need to try on all the dresses and pick the best one," she'd told me. I pulled a chair out from the two-seater table in the kitchen with my foot and dropped into it.

"Late enough," I said.

"What was that kerfuffle with Randy and those guys?"

I took a sip of the strong coffee, wincing as it burned my tongue. "Nothing, really."

"And Will came to your rescue?" Lily turned from the stove, wiggling her eyebrows up and down suggestively.

I shrugged, but couldn't keep a grin from spreading across my face.

Lily laughed. "You be careful. I'm not saying don't. I'm just saying, be careful—"

Boots scraped across the front porch. The front door opened and Will appeared in the entryway. My stomach plunged.

"Will, right on time," Lily said. "Come grab a plate and a coffee."

Dad stepped in behind Will. I'd missed the morning feed and was sure I'd hear about it. But I had to sleep sometime.

"Thank you," Will said, as he walked into the kitchen in his thick grey wool socks. I focused on those, avoiding his eyes as he gathered his coffee and breakfast. In bed the night before, I'd stared at the crack in my bedroom ceiling for what felt like hours, wearing Will's sweatshirt and replaying the kiss over and over. And thinking about Radek. Waves of heavy guilt and light excitement churned in my gut. At least Heather had gotten her single wild oat.

"You're late," Dad said. Lily handed him a coffee and a plate of bacon and fried potatoes.

"Sorry." I moved from the two-seater to the dining room table.

"Too much of the hard stuff last night?" Dad looked more amused than angry. At least I hadn't missed the afternoon chores —those were usually harder on the body, and I wanted to keep Dad away from as many of those jobs as possible. He refused to listen to Lily's and my protests each time he went out to the barn.

"More than enough," I said, and glanced at Will. He focused

on his coffee. What would Dad think if he knew what had happened between Will and me? Likely nothing good. He'd been the closest thing Radek had to a father. I knew Dad wanted Radek and me to "stop messing around and get married."

Sitting across from Will, I kept my eyes on my plate. He probably regretted kissing me. Whenever I glanced up, he wasn't looking at me, not like the past few days at breakfast, where he'd catch me looking at him and smile. He focused on his food, his eyebrows furrowed. All the good thoughts I'd had about the kiss dissipated. Maybe it hadn't been as good for him as it was for me. Maybe he kissed girls like that all the time. Maybe he kissed lots of girls. I didn't know much about him. Did he kiss lots of girls?

Dad talked about the chores for the day, about how he wanted fly masks on all the horses in the paddock, about the colt he wanted me to break along with Whiskey, about the fence he wanted fixed.

"One of Bob Morton's cows all but ruined that fence. Again."

Lily laughed. "Don't be so dramatic! I saw it from the road the other day. It's barely down."

"Down enough," Dad mumbled. "We need to get this place in order. Fall isn't coming any later this year."

Air hissed through my gritted teeth.

"What? You thought I'd changed my mind?" Dad narrowed his eyes at me across the table.

"I swear I didn't pee in his cornflakes this morning," Lily said to Will, holding her hand to the side of her mouth dramatically, as if to tell him a secret. It did nothing to help diffuse the tension between me and Dad.

"If you'd just let me help, listen to my ideas—"

Dad lifted his hand to cut me off. "I told you. The decision is made." He stuck his fork into a piece of crispy bacon, splitting it into two.

Will cleared his throat across the table from me. "With all due respect, she has good ideas. The trail riding one is solid." I blinked at Will, my eyes wide. What. The. Hell. Was. He. Doing?

"Trail riding?" Dad growled at me. "At Stillwater? Ridiculous." He stood and pushed his chair out behind him. "Stop wasting time with your silly ideas and get back to work. You need insurance for that shit, lawyers, waivers. Did you think about that when you came up with your brilliant idea?"

I hunched further down in my chair. Why did Will have to say anything? Why couldn't he mind his own business like I'd been asking him to since the day he showed up?

Dad pulled his faded jean jacket off the hook by the door. "I'm going into town to talk to Marv about the alternator for Clarence's truck. Hannah, you can fix the fence with your biggest fan here." Dad pointed his thumb in Will's direction.

Will winced and rubbed the back of his neck.

"Sure," I said, my voice hard. Another plan good and truly trashed.

AFTER BREAKFAST, Will and I headed to the barn. We'd only gone a few steps before he spoke in a low voice.

"I'm sorry about that. I thought it would help . . ." His voice trailed off as he dragged his hand through his hair, pulling at it near the roots. "Fuck I'm sorry."

I lifted a shoulder and let it fall. In fairness, I had told him it was a plan Dad and I had talked about together. "You didn't know," I said. He opened the man door and stepped aside to let me pass. As my eyes adjusted to the low light of the barn, Will grabbed my hand. I inhaled sharply, heat spreading to my cheeks. He squeezed my hand lightly and I looked up at him. His eyes were trained on mine, waiting. *I'm not sure you know what you want.* I was just a little girl to him. The rancher's daughter. Probably one of many girls he'd kissed. If I kept telling myself that, my stomach might stop clenching every time

Will came within a square mile of me. I pushed my shoulders back and set my face into a blank expression and willed it to stop burning. I looked straight ahead, into the barn, not meeting his eyes. "What?" I said, trying to keep my cool. "I said it was okay."

"Okay, then," he said slowly, releasing my hand.

We didn't speak as we gathered the fencing tools and saddled the horses. But I still couldn't stop thinking about the way he'd kissed me. What *did* I want?

SKOAL KICKED up his heels and shook his head as we got closer to the back pasture: better grass and room to run. Will kept pace beside us, riding Duke, a thoroughbred we'd had for several years. Reliable but spirited, Duke was one of my favourite horses on the ranch. We rode quietly for a few moments, both of us keeping our eyes on the field before us.

"Have you ever told anyone to fuck off, right to their face?" Will asked, breaking the silence.

I glanced sideways at him. "No, of course not. Why would I ever do that?"

He shrugged. "I think you should try it. It might make you feel better." Was he talking about what happened at breakfast, or the kiss? If he thought I had a reason to be mad about the kiss then he definitely regretted it.

"No way."

"You realize you keep saying no to me, before you've even given me a chance?" He smirked at me from Duke's back.

"No I don't."

"You just did. And you said 'no' right away last night, when I asked you to go for a walk."

I glared at him and then sat up straighter in the saddle, lifting my chin.

"Go ahead, try it." He tipped his hat back on his head, rubbing at his sweaty hair. It was still early, but the sun was rising hot and fast.

"Right now?"

He let the reins drop to Duke's neck and held his arms wide. "Sock it to me. You know you want to." He sneered at me like the bad guy in a Western and I laughed despite my anger.

"That's dumb."

"I don't think it is," he said. "Try it. I dare you."

"I don't do dares."

"Perfect Hannah doesn't do anything that requires risk," he said. I sucked in my breath hard and turned my face away from him. Was that why Radek was with Fun Girl? Because she took risks? I'd always wanted to be more like those girls, the ones who were so sure of themselves, so confident. The ones who never worried about outcomes before trying something, the ones who danced by themselves in the middle of the floor with everyone watching. Girls who did things without a plan. Skoal shook his head and pulled at the bit. I pressed my heels into the horse's sides.

"Fuck you," I said, just loud enough for Will to hear. Adrenaline shot through my body, making my limbs tingle. He was right. It did feel good. I clicked at Skoal, urging him into a canter.

"Fuuuuck youuu!" I called. Will laughed behind me as Skoal and I moved across the ground.

By the time Will caught up, we'd broken into a full gallop. I lifted out of the saddle and pressed my chest close to Skoal's neck, enjoying moving across the ground with him, the sense of freedom blooming in my chest. Will and Duke kept pace beside us. Will was a good rider, better than most I'd seen.

"Come on, buddy." I gave Skoal a kick and aimed us towards the back corner of the field. Will hunkered down and sped by, despite my best efforts.

"Nice try," Will said, when Skoal and I trotted to a stop in front of him. He took off his cowboy hat and wiped his forehead with the back of his arm, grinning. "I thought you had us for a minute there."

"You were just lucky." I slid off Skoal's back and untied the tool pack from the saddle. I smiled, glad we'd shaken off the awkwardness, at least temporarily. It was silly, just a silly kiss. If Radek had kissed Fun Girl by now, maybe he felt like this too. *If.* Yeah right. I was sure he'd kissed her by now.

I was supposed to be with Radek—I wanted to be with Radek. Then why couldn't I stop the pang that went through my chest, stealing my breath, whenever I thought about Will? It seemed as though a bigger force were making it happen. Like the lambs that occasionally fell in the creek in the spring, their little legs helpless against the current; I was done for unless someone saved me or I bumped against the shore.

Will and I made our way along the fence, the horses grazing behind us, reins over their necks. I pulled the wire stretcher and pliers from the tool pack and kneeled beside the damaged fence. Dad had wound it around the post, but it wouldn't hold much longer. I untied Dad's temporary fix, attached the wire stretcher and locked it on, and worked the lever up and down. Will picked up the pliers.

"You going to let me do something?" he asked.

"Only if I need something done."

Will laughed and leaned against the fence pole, shaking his head. He took the wire stretcher from me when I stood, and we walked further down the fence line.

"So you're going back soon?" I said.

"Back where?"

"To rodeoing, travelling—whatever it is you normally do."

"Hope so." Will bent down and worked a loose wire until it pulled tight. He stood and brushed off his jeans. "Good as new."

The Jessop rodeo was only a month away. Would he enter? Maybe he wouldn't even stay that long. *If he was leaving, wouldn't he be the perfect person to sow more than one wild oat with? It would keep my mind off Radek, that's for sure*, I thought, looking at Will's T-shirt, drawn tight over his bulky shoulders. I tried to imagine what it would feel like to touch his chest, without his T-shirt covering it, sending a rush of blood to my face.

"I think that's it," Will said, after we'd repaired the third batch of droopy wire. Then he froze, his eyes on something across the field. "Look," he said, his voice low. He put his hands on my shoulders and turned me to face the tree line below the mountains. At first all I could think about were his hands, firm on my shoulders, but then I saw what he was looking at: two grizzlies rolling and chasing each other, swatting at each other's faces. It took me a moment to realize they were adults, not cubs.

"Don't see two adult bears together like that too often. Guess they must have lost their mother young." Will let his hands slide off my shoulders.

The bear, the shed, the blast.

Daddy hopping the porch rail.

Blood everywhere.

"You okay?" Will asked.

"It's my fault she's dead," I said. The words slipped out of my mouth before I had time to think it through.

"I thought . . . Wasn't she shot?" Will moved closer but didn't reach out to touch me.

I nodded. "Yeah, but it was my fault." I took a few steps and grabbed Skoal's reins. The bears disappeared into the dark woods. Why had I opened my mouth? I'd never talked to anyone about this before. Ever. I let out a long breath, steadying my voice. Might as well tell him. It's not like he'd be around long. "The day she died—when Dad saw the bear. I was sneaking candy from her purse. She used to keep these chewy mints in there for when I got squirmy at church." I patted Skoal's neck, rubbing my fingers in the dark hair matted with sweat. "She collected the eggs every day. Every single day. I was so worried about getting in trouble for the candy I forgot to remind Dad that she—" The words came out in a rush. Will reached for Duke's reins and pulled the horse behind him as he came to stand in front of me. His voice was low.

"That's not your fault, Hannah. You were a little girl."

I swallowed hard. "If I'd reminded Dad, everything could have been different. If I'd been good—"

"No," Will said, his voice firm. "No, it wouldn't." He reached his hand out and cupped my cheek, running his thumb along the thin scar under my eye.

I bit into my lip. So many years I'd believed that. How could I ever blame Dad for Momma's death when I was the one who could have stopped it? But now that I'd said it out loud, I realized how ridiculous it sounded. Everything had happened so fast. I couldn't have stopped it. Will let his hand fall to my shoulder. He squeezed and then let go.

We rode back to the barn side by side, not speaking. The sun was overhead now. Sweat trickled down my back and soaked through my T-shirt. Those bear cubs had lost their momma, and I'd lost mine. And if I'd known Momma was in the henhouse, wouldn't Dad have known, too? I needed to find this researcher. He might be the one person who knew more than I did.

$\mathcal{S}$eptember 1991

My tongue stuck to the roof of my mouth like Velcro. I opened an eye and looked around, not moving my head. A nurse with short brown hair spattered with bright blonde highlights appeared at my side.

"Stay still, hon. You've been in a car accident. Your neck is in a brace so you can't move." She pressed buttons on the machines blinking around me.

Pain pounded, dull behind my nose.

"Water?" I said, my voice raspy.

"Not yet. You've had surgery. This is the best I can do." She put a wet cloth in my mouth, and I sucked as fast as I could. The cloth dried on my tongue. I swallowed and opened my mouth for more. Needles and tubes ran into and out of my arms. My chest ached. I could only move my eyes, not my head, so I did my best to figure out what had happened by scanning the room. There were daisies in a mason jar on the shelf by the window, which made me think of Lily. They were her favourite flower. "Not lilies," she'd told me, when she first came to live with us. "That's way too predictable."

"You were in a car accident," the nurse said again. "You went off the road with your boyfriend." My boyfriend? I took a moment to figure out who she meant. I tried to sit up but she pushed me back down, gently but firmly.

"There, there," she said, in a practiced soothing voice. She had wrinkles around her mouth and eyes that made her look puckered and probably older than she was. She attached a new bag of liquid to the hanger beside my bed and hooked it into a tube going into my hand. I wanted to ask where Radek was, but a wave of tired hit me. I felt like I was floating in the water of the canyon, being rocked to sleep.

WHEN I WOKE AGAIN, Dad sat in the chair next to my bed, staring at me. Dark circles hung under his eyes. Who was taking care of the ranch? Where was Lily? Where was Radek?

"Hey now," Dad said, when he noticed me trying to sit up. "They've got you tied down so you can't do that."

Everything ached. My face and chest especially. But the real hurt was in the background, just below the surface.

"Where's Radek?" I asked. A flash of him trying to open the door of an upside-down truck passed through my mind. Was that a dream or was that real?

"He's across the hall. He's fine. The truck's not fine, but he is."

I heaved a breath into my chest, sending a sharp pain rippling through my body. Was Dad going to be mad about the truck?

Dad pushed himself out of the chair and limped to the bed. "You're going to be okay, too," he said. "Your face hit the side of the truck when you drove off the road but the doctor fixed you up last night. Says he put your nose and cheekbone back where they belong and you'll look about the same."

The tears tipped over and ran down my temples. I hadn't cried in front of Dad since I was ten and he told me he wouldn't teach me how to shoot a gun. I wanted more than anything to wipe them away but my hands were stuck.

Dad pulled a handful of tissues from a box by the bed and gingerly dabbed them against the tears. "Er, did that help?" he asked. "Look, I don't care about the truck. We'll find you another one."

"Thanks," I whispered.

"They want you to stay still until they're sure there's nothing wrong with your neck," he said, as if he knew how badly I wanted to move. He stood awkwardly beside me, looking out of place in his cowboy boots, big belt buckle, and worn jeans in the stark white hospital room. He looked rumpled, like he'd slept in his clothes. "You gave us quite a scare, Hannah." His voice trailed off and he squeezed my arm. "I thought—I'm just glad you're alive. You're going to be okay." Dad let his hand drop and looked away. Was he crying?

LATER THAT NIGHT, right before visiting hours ended, Lily pulled open the curtain around my bed. She fed me a few bites of the homemade mac 'n' cheese she'd snuck in before the nurse caught her and made her stop. "She'll likely throw it up anyway," the nurse said, leaning over me to check under my bandages.

"How do they look?" Lily asked.

"I've seen worse." The nurse smiled at Lily and left the room.

"I'll bring vitamin E for you tomorrow." Lily fussed with the flowers on the windowsill near my bed, rearranging them from largest to smallest. How had so many flowers been dropped off in such a short time?

"How did I crash?" I asked her, my voice still hoarse. I'd been trying all afternoon to put the pieces back together, but the nurses would only tell me I'd been in an accident, and to relax.

"You drove off the road and flipped the truck, sweetie." Lily came to sit at my side, taking my hand in hers. She looked at the lines running into my veins and held my fingers softly. "The truck flipped over a deep ditch in the Mortons' cow field. Thank goodness you had your seat belts on."

Fresh tears ran down my face, but Lily didn't seem to mind.

"You missed two oak trees and a fence post. Would you believe it? You're a lucky girl."

"And then what?" I swallowed hard. Everyone had told me Radek was okay, but what did okay mean? They kept telling me I was okay and I hurt so much. Everything hurt in a way I didn't even know was possible, a dull, all-over ache the pain meds couldn't touch.

"And then . . ." Lily stood and moved around the room, pulling at the curtain near my bed, smoothing the blanket over my legs. Her voice was soft when she spoke again. "Radek got out of the truck. His left leg was broken. He tried to pull you out, too, but the door had jammed shut, so he walked through the field on his broken leg —crawled really—and banged on the Mortons' door. By the time they got back to the truck, you had passed out. The doctors said if it had taken much longer you'd be dead. Your left lung is crushed—" My eyes widened and Lily patted my shoulder. "You'll be fine. They say it sounds worse than it is. It'll heal right up." Lily's eyes were damp. "You're lucky to be alive—we're lucky you're alive." She turned away, pretending to examine a machine by the window wall.

Radek had had to crawl on a broken leg to get help. Because of me. If I hadn't had that drink . . . "This is all my fault."

"No! No, Chickadee, it's not." Lily came back to my side, her hand squeezing my shoulder this time. It hurt, but I didn't ask her to stop. "It was an accident. An unlucky accident. Or lucky, considering you're both okay. Your chest will heal, you'll be well again in a few months. We'll make sure your scars aren't too bad. It's going to be okay."

That word again. *Okay.*

"And Radek?"

"He's going to be just fine."

THE NURSE CAME in to administer more pain meds, and I dropped off to sleep with Lily still at my bedside, working on a crossword puzzle.

TWO DAYS LATER, Radek wheeled his way into my hospital room. His broken leg was covered in a cast and stuck out in front of him. He grinned when he saw me sitting up in bed.

"They told me I couldn't see you until you were sitting up," he said, positioning himself so he could get closer to the side of my bed. "And here you are, eating Jell-O."

I'd asked to see him every time a nurse came into my room, but they always told me we weren't ready yet. There were already several signatures on Radek's cast—Clarence had signed it in thick black marker and scrawly penmanship, and I saw Chucker's name too. Had they come in to see me? The days since I arrived in the hospital had been a blur of people coming in and out, of being somewhere between asleep and awake. The Get Well balloons Heather and Chrissy had left at the nurses' station were tied to the drawer handle on the table beside me. A copy of the *Jessop Mercury* with a photo of my destroyed truck on the front and the headline "Two Teens Narrowly Escape Death" sat beside them.

"I'm glad you're okay," Radek said. He had a purple bruise the size of a baseball below his right eye, and he looked tired. "I thought I was going to lose you, Han." His voice cracked. "I tried to get you out, I really did."

I shook my head and put a hand up so he'd stop. I wanted to tell him how sorry I was, how this was all my fault. How I'd almost ruined everything. Would he even be able to play football anymore? I must have been drunk from whatever was in that bottle. How could I have done this to Radek?

"I'm so sorry," I blubbered. More tears. I squeezed my hands together in my lap, pressing them so hard my fingers turned white. Everything still hurt, but the bandages on my face covered the worst of the damage. The friendly nurse with the highlighted hair—Becca—had promised me she'd bring a mirror when they took my stitches out in a few days. *I deserve whatever I get.* Lily had been stopping by to rub my face with vitamin E oil and another potion she'd mixed whenever she could sneak away from work.

"Hey hey hey," Radek said, wheeling closer and angling his stiff leg so he could take my hand. "This isn't your fault. There was a storm, and that old truck wasn't great in the snow."

His hand was warm on mine and I squeezed it, hoping he could feel how sorry I was.

"All that matters is you're safe. You can get another truck. I can't get another you."

I wanted to tell him about the Coke bottle. But he smiled at me and looked oddly happy, given the circumstances, so I couldn't.

"What about football?" I asked, pointing at his plastered leg with my free hand.

"Doc says it'll take a lot of work, but I could be back playing as soon as this summer."

"You'll miss the playoffs."

He shrugged. "There's always next year."

I looked at the cast, reading more of the names. Heather and Chrissy had signed their names close to each other. And there was Olivia's signature too, written in pink marker with two neat hearts over the *i*'s. I guess she'd gotten over Radek's pointing at me at the game pretty fast.

Becca came into the room and shooed Radek out. "Time to check her vitals," she said. Radek turned his wheelchair around, joking familiarly with her as he wheeled away. He must have been awake longer than I had. He was okay. Radek was okay.

une 1996

THE NEXT MORNING, I was up and out of the house before anyone else. I'd told Dad I'd miss the morning chores because I had to help Heather set up her new apartment, and he'd seemed fine with it—Will was there to help him. I needed to get away from the ranch, to clear my head of the swirling cloud of Radek and Will, and to figure out what happened to Momma.

"No small task for a Saturday morning," I mumbled to myself as I started my truck. I pushed it into gear and followed the road into Jessop, but instead of turning left to go downtown, I drove straight. I had at least an hour to burn before the library opened. Momma was buried behind the church. Dad's family was from outside Bozeman, Montana, and he wasn't about to ship Momma's body back to England, where her mother lived, so he'd taken all of his savings and bought her a plot at the edge of the graveyard, under the shade of a broad fir tree. Dad had never told me any of this—Mere had been the one to answer my questions about Momma over the years. Why hadn't he buried her on Blueberry Hill? It was her favourite place to paint, as far as I could tell from the few paintings of hers Dad kept. Maybe he didn't want her ghost there any more than it already was.

I pulled the truck, new bumper in place but the windshield still cracked, into the church's deserted parking lot. The wet grass stained my boots as I walked through the graveyard. For the first few years after Momma died, Mere had taken me to visit the stone on the anniversary of Momma's death. She'd help me collect flowers from the field beside her house, and would say a few words of prayer after I laid them beside the grave, but at some point we stopped coming. I couldn't ever remember Dad coming with us. It never felt like Momma had anything to do with the cold, grey stone at the head of her grave anyway.

I stood in front of Momma's stone, careful not to step where I assumed she was buried, under the dewy grass. What did her body look like now, fourteen years later? Did she still have skin, or was she like the mummies I'd seen in our history textbook? Was her hair still clinging to her skull, ragged with age? She'd had long, dark hair—I remembered her brushing it, sitting on the edge of her bed. After she died I'd tried to commit to memory every little thing about her—the freckles on her cheeks, the way her eyes crinkled when she smiled at me, her crooked front tooth, the way she smelled like flowers after she took a bath. I'd lie in bed trying to create her from head to toe, begging myself to remember it all so I wouldn't forget her. But over time the memories had become fuzzy and frayed around the edges, and now I wasn't sure if how I pictured her in my mind was how she'd been, or something I'd made up.

The gravestone was simple, grey granite laid on the ground. Nondescript flowers curled around the edges of the lettering.

Elizabeth Cumberland Tatum
April 25 1945 – July 20 1981
Loving mother. Wife.

MY BREATH CAUGHT in my throat. Loving mother *period* wife. I walked along the row of stones, scanning the inscriptions. Most of them were names and dates—no extra information about who lay below. Some of the larger, upright stones had a few lines of poetry. One stone a row over read, "Loving mother, wife, nanna, and friend." I rubbed my hands up and down my arms, chilled despite Will's warm sweatshirt. I made my way back to the truck, weaving between stones. Another vehicle sat in the church lot— Mere's pristine Cadillac. I hurried to my truck, hoping she was already inside the church.

"Hannah?"

Shit shit shit. I turned, wiping the grimace from my face. She stood at the church's basement door, a tray of cookies in one hand, a ring of keys in the other. Her lips pursed together with a look of concern. "Are you okay?"

"Yes, I'm fine." I hurried to help her, taking the tray from her hand. She unlocked the door and opened it; the basement's musty smell floated up the stairwell. It felt as if I'd been caught doing something bad, like when I was eleven and the librarian caught me sitting behind the magazine rack at the back of the library flipping through a romance novel, looking for sex scenes. I tried to think up a reason for being there, but nothing came. I couldn't say I was there to see Momma, not after all these years, not when I'd never come by myself before. If I told her that, she'd want to know why, and I'd have to tell her about Dad, about the ranch, about the researcher asking questions. Mere's eyes moved over me. They landed on Will's sweatshirt. My face flushed. Would she recognize it wasn't mine? Before she could ask questions, I

149

walked down the stairs to the kitchen. "I've got to get going," I said, my voice reedy and strained as I moved through the dimly lit hallway. "Dad needs me back before lunch." A lie, but a harmless one. Or was it? Were there harmless lies?

"Oh, okay." Mere followed behind me, her long skirt swinging. I set the tray on the spotless counter in the church kitchen.

"Ladies auxiliary meeting today?" I asked, hoping to distract her. It worked. Mere talked for a few minutes about how they'd called an urgent meeting to discuss how to best support one of their members, whose husband was ill. She bustled about the kitchen as she talked, boiling water for tea and setting out cups. When she took a breath, I cut in.

"I've got to get going," I said again. For a moment, I considered asking her about Momma's gravestone. Had Dad ordered it or had she? "Chores," I added with a shrug.

"Always such a good girl." Mere came to stand in front of me. I crossed my arms over my chest, covering the John Deere tractor. Maybe she'd assume it was Dad's. She brushed back a strand of hair that had come loose from my ponytail, and let her hand rest on my cheek for a moment. "Your Momma would have been so proud of you," she said. Her eyes glistened like she might cry. I shifted in front of her. She knew I'd been at Momma's grave.

"Were Momma and Dad happy?" I blurted.

Mere raised an eyebrow. "Happy?"

"Yeah. In love." *Loving mother* period *wife.* Had she not been a loving wife?

The basement door opened and shut, and the sound of women's voices and shoes clicking along the hallway's cement floor rang out.

"Some things are best left in the past," she said, her voice low.

ALONE IN THE LIBRARY CARREL, I flipped through pages of the

Jessop Mercury from the month of Momma's death. Augusta Walker, the portly librarian with a big white goose stitched on her sweater, had found the right reel for me and set me up at the microfiche reader. I had no idea what I was hoping to find. I'd found one newspaper article announcing Momma's death, and her obituary; neither told me anything I didn't already know. Charges had never been brought against Dad, so I couldn't imagine there would be much else. I sighed and stretched my arms overhead, leaning back in my chair. Whatever had happened, I wasn't going learn the truth through a newspaper. Besides, as much as I tried to forget it, I remembered that day.

Long claws. The acrid smell after the shotgun goes off. Blood on Dad's face. I snapped forward, almost falling off my chair. I flipped the film back to the article announcing Momma's death and scanned it again. There it was. The RCMP guy's name. Harlon Schultz. Why hadn't I thought of that earlier?

BACK AT THE CIRCULATION DESK, Augusta sat with her back straight as a ruler, flipping through an issue of *Homes & Gardens*. She glanced at me over the edge of the magazine as I approached the counter.

"Need something else?" she said in her soft voice. She didn't look as if she minded the interruption. The library was empty except for a guy hunched over a low table with what looked like textbooks spread over it.

"Do you remember an officer named Harlon Schultz? RCMP?"

Augusta leaned forward. She was an ever-present fixture in the library, much like the wooden card catalogue that had been there since the library opened. She'd caught me with the romance novel so many years ago, although she wasn't as grey then. "You're really getting into your research," she said. "This is for a paper you're writing?"

"Yes." As if I would tell her I was trying to figure out whether my father had murdered my mother. In my third lie of the day, I told her I was working on a paper for a school application. I didn't even know if you had to write papers for school applications, but she seemed to believe it.

She set the magazine down and came around the desk to stand in front of me. "He left town after . . ."

After Momma died.

"Do you know where he went?" I asked. I tried to remember what Mere had said. Somewhere in Montana.

"Billings."

I nodded. "Thank you." I hoped she wouldn't tell anyone I'd been asking.

"You aren't the only one researching this, you know," she said. My whole body stiffened. The student—the researcher Lily had mentioned. Of course he'd been to the library. "That fella over there is too." I followed her finger as she gestured towards the guy bent over the books. He looked up, his eyes scanning the nearly empty library. He noticed us staring at him and gave a short wave.

Now that I was paying attention, I couldn't believe I hadn't taken note of him sooner. He looked woefully out of place with his smart suit jacket and thick-rimmed black glasses and longish hair that looked as if it hadn't been brushed in days—not like someone from Jessop at all. I thanked Augusta and walked to his table, my heart pounding. I stood before him, suddenly realizing I had no idea what to say.

"Can I help you?" he said, looking up at me. He sounded younger than he looked. Tentative, maybe a little bit afraid. It helped.

"I'm Hannah," I said. I pulled out one of the padded chairs at the table and sat, careful not to disturb any of his books. The table and chair were so low I felt like I was chewing on my knees.

"Hannah Tatum," I said. His eyes widened and he cleared his throat.

"Look, I mean no harm. If your father sent you—"

I cut him off with a wave of my hand. "Just tell me why." Might as well get right to the point. We were far enough away from the circulation desk that I didn't think Augusta would be able to hear us if we kept our voices at a reasonable level. Why would he be looking into Momma's death? There had never been a court case, charges, anything. How did he even know about Momma?

I listened as he told me about his PhD dissertation. He was studying psychology, planning to become a doctor. His name was Roger.

"Uxurocide?" I repeated after him.

Roger shook his head. "Close. Uxoricide. Killing one's wife." His cheeks reddened. "I found out about your mother while digging through newspapers. It's an exceptional case . . ." His voice trailed off and he looked at me, his serious brown eyes meeting mine. He pushed his glasses up on his nose. "Not many of these cases involve a bear. None of them, in fact."

"But it was an accident," I said firmly. *Please say yes.*

He shuffled the papers in front of him into a neat pile and nodded. "So everyone says."

I opened and closed my clammy hands at my sides, wishing I could rub them along my jeans without him noticing. "You've been asking people?"

"Er, yes." He shifted, and pulled at his collar, as though it were too tight. "I was trying to find the investigating officer, the one who worked on your mother's case. But he's long gone."

"Harlon." Flashes of the tall sergeant with curly brown hair flitted through my brain. *The Mountie on our lawn, touching Momma's cheek. The Mountie behind the barn with Momma, giving me his badge. The Mountie at the wake, asking me if I knew where Momma had been that morning.*

153

"Anyway, I can't use your mother's case for my paper. I'm analyzing uxoricide committed by men with previous offences. I may even have to expand it to include all intimate femicide." He noticed the look of confusion on my face and continued. "Cases where women were killed by intimate partners—boyfriends, lovers, ex-lovers—not only husbands."

"That's really interesting." I liked that he was talking to me as if this were a topic I could understand, something I'd know about. Dissertations. Papers. PhDs.

Augusta rose from the circulation desk and disappeared into the stacks, pushing a cart of books ahead of her.

"Do you go to school?" Roger asked.

"No." I crossed my arms over my chest. What would a scholarly guy like Roger think about me, a girl who'd done nothing since high school?

"Do you want to?" His eyes were kind, his face pleasant. I paused for a moment before answering.

"I used to want to." I told him about Lily's memory book, about how I'd always wanted to be a scientist. "A biologist, or a botanist," I added.

"They have scholarships. That's how I started. That's how I'll finish, too, if I ever get this dissertation done. Did you have good grades?"

I let my hands drop to my lap and nodded. Straight As. Not that it had helped me with ranching, or saving the ranch. Had Roger's asking around made Dad worried the investigation into Momma's death would be reopened? That seemed far-fetched, after so much time. But it would explain why he wanted to sell.

"Did you talk to my Dad?" I asked Roger.

He rubbed his eyebrow and grimaced. "I tried."

"You're a brave man," I said, smiling. "What happened?"

"He threatened to shoot me if I didn't get off his property."

"Sounds about right." I grinned, imagining Dad with his shotgun out, standing on the porch. It wasn't the first time I'd heard of him chasing away a visitor with a threat like that. There was a reason we didn't get calls from religious types or knife sharpeners or travelling salesmen. And a reason he didn't want me running a trail riding business. Dad wasn't fond of visitors.

Roger glanced at the faded leather watch on his wrist. "I've got to get going. I'm due back at the university for class on Monday."

I waited as he gathered his papers and put them into the briefcase beside him.

"It was nice to meet you," Roger said, holding out his hand.

I shook it, noting how soft his skin was. "Not a day of hard work in his life," Dad would have said.

"You too."

He walked a few steps and then turned back to face me. "Hannah?"

"Yes?"

"Do you think he did it on purpose?"

I blinked. No one had ever asked me directly. They'd called him a murderer, told me he killed her, assured me he hadn't, asked about the bear and the henhouse and the eggs and the weather—everything you could imagine. But in all the years since Momma's death no one had ever asked me if I thought he'd done it on purpose, as though I might have known what had been going through his mind that day. Part of me wanted to tell him to fuck off—Will was right; it did feel good. Part of me wanted to ask him what he thought. Another part of me wanted to cry. Instead, I shook my head and walked away, drawing my shoulders in to protect my heart.

ay 1981

MOMMA GIVES me a cup with red Kool-Aid and a bendy paper plate with a hot dog in a bun. "Go find Radek." She smiles and pats my hair. My momma is the prettiest momma at the party. Her dress is blue like the sky and has white buttons down the front and white lace at the top. She let me brush her hair today in her bedroom, and then she gave me two squirts of perfume.

Radek is sitting at the kids' picnic table. "You smell like an old lady," he says. I stick my tongue out at him. All the other kids are done eating. Their plates and cups are all over the table. I don't want to get Kool-Aid on my dress so I sip carefully.

The grown-ups sing to Mrs. Bailey: "Happpppy birthdaaaay to yoooouuu." When we're done hot dogs, we wait in line to get cake. Momma and Daddy stand with the other grown-ups. The cake has white icing and blue letters. Mrs. Bailey puts a slice on my plate. "A sweet piece of cake for a sweet little girl," she says, and tickles my belly.

"How old is your momma?" I ask Radek when we get back to the table.

"Older than your momma," Radek says.

The sky is getting black now. The grown-ups are louder and a few are dancing and they are all drinking out of red cups but I don't think it's Kool-Aid. Radek and Brandon Morton and I play cops and robbers. I am the cop and they are the robbers. They rob my pretend store and I pretend I'm in a police car and I *vrrroooom* after them. Radek heads away from the people and behind the barn, yelling, "Catch me if you can, copper!" I make my legs go fast.

"Hannah!" Momma yells as I zoom by. "You scared me!" She is standing with a man behind the barn—the RCMP man I saw on the lawn. He's the *real* police.

"I'm a pretend police," I say. "Radek's the robber." I point to where Radek ran off, towards the water troughs. "I gotta find him."

"Well he's not back here, kiddo," the man says, leaning against the barn. Momma's face is all red, but not like a crying red.

"Look at your party dress," she says. "Mud everywhere."

Momma brushes at the stains. I had to do a slide to catch the robbers the last time they robbed my store. I pull away from Momma. The man tugs at his moustache and then reaches into his back pocket.

"You want to look like a real police officer?"

I glance at Momma and then nod.

He hands me a metal badge attached to a wallet, like the ones the police have on TV. "You be careful with this—I need it back." Momma smiles at him, a big smile with her crooked tooth showing. I only see Momma smile like this when she gets a letter from England.

Momma pats my bum. "Well you'd better go catch those robbers."

I hold the badge in my hand and walk to the water troughs. Radek is lying on the ground behind them.

"Why's your momma talking to the RCMP man? Is she in trouble?"

I hold out the badge. "You're under arrest, robber!" I say. The wallet is warm in my hand from the policeman's pocket.

"Woah!" Radek jumps to his feet and tries to grab the wallet, but I hold it high where he can't get it. I'm only a little bit taller than him, but it's enough.

"Let me see!" he whines, but I run off. I'm faster than Radek, so I make it back to the parents before he can catch me. Daddy is standing with Mrs. Bailey, so I go beside him and wrap my arms around his leg. I want to tell him about the badge but they are talking about the hay harvest and I know Daddy will get mad if I interrupt. Finally Daddy looks at me when I squeeze his leg harder, and I let go and hold out the wallet, flipping it open so he can see.

"Look, Daddy!"

Daddy's eyes go small. He's not excited I am a real police. "Where did you get that?" he says.

"From the RCMP man," Radek says, coming up beside us.

Mrs. Bailey's mouth turns down. "Let's get you two cleaned up for bed." She takes the badge from me and puts it in her dress pocket and then takes our shoulders and pushes us towards the house.

Daddy stays in the same place, staring at the campfire.

AFTER IT GETS DARK, all the little kids who are sleeping over go in Mrs. Bailey's bed. "Time to sleep," Mrs. Bailey says, and she turns out the light. We're on top of the grown-ups' jackets. I find Daddy's brown jacket that he only wears for visiting and pull it over me. I put my hands in the pockets and sniff his barn and soapy smell. I'm almost asleep, but then—

Yelling.

I sit up. Poke Radek with my fingers.

We go to the door and creak it open. The window at the end of the hall is lifted, so we press our noses against the screen so we can see out to the backyard.

"Your daddy is mad," Radek whispers.

Daddy waves his arms and yells, but I can't hear all the words so far away and with the music still playing. The grown-ups are standing in a circle around the fire pit. Momma is across from Daddy, her hand on her heart place.

"I saw you with him!" Daddy yells so loud the music doesn't matter.

With who?

Momma shakes her head and hugs herself with her arms. Mrs. Bailey puts her hand on Momma's shoulder.

Momma says something and Daddy moves towards her. Men grab him. "Hey hey hey," a big man in overalls says. It's Mr. Morton who has the cows. "Let's go have a breather, Luke."

Where's the policeman? Maybe he could fix things. I hope Mrs. Bailey gave him his badge back.

Radek and I stand in the hall. "When we get married, I won't yell at you," he says, and he holds my hand. I usually don't let him, but this time I do.

ctober 1991

"Lunch time!" Mere called from the kitchen. Radek and I pulled ourselves up from the couch. I moved with more ease and my scars had begun to heal. The accident had broken my nose and cheekbone and cut a long slice over my left eyebrow and a deeper, shorter slice under the same eye. The cuts were clean, though, and thin. My breathing had returned to normal. Who knew a collapsed lung would heal faster than cuts?

Radek balanced himself with his crutches as I turned off *The Price Is Right*. We'd been off school since the accident, over three weeks. The doctors said we could both go back after the Christmas break. Radek had broken his leg in three places; the doctors screwed it back together with a plate. They told him if his leg didn't heal well, he might not play football again. "Of course I'll play again," he'd said. "What else would I do?" I believed him. Mere drove him two towns over once a week to see a therapist who helped him strengthen his leg, even as it pulled itself back together. I never went with them. They never asked, and I couldn't bear the thought of watching Radek in pain, trying to fix something I'd broken.

Mere had set out two bowls of tomato soup and greasy BLT sandwiches and then left to go into town to rent a movie for us.

Radek finished his second sandwich then hobbled to the fridge using one crutch. He took out the two-litre jug of whole milk and tipped it into his mouth while leaning against the counter. He wiped his mouth with the back of his hand. "Back to the couch?"

It was my fault this had happened. My fault Radek might not play football again, my fault my truck was toast, my fault my face might be scarred forever. My fault Dad looked so sad. It was ridiculous to be dwelling on it, but I couldn't stop.

On the couch, I shimmied over to make sure there was distance between us. Since the accident, we hadn't talked about Olivia or anything to do with school. It wasn't that we were avoiding it, but between making sure Radek had time to get his physiotherapy exercises in and being immersed in the day-to-day of the Baileys' ranch (not that we were doing any chores), school and Olivia didn't seem to be important. Our teachers had been understanding—we'd be given the grades we had when the accident happened and would start school fresh in the new year. It seemed as if we'd gone back to normal, as if Radek had never rested his legs on my lap, or acted weird when we were together. I wasn't even sure why he was still my friend, after what I'd done. I was surprised he'd even talk to me, let alone spend all of his time with me.

He gave up changing channels and left the TV on a soap opera, the only thing on besides the weather. I tried to force myself to stop thinking about the accident, so I wouldn't cry. Tears ran down my cheeks anyway.

"Hey," Radek said, putting a long arm around me and pulling me into his shoulder. "Come here."

I let myself lean into him. He smelled like fresh laundry detergent and milk. I dried my cheek on his shoulder and let the warmth of his arm soothe me. He used his free hand to tip my face up to his. My stomach flipped. We didn't touch, not unless we were wrestling or goofing around, and not like this.

"It's not your fault," he said. "You've got to let it go." We'd had this conversation almost every day since the accident, but I'd never told him about the Coke bottle.

"But it is." The words brimmed, desperate to come out. "I-I was drinking that night."

"What do you mean?" His eyes turned serious.

"Chrissy's sister's friends were passing around a Coke bottle. It was spiked with something. I drank it."

"How much?"

"I don't know how much was in it." Fresh tears poured down my face. I couldn't meet his eyes.

"No, I mean how many sips?"

"Maybe three? Definitely two."

Radek leaned back, his face breaking into a smile, the tension eased. "You can't get drunk from a few sips of alcohol in pop."

"But what if it was strong?"

"Even if it was strong."

"This is all my fault." I pointed at the cast on his leg, resting on the coffee table.

"Bullshit. There's no way you were drunk. I was with you—you weren't even close to being drunk. It was an accident. It's not your fault."

I winced and bit my lip, squeezing more tears out of the sides of my eyes. I'd taken the bandages off my face to let the cuts heal, but I was all too aware of the itchy red line under my eye.

Radek ran his fingers over my face, wiping the tears away. The bruise on his cheek had faded and he looked like himself again. Our eyes met. And then it happened so fast. He leaned closer and I closed my eyes and his lips touched mine. He kissed me gently but confidently—nothing at all like our kiss behind the barn in grade six.

I stopped and pushed him away. "What about Olivia?"

He shrugged. "What about her?"

"You're sure you don't blame me?"

"I don't blame you." He grinned beside me on the couch.

The belt of worry that had been wrapped around my chest since the accident loosened a notch. He leaned over to kiss me again, and his cast-covered leg slid across the coffee table and knocked off an empty bag of Oreos. We both laughed. This time I kissed him back.

"I ONCE READ an article in a magazine about what happens to kids who lose their parents young," I said.

Will stuck his shovel into the ground and stood straight to tip back his hat and wipe his forehead. We'd been fixing the irrigation ditch in the field closest to the house for days. The rain had started the afternoon I got back from the library and hadn't let up for three days, causing minor flooding near the creek and taking out part of our irrigation system. My wrists and arms ached at night from the shovelling, and the blisters under my gloves had burst into bloody sores. The extra work had meant extra time with Will—time we'd spent quizzing each other about our lives, talking about anything to keep our minds off the work. And each other. "Oh yeah?" Will said.

I nodded, my eyes trained on the ditch in front of me. "It said losing a parent at a young age changes a person at the cellular level, like your actual bones and brain change."

"You think it changed you?"

I dug into the wet mud with my shovel, ignoring the pain in my hands. "I don't know." Will waited for me to say more. "Sometimes I wonder what I'd be like if she were still here."

"Do you miss her?"

I stopped shovelling, considering.

"I don't remember much about her, only a few things, little stories and stuff." I took a deep breath. "I think she might have been having an affair." My shoulders slumped forward. Saying it out loud sent relief flooding through my tired limbs.

Will leaned against the shovel's handle, his eyes trained on mine. "How come?"

"Well I remember a few things, little snippets of her and this friend she had—an RCMP officer."

"Shit."

"Yeah." I picked up the shovel again and rammed it into the muck, sending a shock of searing pain into my hands.

"Where'd the guy go?" Will asked.

"Billings."

"Have you tried to find him?"

I threw a shovelful of dirt over my shoulder. "No, that's crazy. Momma died years ago. I can't go stalking a random guy based on these childhood memories I have." *But what other lead did I have?*

Will shrugged and picked up his shovel and started back at the ditch. "You want answers, don't you?"

I took a swig out of the water bottle we'd brought with us. The sun was high in the afternoon sky, pounding down on us. The grass had turned green again, thanks to the rain. Everything was more vibrant, alive. I watched Will's bare back as it strained with the effort of lifting the heavy mud. He'd stuck the tail of his T-shirt into the waist of his jeans to keep it from getting soaked with sweat. I swatted at a fly that buzzed around my face. Digging irrigation ditches was my least favourite chore. Having Will with me made it a whole lot more bearable.

"Do you want to go to the rodeo with me?" I asked. The Jessop rodeo was a week away. I went every year, usually with Radek. But he wasn't here. And I hadn't talked to him in ages. *Likely hanging out with Fun Girl*, I thought bitterly.

Will stuck the shovel into the muck by his feet and looked at me. I could have sworn he looked surprised.

Why was he taking so long to answer?

"We could go on the Saturday or something," I continued. My stomach rolled. Ever since the kiss I'd been wracking my brain to come up with reasons not to hang out with Will. I'd even gone as far as calling Heather and telling her about the whole thing.

"He doesn't think of you as a little girl, you doofus," she'd said over the phone when I'd called her the night before. "He said he didn't want to hook up with you if you weren't sure. Basically, he's telling you he's a good guy. I swear, for a smart girl, sometimes you analyze yourself into a corner. Remember what Mr. Simpson said about assuming?"

"It makes an ass out of you and me," I'd mumbled into the phone receiver. "Okay. Fine." It was serious when Heather was quoting Mr. Simpson—she hated grade twelve bio.

Being around Will more was only part of it. Radek had stopped calling. We usually spoke at least once a week, but I hadn't heard from him since the conversation at his mother's house. I fanned my shirt, trying to bring cooler air onto my sweaty stomach.

"Yeah," Will said. "I'd like that." He picked up the shovel again. "It's the guy's job to ask the lady out on a date though." A date. He called it a date. Maybe Heather was right.

I laughed, my aching hands forgotten. "Well, if the guy takes too long to ask, the lady needs to take matters into her own hands."

. . .

AFTER DINNER THAT NIGHT, Dad and Lily went over to Mr. Morton's for a visit. Will and I sat on the porch alone. He smoked while I rubbed Mickey Two's belly with my bare toe. We talked easily about the ranch, what we needed to work on the next day, the horse that'd gone lame but was recovering nicely. In a movement that had become familiar over the past few weeks, Will stubbed out his cigarette in the sand-filled planter and stood, stretching his arms above his head and letting out a breath. "What do you say we go for a walk?"

"Okay," I said, unable to bite back my smile.

"Mind if I use your phone first?"

Will had never asked to use the phone before. Most ranch hands called home once a week or so, to let their families know how they were doing or when money was coming. But never Will.

"Sure." I pointed towards the kitchen and then realized Will would of course know where the phone was by now. He nodded and walked inside the house. I waited, and then heard only a low murmur. He didn't want me to hear what he was saying. Who was he talking to? He'd told me snippets about his parents (wealthy ranchers), his brothers (one a rancher, one a lawyer), how he'd gone to boarding school, a few of his adventures on the rodeo circuit, but nothing else about his past. I didn't even know if he had plans to go back to Nevada after the summer.

"You know I can't do that." Will's voice rose. I craned my neck to look in the door and then snapped myself back into my chair before he saw me. It was like I was eavesdropping on one of Dad and Lily's fights, like the one they'd had the night before. They'd had a few drinks after dinner, and by the time I got back from the barn they were yelling at each other full tilt. I'd asked Lily about it in the morning—she told me she'd put her foot down about Dad marrying her and he'd flat-out refused. "I even told him we

168

could just go to the courthouse," she said. "I'd give up the big, fancy white wedding. But no. He won't budge."

Mickey Two stood and scratched at the door, whimpering.

"Come here, boy," I said. He looked back at me but didn't move. Will's voice rose again, but I couldn't piece together what was going on by the small bits of the conversation I caught.

"No, I told you—I don't know why you won't let me see . . . We already tried that. I know he—"

Will cursed and then there was a thump and a smash of glass. I stood and opened the porch door, and Mickey Two ran into the kitchen, head down and tail wagging nervously. Will picked pieces of glass off the floor.

"Stay there," he said to Mickey, pointing at the doorframe. The dog stayed.

Will turned to face me. "Sorry about that. I'm a fuck-up." His face was red but he looked more sad than angry. "I knocked one of Lily's glasses off the counter."

"That's okay, it's an old glass." I opened the door to the cupboard under the sink and pulled out a plastic grocery bag for him to drop the shards into. I wanted to ask who he'd been talking to, but didn't. "Are you bleeding?" I said.

He held up his hands to show me, as if he were surrendering to the police. No blood.

"I hit the counter and the glass fell off," he said. "Stupid."

"You're not stupid." I tied the top of the grocery bag, dropped it into the garbage can, and grabbed the broom and dustpan from the corner. Will kneeled down to pet Mickey to keep him still as I swept up the remaining bits of glass. When I turned back after replacing the broom, Will's eyes looked darker.

"Do . . . do you still want to go for a walk?" I asked.

"I think I better skip it." Will stood and gave me a weak smile. "I'm going to call it a night before I make any more mistakes."

I stared at him, unblinking. Was I a mistake?

"Shit, I didn't mean it like that. I can't do anything right today." He rubbed his hand across his forehead, pressing at the lines of tension there. "Why don't you come down to the cabin? We can have a fire."

WILL HAD ALREADY SPLIT several pieces of wood and piled them on the cabin's porch, so it didn't take long for him to get the fire started. I sat on a log by the fire pit while he stacked the wood into a teepee shape and then used little sticks, dried leaves, and his Zippo to light the logs. The sky had darkened to a bruised purple, and the stars were starting to prick their way through the clouds.

Who had Will been talking to? He'd changed his mind so quickly about hanging out with me. He stopped poking at the wood and sat on the log beside me, then opened his hands to the fire to warm them. I wanted him to reach his arm across my shoulders or grab my hand. I hadn't come any closer to figuring out what to do about Radek—but Radek felt so far away. Besides, he was the one who'd said we should see what else was out there. I wasn't doing anything wrong by thinking about Will, was I? I wanted to be the kind of girl who would have a summer fling with a guy like Will. Deep down I knew that wasn't me. Why couldn't I convince my body of the same thing?

Will cleared his throat. "Look, about that phone call . . ." He looked straight at the fire, but I watched him out of the corner of my eye. I felt like I'd known him forever, or before, even though he was one of the only people I knew who wasn't from Jessop—and even though I knew so little about him. He seemed to understand me.

"I guess things are more complicated back home than I've let on," he said.

Hot fear shot through my belly. He'd said he didn't have a girlfriend. All these weeks I'd been worrying about Radek. Maybe

Will was worrying about a girl back home. "You can tell me," I said, my voice quiet with dread.

"I don't want to. I like what's going on here." He used a long stick to push at the logs in the fire. "Whatever that is." He smiled at me and my breath caught in my chest.

He liked me. I wasn't imagining it. He wasn't being nice to me only because I was the rancher's daughter.

"I'm not a great guy," Will continued. "If you knew more about me . . ." The fire let out a loud crackle as a log split, and I jumped a little.

"That's not true."

"You can't say that without knowing what I haven't told you."

"Well then tell me and let's see."

He leaned forward, his elbows on his knees, shaking his head. His hair hung around his face, the firelight casting flickering shadows so I couldn't make out his expression. "Fine. I was arrested once."

The weed. Was he going to tell me about the weed? I'd tried not to think about the coffee tin the past few weeks. From everything I'd seen of Will, he didn't seem like the kind of guy who was a drug dealer, but what did I know about that? Will stood and adjusted the logs again.

"For what?" I asked, squeezing my hands together in my lap.

"Mischief. My brother Greg and I threw a whole basket of eggs at an old guy's house. He'd backed out of a deal with my dad that cost us a bunch of money."

"How did that possibly get you arrested?" So not the weed.

"We got caught. And the old guy was also the mayor."

"That isn't that bad."

Will sat back down beside me, close enough that I could feel the warmth of his body. "That's only one story," he said.

I tried to commit every detail to memory. The crackle of the fire. The smell of the burning wood mixed with Will's soapy scent. The stars over our heads in the cool air. Will's face, looking down at me with a half smile. Every detail. Just in case.

"Things are complicated here too," I said.

He took a deep breath and let it go slowly, shifting so our thighs pressed together. "Yeah, they are."

I licked my lips, not meeting his eyes. So much of me wanted to assure Will it was okay, that we could do . . . something. But the big lump of guilt in my stomach, and the girl who followed the rules and did what other people wanted her to, won out. I said nothing. After a few minutes, Will reached his arm around me and rubbed my bare arm, sending a jolt of electricity into my chest.

"You're freezing. I swear you're just using me for my sweaters," he joked. I looked at his hand on my arm, wishing I had the guts to kiss him again. Before I could do anything, he let his hand drop and stood. "I'll get you a blanket."

I stared at the fire as Will walked into the cabin. The creek, now swollen from the rain, rushed by in front of me. When I was younger and didn't know what to do, I used to wonder what Momma—the woman who made me, who was part of me, who shared my DNA—would have said. Sitting there, staring at the fire, I would have given just about anything to know. Would she have told me to let go of Radek? To give things with Will a chance? To trust my gut and continue to believe Dad hadn't done it on purpose? To go along with selling the ranch and leap into an entirely new life? I tilted my head back to look at the sky. A billion trillion stars. A billion trillion choices. If I couldn't know what Momma would have said, at least I could find out what really happened to her.

ay 1981

MOMMA'S under her quilt with the birdies, lying on her side. Rain splatters the window in her bedroom. I stand by her face and pet her hair. She says, "Momma is sad, love." Momma forgot I can't reach the cornflakes and milk without her help or standing on a chair, which she says isn't safe. She pulls her quilt up to her ears and I wait by her bed. Momma told me *her* momma made her the quilt for her wedding to Daddy. Her momma is my grandma, but I've never met her 'cause she lives in England.

"Why are you sad?" I whisper. When Momma is sad she likes it if I whisper, quiet as a mouse.

"My heart hurts," she says. Her voice sounds like she's crying. I don't like it when Momma cries, so I go downstairs.

Daddy is in the barn. Maybe I could help him with the chores. He likes me to help sometimes. He tells me about the different parts of the saddle as I polish it, or he lets me pour the grain in the horses' bowls.

But today I am home with Momma. When I am sad because I'm not allowed to go out and play or because I miss *Mr. Dressup*, Momma makes me chocolate chip cookies. I will make Momma cookies.

I go into the kitchen and pull a chair to the counter. Then I climb on the counter to get the chocolate chips. While I'm there, I pull out the flour and then drag the chair to the fridge to get the butter and the milk. That's all I can remember that goes in cookies. I crawl into the cupboard below the counter and find the big green bowl. I scoop the flour out of the bag with my hands and put it in the bowl on the floor. I only spill a little bit but the little bit goes poof! White everywhere. I pour in all the chocolate chips and all the milk and it makes a chocolate chip soup. I can't get the spoon drawer open so I mix with my fingers. The bowl is tippy and I spill on the floor. It's slippery and I mush it around with my toes.

The porch door opens and Daddy stomps his boots on the mat to get the mud off. His jacket is dripping on the floor— Momma better not see that. He looks into the kitchen.

"What are you doing?" Daddy says. And then, "Where's your mother?"

"I'm making cookies for Momma. She's sad today." Daddy will get mad. He hates messes almost as much as Momma does. He takes off his boots and comes into the kitchen and picks me up. He washes my hands and feet in the sink and I giggle. Momma would never do that. The water is too cold and my clothes get all wet. Then Daddy and I wipe up the floor with one of Momma's dish towels.

"Are you hungry?" Daddy asks me.

I nod and he pulls out a bowl and fills it almost to the top with Rice Krispies. He gets out a new milk for me. "Can you pour this?"

Momma never lets me pour the milk. I do it though, and only spill a bit.

I kneel on a chair and eat my cereal while Daddy goes upstairs. Out the kitchen window two magpies are fighting over a worm on the lawn. Upstairs Daddy is yelling a little, but not too loud like sometimes.

"She hasn't eaten," he says. His voice sounds like gravel hitting the side of a truck.

I can't hear what Momma says. Did I get Momma in trouble?

That afternoon, after it stops raining, Momma stays in bed and I get to help Daddy work on a tractor. I hand him the tools and he fixes.

 ebruary 1992

AT FIRST RADEK wanted to wait until we got married. He kept telling me we should wait, that his mother would be disappointed if she found out we hadn't waited, that there was no rush. But since the accident we'd spent increasingly more time in the basement, "watching movies." No one had been surprised when we came back to school in January as an official couple. Even Olivia Murphy hadn't seemed to mind.

A month after we celebrated my seventeenth birthday—dinner at the Italian place in town, just the two of us: our first official date—I spent the weekend at the Baileys'. Radek and I helped Clarence fix a wall of the sheep barn that was falling in. After dinner on the Saturday night, Radek and I retreated to the basement with a bag of sour cream and onion chips and a big bottle of Pepsi. Radek put a movie in the VHS player and pressed Play. He turned the volume up to thirty-one—any louder and Mere would come down and check on us. We had a condom

Radek had bought from a vending machine in a truck-stop bathroom. We'd been hiding it in a plastic Hubba Bubba gum bucket in the basement for a few weeks.

Radek and I lay on the couch, my back to him. He kissed my neck and ran his hands over my boobs. Chrissy had recently told Heather and me she'd lost her virginity to a hockey player from Cardston. She met him at the arena after one of her brother's hockey games, and they'd been seeing each other every few weeks. Heather had been sleeping with her mom's boyfriend, Avery, since the summer between grades nine and ten. It was only me left, behind everyone else, as always.

Radek let his hand move under the waistband of my jogging pants. What would it be like when we had sex? Would it hurt, like Chrissy said? Would it be amazing, like in *Dirty Dancing*? Or would it only be "okay," like Heather told me her first time was? Whichever it was, I was ready to find out.

I rolled to face Radek and undid the top button of his jeans. He sucked his breath in hard, watching me. Normally he'd push my hands away at this point, saying he couldn't stop himself so we'd better not. This time he didn't. I stood up in front of the sofa and pulled my shirt over my head, resisting the urge to cover my bare chest with my hands. I rarely wore a bra; I didn't need one. Radek sat up and took off his shirt as I bent to pull off my jogging pants.

"So we're really doing this?" he asked, dropping his shirt on the carpet.

"I don't want to wait anymore." I wanted to get it over with, to get past the awkward part and to the good part. I needed to know. My heart raced in my chest. I told myself I was shivering because of the cold basement, not because I was nervous. It felt surreal, like I was watching a movie of myself, standing in the basement, about to change my whole life.

Radek grinned at me. "Okay." He kicked off his jeans, struggling with the left leg; his knee was still stiff. Even in the low light I could see the deep scars from the surgery. I lay on the scratchy green carpet and quickly pulled the couch blanket over me. It was cold and the basement smelled a little bit like mildew and a little bit like chips. Radek lay beside me.

We stayed there, side by side, for a few moments, looking up at the panelled ceiling, listening to the movie play, not really sure how to start.

"Your boobs are exactly how I imagined them after the canyon," he said. Even though we'd been fooling around in the basement for months, we'd never been fully naked in front of each other.

I elbowed him. "Oh my God you are such a loser," I said, but I was smiling. He moved his hand under the blanket, letting it rest on my upper thigh. He rubbed the soft skin there, moving his fingers in circles, getting closer and closer to the elastic of my underwear.

I looked at him. "Are you sure?"

"Yeah, why not?"

"Are you nervous?"

He smiled. "Aren't you?"

"Stop answering my questions with questions," I said. I pulled the blanket up closer to my chin.

Radek reached his long arm out and took the Hubba Bubba container from under the coffee table and dug around in the gum until he found the condom. He fumbled with the wrapper, blushing. "Just like Ms. Peterson showed us in sex ed," he said, trying to ease the tension. I wiggled out of my underwear and looked around the basement as he moved on top of me. *I should remember this moment*. The VHS tapes lined up on the shelves below the TV. The basement carpet, already making my back itch. The quietness of the house, dark behind the final scenes of *Indiana Jones and the Last Crusade*. Radek's face above me, so serious and not Radek-like.

I winced.

"Is that okay?" he asked, his voice husky.

I nodded and tried to smile. It was and it wasn't. It hurt, but not the way I'd expected it to. It was sharp pain and then achy. I could tell one day it might feel good, but right now I wanted it to be done.

After, we looked at each other in the flickering light from the TV. Radek rolled onto his back beside me, his eyes on the ceiling above. I thought about what people on TV did after sex scenes: looked longingly into each other's eyes, put a hand to their lover's cheek, had a heart-to-heart, said 'I love you', smoked a cigarette. None of those things felt right. Radek cleared his throat.

"Was it . . . good?" he asked.

I glanced over at him. I'd never seen him doubt himself before. "Of course—yes." I kissed him on the cheek. "We'll practice." He smiled back at me.

I EXPECTED to feel different right after. Older or more like a woman or closer to Radek. But nothing changed at first. Heather could tell right away when she saw us at school on Monday. "Did it hurt?" she asked as soon as we were alone outside the Chemistry lab.

"Not really," I said sheepishly. "How did you know?"

"You can always tell by the way two people look at each other after. Something shifts. It's different. Do you feel different?"

"Maybe a little."

Heather nodded wisely. "It gets better." She winked at me. I punched her lightly in the arm and followed her into the classroom. I hoped she was right. She was right about one thing: it had changed things with Radek. Us being together felt real, solid, secure. We were doing what we were supposed to be doing. We were growing up.

uly 1996

THE DINER SMELLED of fresh coffee, warm donuts, and last night's leftover chili. Heather stood at the counter rolling cutlery into napkins and placing them in a neat pile. Pictures of American presidents hung behind her. Most of the photos were old and yellowing, their corners peeling off the smoke-streaked walls. Dolly, the diner's owner, had moved from Montana to Jessop and was very proud of her American heritage.

"Your dad will flip," Heather said. She stopped wrapping cutlery long enough to fill a to-go cup with coffee and a generous dollop of cream and slide it across the counter. I sipped it as she dropped mini sugar donuts into a white paper bag. The smell of them reminded me of the rodeo, and Will. He'd told me he'd distract Dad as best he could. And he'd given me a crinkled map of Montana he'd found in the back of his truck.

"That's why he's not going to find out. I left a note saying I'm at your place."

"Don't make me part of this!"

An elderly couple at the corner table across the room looked at us, and Heather lowered her voice. "I'm your dad's favourite, remember?"

"Look, he won't know anything. He won't call."

"I don't know, Hannah." She pulled her apron strings tighter around her waist. "It's been almost fifteen years. You don't even know if this guy is still alive."

She was right. I also didn't know if he still lived in Billings. I'd wanted to look up his phone number the night before, but the library was closed so I couldn't find a Billings phone book. But now that I had the idea, I couldn't wait another second. "Either way, I need a drive." I needed time to think, and with over eight hours of driving ahead of me, time would be one thing I wasn't short on.

Heather put her hands on her hips and cocked her head to the side. "Who are you and what have you done with my best friend?"

"Nothing," I snapped.

"It doesn't sound like nothing." The bells chimed as another customer came through the door and took a seat by the window.

I took a sip of the coffee, savouring its familiar almost-burned-but-saved-by-the-heavy-cream taste. Heather, Chrissy, and I had spent many mornings at the diner recovering from the night before. I thought about what Roger had asked me. Had Dad done it on purpose?

"Really, nothing," I said. "I just need to know what happened to her—what really happened to her." I gripped the coffee cup so hard the paper sides squished in. I could do this. I'd been across the border once before, when Dad and I went to look at a horse in Eureka. How hard could it be?

"Does Will have anything to do with this plan?" Heather asked. The new customer cleared his throat, irritated he hadn't yet been served in the almost-empty restaurant. "We'll talk about this later," Heather said. "Call me when you get there tonight. And be careful."

"Thank you." I took the bag of donuts and the coffee from the counter. "For everything."

I TURNED onto the highway lost in thought about the night before —Will by the fire, the clenching in my belly when he looked at me, how much I wanted to be with him. In some ways, it seemed my whole life had rolled out in front of me after Momma died, that I'd never had to make a real choice before. I'd been so busy being a good girl for Dad, unnoticeable in school, Radek's perfect girlfriend—anything to not be the girl whose dad shot her mom —I'd forgotten to make any decisions about how I wanted my life to be. I'd driven straight down a well-worn road at a safe speed, abiding every traffic sign and law of the land, and had expected everything would work out.

I glanced over at the map on the passenger seat. A long red line ran from Jessop to Billings, an almost straight shot down the highway. If I was lucky, I'd get there by nightfall. Had Momma driven a straight line in her life? I didn't know much about her life before she met Dad. I sat back in my seat and trained my eyes on the road. Maybe I'd know more soon.

DESPITE MAKING three wrong turns and travelling forty-five minutes in the wrong direction, I made it to a motel on the outskirts of Billings before nightfall. I'd taken three hundred dollars from my Crown Royal bag. Hopefully it would be more than enough to get me through one night and two days of travel. The blue-haired woman behind the counter didn't ask me any questions about where I'd come from or why I was travelling alone, and she took my Canadian money, although I guessed I was overpaying with the exchange rate. She handed me a key attached to a plastic tag with my room number on it. I trudged across the parking lot to my room and closed and locked the door behind me. The small room smelled of mildew and stale chips—reminding me of Radek's basement—but the sheets on the double bed appeared clean in the low light. I called Heather and nearly fell asleep while talking to her even though it was still light outside. Then I clicked on the small TV to find only static. I fell asleep to the sound of vehicles whooshing past on the highway.

The next morning, I handed in my key at the front desk. The same woman took the key and asked where I was off to. She'd applied fresh blue eye shadow and bright pink blush but her hair looked exactly the same as when I arrived. I considered asking her about Harlon, but I knew Billings was a whole lot bigger than Jessop.

"If you're stayin' for breakfast, you should try Betty Jane's. It's on Second Avenue, near the Babcock Theatre," she said.

I thanked her and followed her directions into town. As I drove, my eyes darted from side to side, taking in the city. Billings was the biggest place I'd ever been. There seemed to be people everywhere—cars, trucks, pedestrians. And no one I recognized. I bit back the wide grin spreading across my face, feeling a little light-headed as I pulled the truck into a street parking space. No one knew me here—except maybe Harlon, if I could find him.

AT THE CAFE, I ordered a breakfast called the Rail Car and sat in a window seat watching people walk by, duck into stores, pull children behind them, rush off to work or school. What would it be like to wake up in a city every morning, to not have horses to feed, stalls to muck, fences to be fixed? I almost choked on my toast when a tall guy with dark brown hair walked past. His head was turned, his face shielded from view. He had his arm around a woman's waist. Her long, curly blonde hair bounced on her shoulders. For one wild second, I thought it was Radek and Fun Girl, and my brain chugged desperately, trying to make sense of it. I stood, half out of my seat, before the guy looked over his shoulder and I spotted his scruffy brown beard—not Radek. I dug my fork back into my potatoes and ran them through a streak of ketchup before pushing them into my mouth. It wasn't quite jealousy I'd felt when I saw the guy, but something closer to surprise. What if Radek was right? What if we should be exploring things with other people, to be sure? I washed the potatoes and the lump in my throat down with a gulp of coffee. There was a problem Radek and I hadn't talked about—what if we ended up liking the other people more?

IN THE CAFE'S front entryway, I found a tattered phone book hanging by a wire from the pay phone. I flipped to the S's, my heart racing. There it was. Schultz, Harlon. I held the page with my finger and folded the book to check the year on the spine. 1993. Three years ago. Sweat prickled my armpits. He was likely here. All I had to do was find him. I considered going back into the diner and asking the waiter who had served me breakfast if he knew a Harlon Schultz, but decided against it. If he knew Harlon, I'd have to make up a story about being a long-lost niece or something. Or even worse, if he didn't, he'd think I was a country bumpkin who didn't understand how big the city was. I could call the number, but what would I say? What if he refused to see me? I had no idea why he'd left Jessop or how things had really been between him and Momma. He could hang up on me right away and I'd have come all this way for nothing. I imagined driving back to Jessop not knowing anything more than I had when I left. This was my only lead—I couldn't mess it up. I'd go with the best option: the truth.

I lifted the receiver off the hook, pumped a quarter into the phone, and dialled the number. My heart thumped with each ring. I hung up after nine. No answer. I blew air out through my lips and let my finger slip from the phone book. Of course it wouldn't be that easy.

I GOT in the truck and leaned my head back against the seat. People ambled by on the sidewalk. I thought of the old Westerns I'd watched. The good guys always found their man, and usually by accident. Someone walked into a saloon. Someone rode through the middle of town. Someone happened upon the bad guy's hangout. I rubbed my hand across my face and sat forward. I'd have to ask. I put the truck in gear, deciding to drive back to the motel. And then I saw it. A giant billboard, right there on the side of the diner's brick wall.

Schultz's Quality Office Supplies & Equipment
For all your office needs.

HOW MANY SCHULTZES could there be in Billings? But how did one go from law enforcement to office supplies? I put the truck back in Park, pulled out Will's map, and folded it to the magnified Billings section. The address listed on the sign was only a few minutes away. My hands shook as I reversed onto the street. What would I ask him if I did find him? *Did you love my mother? Was she happy? Oh, and do you think my dad meant to kill her?*

I pulled the truck into a space right in front of the store and took a deep breath before opening the door. The store was beside a doctor's office, in a building with dark brown gingerbread trim and off-white brick walls. It looked a bit like a Swiss cabin. "Since 1923," the sign hanging in front said. Chimes rang out as I stepped inside. Fluorescent lighting buzzed above me. The store was a garish mix of old and new: harsh lights, worn wooden floors, steel shelves, and a long counter that looked more like a bar than a checkout. The back wall was lined with desks, bookshelves, and filing cabinets—floor models, I guessed.

A large man with greying curly hair came out from behind a stack of paper reams. "Can I help you?" He walked towards me and I froze, my mouth hanging open. *The badge. His hands brushing away Momma's hair as they stood on the lawn. His red eyes, level with mine in the kitchen after the funeral.* He had aged, but it was him.

"Miss?"

I cleared my throat. I hadn't bothered to come up with a cover story.

Harlon's eyes widened. He ran a hand through his hair, setting it on end. "You look like her," he said, finally.

I was too surprised to stop myself. "I do?" Mere had told me we shared the same long hair and lanky frame, but I'd never thought I looked enough like her that a stranger could see the resemblance.

He moved around the counter and ripped the tape off a cardboard box. He piled packages of pens on the counter, sorting them by colour. Red, black, blue. I waited for him to speak again, watching his face as he focused on the pens, never looking up at me, never meeting my eyes. He had wrinkles around his eyes and his skin was pale. He had shaved off his moustache. Had he married after he left Jessop? Did he have a family at home?

"What do you want then?" he asked gruffly.

I came to stand at the counter. "I want to know what happened to her." And what she was like—what she was really like. I wanted to know everything.

He shrugged. "You were there."

My throat felt thick. I swallowed hard. "I was a kid," I said quietly. Dust motes floated in the light from the high windows behind the counter. Now that my eyes had adjusted, I could see that the store was crowded and a little bit dirty, and a lot messy. He followed my gaze to a stack of old newspapers piled in the corner, behind the door.

"I inherited this place," he said. "Don't give a damn about office supplies."

I looked at him, trying to imagine what Momma had seen in this man, what he had given her that Dad couldn't.

"I've got a lot to do here," he said, gesturing to the stack of boxes behind him. His voice sounded sad. "Better get on with it."

"Was she happy?" I asked.

He met my eyes for the first time. "How could she have been?" He straightened the piles of pens in front of him. "She was always too big for that town. She should have been in the city, showing her art in galleries, living the life, not stuck on that damn ranch with your father, not the way he treated her."

"What do you mean?"

He shook his head. "Doesn't matter. You must have seen the reports. His name was cleared. That's the way the justice system works. Part of the reason I'm not in it anymore, if you want to know."

"You think he did it on purpose." I clenched my clammy hands into fists at my sides.

He leaned forward, resting his hands on the counter. "I didn't say that."

"You didn't have to." I let out a breath I didn't know I'd been holding and turned to leave.

"Look."

I stopped, my hand on the doorknob, and turned back to him. His expression was slack, his eyes dull.

"I couldn't prove it. Why don't you ask him? He's the only one who knows the truth."

I LEFT RIGHT AWAY, not bothering to call Heather to tell her I wouldn't be staying another night. On the way home, I didn't make any wrong turns. I opened the driver-side window and let fresh air fill the cab. I thought about Harlon's eyes, their haunted, faraway look. He had loved Momma. *You look like her.* He'd never let her go. Was that how it would be if things didn't work out with Radek and me? I couldn't imagine my future without him—what would I do? Leave Jessop? Move to a city like Billings? Become one of those people in the crowd on the street? My life and Radek's were so entwined. Braided like a rope. But I had seen old ropes unravel.

29

June 1981

"WELL, all I know is what people are saying, because you're not talking," Daddy says.

I sit at the top of the stairs. I hold my doll, Marianne, close.

"I'm talking to you," Daddy says to Momma, his voice quiet. "Why won't you talk to me?" I've never heard Daddy's voice like this before—soft and crackly, like he might cry. I can't see downstairs, but Daddy must be in the dining room because he sounds far away. I scooch down a few more stairs so I can see Momma on the sofa.

Momma is fixing a hole in one of my socks, the blue ones with the red and pink hearts on them. My second-favourite socks, after the light blue ones with the pink bunnies. I stare at Momma, hoping she'll turn and smile at me, and then I'll go back to bed. Instead she keeps her eyes on my sock.

Daddy walks in front of the sofa. He raises his arms and then lets them drop. "Lizbeth, please . . . just tell me if what they're saying is true. I know it's been hard for you here. I know you're homesick. I know there's not fancy art like you want there to be." Daddy sways back and forth, like a horse when it falls asleep standing up.

The little clock with the wooden birds on top that sits on the mantle goes *tick, tick, tick, tick*. I listen so hard the sound of the clock mashes in with the buzzing of the bugs outside until I can barely hear anything anymore.

There is a smash, like breaking glass, and Momma screams. I gasp and scoot back up the stairs, pulling Marianne with me. I bury my face in Marianne and squeeze my ears between my knees. I wait and then lift my head. The clock is ticking again, and the bugs are chirping, and there is something else. When I walk back down a few steps Daddy is pulling Momma by the arm across the living room, like she's been bad and he's taking her to her room. Momma stumbles behind him. My sock is on the floor in front of the sofa. Where did the needle go? Momma said the first rule of sewing is to always know where your needle is.

"Tell me!" Daddy yells. He holds Momma by the top of her arms.

Should I go down?

"Tell me. Did he kiss you? 'Cause that's what everyone's sayin.'"

Momma cries, cries like the dogs do, a quiet cry. "Let me go, Luke," she says. "You're hurting me."

"I'm not myself—this is making me crazy," he says, his voice quiet again. His hands let go of Momma and hang by his sides.

Marianne and I run back to my room.

30

July 1996

LILY PUT on her peach blouse, teased her hair, and spritzed herself with perfume that smelled like baby powder and sweetness. While she got ready in the bathroom, I sat on the end of her and Dad's bed and looked at the watercolour painting above it. Momma had painted it: a field of daisies, probably near the mountains. *Leucanthemum vulgaris*—Lily's favourite flower, ironically. Did Lily know Momma had painted it? It was as if Momma was there with them, right in the room all along.

When I got back from Billings, Lily and Dad had been distracted. No one asked why I'd been at "Heather's" all weekend. Part of me was relieved not to have to tell more lies, but another part was worried. What could be so distracting they didn't notice my being away for two days?

"Hey, Chickadee. What do you think?" Lily spun in a circle, her hair billowing out around her. She'd put on makeup, including bright red lipstick, but for the first time I noticed the creases around her eyes. My shoulders slumped.

"Why so glum?" Lily said, and sat beside me on the bed.

Because of everything. Radek. And Will. And what I didn't know about Momma and Dad. And there was no one who would tell me. Not Harlon, that I knew for sure now. The harder I tried to figure it out, the further away it felt.

Lily put her arm around me and pushed my hair behind my ear.

"Do you ever regret anything?" I asked her.

She patted my hair and I laid my head on her shoulder. We sat facing the bedroom door, looking out across the hall at the linen closet. The late afternoon sun was on our backs, hot even through the window behind us.

"Yeah." Her voice came out in a whisper. "I regret lots."

I picked up my head and looked at her.

"Like what?"

She rolled her lips together and shook her head, resting her hand on my knee. "We live with the choices we make, don't we?" Her voice turned hard. "Like I always tell you, you always have a choice. You get to look at all the dresses and pick the one you want." Lily looked right into my eyes. Did she know about Will?

LATER THAT EVENING, I pulled Momma's box down from the top shelf in the linen closet and opened the lid, sending up a puff of dust. I laid each item on my bed, just like I used to. A compact with a mirror and cracked powder and lipstick. A small note-book with a black cover. A silver hairbrush with an elaborate flower pattern on the back. I picked up each one, turned it over in my hands, and tried to imagine what she'd been like. What she'd been thinking, feeling. What she'd wanted. If she'd been happy. There were a bunch of handwritten notes. Grocery lists, chores to do around the house, calculations that looked like budgeting for the ranch—always ending in negative numbers. I'd found the shoebox in the linen closet in grade four when I was looking for the memory book Lily made me fill out each year. The faded white box had been pushed to the back of a shelf behind a stack of wool blankets. I'd rummaged through the box quickly that first time, hoping for a photo, a journal, a note— anything that would tell me more about who she was and what had happened to her. But everything seemed to be a remnant of a normal life: things Momma had kept in a shoebox that Dad hadn't bothered to go through after she died. I hadn't opened the box in years.

I turned each paper over after I read it, making a neat pile. I smiled when I read a shopping list that said *New dress for H* right above *Long socks*. I must have been *H*. When I flipped the small piece of paper and placed it on the pile, I noticed faded print on the back for the first time. I took it to the light on my bedside table and squinted at the type. Parts of it were smudged, but I could make out most of the words:

July [smudge] 1981
Jessop to Calgary
Departing: 10 [smudge]
1 Adult
$22.50

WHY WAS she going to Calgary? The month she died? I shuffled through the rest of the papers, looking for another one the same shape. Why was there only one ticket?

DAD SAT in his easy chair, legs kicked up on the footstool.

Condensation from his glass pooled on the table beside him, staining it. "Dad."

His eyes were glued to the hockey game. The Flames were playing. Their red-and-white jerseys whizzed around the ice. Outside it was still summer. An old game.

"Dad. Did you know about this?" I handed him the paper, bus-ticket side up, and then stepped back. He glanced at it and flipped it over. "*Dress for H*? No, should I?"

"It's a bus ticket. To Calgary. For the month Momma died."

Dad flipped the paper over again. Slowly. His face drooped and then, after a moment, his shoulders clenched and rose towards his ears.

"This doesn't mean anything," he said, and thrust the paper back at me.

I reached out to take it as he took another sip of his drink and turned his eyes back to the TV set.

"I want to know."

"What's there to know?" he said, his eyes still on the TV.

I took a deep breath and looked at the side of his face. "Was she going to leave us?"

"If she was, I didn't know about it," he mumbled.

He took a long swig from the glass before letting the cubes clink back to the bottom. I glanced into the kitchen and could see the almost-empty whiskey bottle on the counter. He rarely drank so much this early. Lily had only been at work for a few hours.

"Was she having an affair?"

Dad stood up quickly, directly in front of me. The footrest snapped back into his lounger. His face was red and blotchy. For a moment I thought he might hit me, even though he'd never so much as spanked me when I was a child. He balled his hands into fists at his sides. "No." He pointed his finger at me, inches from my face. "Don't you dare speak of your mother that way." His lips were pulled back and white. "Ever." He punctuated it with another jab of his finger.

I stepped back, my heel bumping painfully against the leg of the coffee table.

We looked at each other for a moment before he turned and walked around the other side of the chair, glass in hand.

Something inside me snapped. Like Harlon had said, Dad was the only one who knew the truth. "Why don't you just tell me?" I yelled. "Tell me, Dad!" My whole body vibrated with white hot fury.

Dad slammed his glass on the dining room table. It hit the edge and smashed into shards that littered the floor. The second broken glass in a week. We both looked at the mess, at the bits of glass sparkling in the light from the dusty chandelier over the table. Dad hung his head. Mickey Two whined and scratched at the porch door outside.

"Is this why you're selling the ranch?" I said, my voice quiet. "Because that researcher was asking questions?"

Dad's head snapped up and his eyes met mine. "That's what you think?"

"Why else would you be doing this?" The hockey game echoed behind us, the only sound in the house. I held my ground, my legs planted wide. I would not let him get away without answering this time.

Dad took a deep breath and rubbed a hand across his face. "I'll clean this up."

"That's it?" I demanded.

"That's it."

White dots exploded in front of my eyes. I pushed by Dad and forced my bare feet into my rubber boots. I left without grabbing a jacket, slamming the porch door behind me. I gave Mickey a clipped "Stay," and he lay down and let out a sigh, his head on his paws. I walked so fast my breaths came ragged, burning. I wiped at the hot tears running down my face.

I didn't think about where I was going, but a part of me must have known because I ended up pacing in front of the cabin by the creek. The kitchen light was on but I didn't go to the door. I strode back and forth in the dying light, periodically reaching up to rub away the tears that wouldn't stop. Why wouldn't he just tell me? I of all people deserved the truth. She was my mother. I couldn't conceive of my dad as a killer. If he had done it on purpose, my whole life was one long lie.

"You're going to wear a hole in my lawn," Will said. He stood on the porch, his head surrounded by a halo of light from the kitchen behind him. The red ember of his cigarette glowed in the darkness. I hadn't even heard him come out.

"Sorry," I said. The ember grew brighter and then went black. I heard Will's footsteps on the porch stairs.

When he got close enough to see my face in the moonlight, he stopped.

"I don't know why I'm here," I said. More tears poured down my face and I didn't bother to wipe them.

Will pulled me close. My face fit into the firm space between his shoulder and his collarbone. "It's okay," he said.

"I'm sorry." I continued crying into his flannel shirt.

"Don't say sorry." He rubbed his hand up and down my back. He didn't ask what was wrong; he just waited.

I pulled back and took a deep breath.

His eyes moved over my face. He reached his hand up and clasped my chin, turning my head side to side.

"Did he hurt you?" he asked, his voice gravelly.

I shook my head. "No, never. Never like that."

His face was close. His eyes stared into mine as if he were trying to read something, searching. I looked at his lips, the stubble across his jaw. More than anything I wanted him to kiss me. I needed him to.

"Hannah, I don't know what to do with you. There are things I haven't told you—"

I cut him off. "You said I needed to figure out what I wanted. And

I did. I figured it out." I stepped back from him and crossed my arms over my breasts. A fiery mix of anger and attraction rose from my belly, sending tingles of excitement through my limbs. I narrowed my eyes at him, daring him to tell me I didn't know what I wanted.

He let out a noise that sounded like a snort. "Do you now?" he said. "And what's that?"

Turning to look out across the creek, I sucked the cool night air into my lungs, my arms still tight against my body. The full moon hung high over the mountains. I glanced at the aspen grove to our left, the trees clear in the moonlight. Was I going to do this? Would he?

"I . . . I want you," I said, my voice quiet. I kept my eyes on the creek. Will didn't move.

"What about Ra—your boyfriend?"

I squeezed my eyes shut and shook my head. His rough hand gripped mine.

"Okay," he said.

My eyes snapped open and I tried to pull my hand away, but he held it tight. "Okay? Only okay?"

He pulled me back into his chest, hard enough that my breath came out of me. "I mean I believe you," he said, his mouth close to my ear, sending shivers down my spine. "I've been thinking about this since that first night I saw you," he said. "Ever since you tried to convince me to leave."

I reached up and wrapped my fingers around his neck, pulling his mouth to mine. We grabbed at each other, hands reaching to pull off shirts and struggling with buttons even as he lowered me to the grass. He yanked at my bra, unhitching it with an ease that told me he'd done this before. I kept fumbling with the button on his jeans until he finally undid it himself and kicked his pants off, desperate for hot skin against hot skin against cool grass. His mouth moved from my lips to my neck, devouring the space between my breasts, moving ever downward. When he reached the place between my thighs, I jolted, my breath catching in my throat.

"Is this okay?" he asked, looking up at me, his long hair tickling my thighs. This. This was exactly what I needed. Under the full moon, beside the creek, miles from anyone else. I couldn't continue the way I had—doing everything right, everything everyone else wanted me to do. I had to do the things I wanted to do.

And I wanted this so much.

I pulled his face up to mine and thrust my hips against him, urging him to continue. He reached down and removed my underwear. "Don't stop." My breath came out in a whisper. I reached my legs around his back, pushing him into me. He groaned. It wasn't like this with Radek. With him it was clinical, pure biology, mating, action and reaction. With Will it was two bodies melding into one, fire before sparks, tornado before funnel cloud, thunder before lightning. None of it made sense, none of it was figure-outable. But every part of me was thrumming with life, alive, buzzing. I felt wild with need, desperate to hold on to part of him, to keep him with me, in me. I raked my hands down his back, pulling him deeper into me, his skin slick against mine as we moved together.

"Fuck." His breath was hot on my cheek as we climaxed together, our bodies moving themselves, far outside our control.

He fell heavy on top of me, pressing me into the ground. We heaved for breath. After a few moments, he rolled to the side.

"That never happens," I said. It never did.

"Mmm?" He moved onto his elbow and looked at me, brushing my damp hair off of my face. I could see all of him in the moonlight, the bump of his broken collarbone, the hardness of his stomach, the defined muscles surrounding his hips.

"Nothing." I reached my mouth to his, smiling. Nothing at all.

WILL WOKE me when it was still dark. He stood beside the bed with only his jeans on, nudging my shoulder. During the night we'd moved inside to the twin bed and slept curled together so we wouldn't fall off.

"Won't your dad be getting up soon?"

I stretched my arms above my head and pointed my toes. My feet hung over the end of the bed. The sky glowed red outside the little bedroom window.

"Yeah, soon." I pulled the sheets to my chest, shy, even though he'd seen every part of me the night before.

Will picked up my jeans and crumpled T-shirt from the floor and laid them at the end of the bed. He pressed his messy hair behind his ears and looked down at me. The warm air in the room smelled of stale laundry and deodorant. Not entirely unpleasant. "There's coffee, when you're ready," he said with a smile. He walked to the kitchen. I watched through the bedroom doorway as he poured two mugs of coffee and then leaned against the counter to take a sip from his. Light-brown hair covered his chest. Radek had only ever had fluff there. My stomach lurched. Radek.

"THANK YOU," I said, joining Will in the kitchen and taking the mug he handed me. I leaned against the counter beside him and looked out the window towards the creek. He moved his hand over mine and rubbed his thumb back and forth across the back of my hand, but his eyes stayed forward.

"Are you . . ." Will looked at me sideways, concern on his face. ". . . on the pill or anything?"

Everything had happened so fast the night before, we hadn't used a condom. I smiled. "Of course, yes." I'd been on the pill since Lily took me to the doctor and demanded it when I was in grade eleven, a few weeks after the accident. Before Radek and I had even kissed. It was like she'd known all along what would happen. But not using a condom had been stupid.

His face relaxed into a grin. The invisible tension between us eased. "Phew. In that case, we should try that at least one more time," he said, taking the mug from my hand and turning to face me. He put his hands on my hips, pulling at my shirt. I squirmed to get away from him, a wide smile on my face.

"Dad will be awake soon, if not already," I said, laughing. I let Will catch me and kiss me.

"Fine, fine. But I can't wait too long. Not anymore."

Me neither.

Will followed me onto the porch. Just like in the girly movies Heather and Lily loved so much, he held my hands in front of me and then kissed me softly, his lips still hot from the coffee. I waited for him to dismiss what had happened, to tell me it was a mistake, to apologize.

"See you at breakfast," he said with a grin.

I circled around the cabin and through the field that bordered the Baileys' ranch rather than taking the shorter way back, by Blueberry Hill. If Dad saw me he'd think I was coming from Mere's, that I'd slept in her spare room after our fight. As I walked, I thought about the night before. The intensity between Will and me, something impossible to resist—as though it wasn't our choice to be drawn together like that. When I got to the porch, I ran my hands through my hair and took a deep breath. I smoothed my T-shirt and opened the porch door.

Dad and Lily were sitting at the small table in the kitchen, sipping coffee. They both looked tired. Had Dad told her about our fight last night? Probably not.

Lily forced her face into a smile. "Morning, sunshine." She stood and poured me another cup of coffee. Again, no one asked where I'd been.

3 1

une 1993

I FOUGHT my way into the dress Chrissy and Heather had helped me pick out at Charlotte's Closet in town, and let Lily curl my hair into ringlets. The dress was too tight, too short, too pink—too much. But they'd convinced me it would be perfect for prom. Lily sprayed what felt like a full can of hair spray into the bathroom, until the curls crunched when I pressed down on them. When I tried to pull away she put her hands on my shoulders, holding me steady.

"Your hair isn't easily tamed," she said. "Stay still." She took out a tube of cover-up and dabbed it across my scars. "These healed up well."

It had been over a year since the accident. The scars were only thin lines now. I often forgot they were there, but the one below my left eye was still noticeable. Lily smeared pink lipstick over my mouth and made me press my lips onto a square of toilet paper.

She took my bare shoulders and turned me around. "Take a look," she said, stepping back in the small bathroom. I hardly recognized myself. Lily smiled. I could see her in the mirror behind me. "There. You're perfect."

"Did you go to prom?" I asked. Lily rarely talked about anything from the time before she met my dad.

"I did. Twice." She grinned at me. "Grade eleven and twelve. Two different boyfriends."

"I should have known." I smiled. "Are you sure I look okay?" I turned in front of the mirror. I looked different. Softer.

"Better than okay." Lily ran her fingers along the top of my dress, tugging it up to cover my chest. She readjusted the bow. I raised an eyebrow at her.

"Since when do you want me to cover my chest?"

"Since your dad is downstairs with Radek, waiting to make sure you look like a presentable lady before letting you go to prom."

I laughed and followed Lily down the stairs. I felt a little embarrassed and a little pleased when Dad and Radek both stood as I entered the living room. Thank goodness Chrissy and Heather had let me buy flat shoes so I wouldn't break my neck on the stairs.

"Woah." Radek's eyes were wide.

Lily pushed me towards Radek, who was wearing a dark blue suit. It was strange to see him in clothes other than jeans and a T-shirt. He'd slicked down his hair. "I told you she'd clean up nice," Lily said. "R.W., get that flower on her."

Radek fumbled with the plastic case for the corsage he'd brought for me while Lily retrieved his boutonniere from the fridge. I tried to remember the scientific name for roses as I waited. *Rosa* something? I gave up when he snapped the elastic a little too hard on my wrist. After Radek and I made several pathetic attempts, Lily ended up pinning the boutonniere on Radek's lapel.

We stood together in front of the fireplace while Lily took photos. Dad clapped his hand on Radek's shoulder. "Bring her home at a reasonable hour."

I could have sworn he winked at Radek. Then he turned to face me. "You look beautiful," he said. He pulled me into a hug, patting me firmly on the back three times. I remembered the last time Dad had hugged me: the day I got out of the hospital.

When we were finally alone in Radek's truck, we both let out big sighs of relief. "That was intense," I said.

"Yeah. You're telling me. I can't believe Luke didn't give me a talking-to about what time you needed to be home by." Radek started the truck and revved the gas a few times before reversing out into the laneway. We'd planned to leave the truck in the school parking lot and pick it up the next day. The school had hired buses to run kids out to the country once the dance was over. "You look . . . good. Really good."

I scrunched up my face and punched him in the arm but said thanks. As he drove, we talked about who would be at prom, who hadn't found a date, who we thought would get kicked out for drinking too much. When Radek pulled the truck to a stop in the parking lot he leaned across the bucket seat and gave me a peck on the mouth.

"Wait." I pulled him back, kissing him hard. He pushed away and turned his face from me to look out the truck window. "What?" I asked.

"Someone might see."

"So?"

"So, I don't want people watching us kissing."

"Aren't you supposed to want to kiss me?" I crossed my arms over my chest, careful not to squish the corsage.

"I want to kiss you, just not here, in the parking lot, when we should go in."

"Fine." I opened the door of the truck and stepped out. He always acted like that, worried about what people would think. It reminded me of his mom and her deep fear that leaving the house without pearls on would make the town newspaper.

Radek came around the truck and brushed dust off his suit jacket. His cowboy boots peeked out from under his dress pants. "You sure this suit fits me?" he asked. It was Clarence's, and a little too tight across the shoulders.

Before I could respond Heather jumped on my back, forcing me to take a few steps forward to keep from falling. "Heya!" she yelled. "You two ready to par-tay?" She dropped to the ground and I pulled my dress up, wiggling to loosen the fabric. Chrissy followed with her date, a guy named Matt who was a grade behind us. Chrissy didn't like him, but she needed a way into prom and had refused to come on her own, unlike Heather.

We filed into the gymnasium. Crepe paper hung from the ceiling, and the chairs were draped with white covers tied into bows at the back. It reminded me of one of Radek's cousin's weddings that we'd gone to the year before, except for the huge "Class of 1993" sign that hung over the stage. Girls stood in small circles at one side of the gym. The boys stood near the makeshift bar area. The Prom Planning Committee had borrowed a booth from the drama club and hired two bartenders to serve drinks to those of us who were already eighteen—although even those of us who weren't, like Radek, found drinks.

Radek squeezed my arm above my elbow before heading towards the bar, high-fiving guys from his team as he passed. This year, Radek had not only been the starting quarterback, but also team captain. When we entered a room I disappeared. It seemed like all anyone could see was Radek. Over the past year I'd gone from being Hannah, the awkward ranch girl who was good at school and kept to herself, to being "Radek's girlfriend." I followed Chrissy and Heather to a table in the corner of the room and waited until Matt and Radek returned with their hands full of plastic cups.

"It's not so bad without a date," Heather said, taking the cup Radek handed her. "Who needs a date when you have good friends?"

We tapped our cups together over the centre of the table and turned to watch our classmates trickle into the middle of the gym to dance to Billy Joel's "The Longest Time."

Radek looked over his shoulder every time a new person walked into the gym. It reminded me of Mickey Two lying on the porch and lifting his head each time a car passed. Eventually Heather and Chrissy pulled me onto the dance floor and Radek went to stand with a few guys from his team in front of the bar.

WHEN THE LAST song of the night came on, Radek found me on the dance floor.

"So, was it as bad as you thought it would be?" he asked, pulling me in close. Radek, Heather, and Chrissy had spent weeks convincing me it wouldn't be nearly as awkward as I imagined.

"No, not terrible," I admitted. As we swayed, I looked around at my classmates, the people I'd spent my whole childhood with. How much would I see of them after school ended in a week? Everything would be different. Or would it? I hadn't sent away any applications to schools, even though my grades were more than good enough. "What's the point?" Radek had said, when I'd been debating about applying. "You don't need a degree—I'll take care of you. And besides, you can read your magazines to learn more science stuff." At the time, I hadn't disagreed with him. The only classes in the fat course books in the counsellor's office I was interested in were biology ones, and what good would those do me in Jessop? I already knew everything I'd ever need to know about the ranch. Paying thousands of dollars to get a degree when I could save that money and put it towards Radek's and my future together was the right thing to do.

Radek pulled me closer, his mouth by my ear. "Maybe the next time we dance like this it will be at our wedding."

My stomach went rock hard, the room suddenly too loud, everything spinning around me. This was what I wanted, right? I gave him a weak smile and then focused on the floor, watching crepe paper blow around the dancers' feet. Maybe this was just happening too fast.

"I already asked your dad for permission," Radek said. He sounded a little drunk, his voice drawling and thick.

"What?" I stopped in the middle of the dance floor and pushed him back to look at his face. "When did you do that? No you didn't." I couldn't imagine Radek talking to Dad about me, about our future. They talked about football, the latest Jays game, when the hay would come in, the horses. But not about me. Right?

He shrugged and grinned.

"Well what did he say?"

Radek spun me around and dipped me over his arm, then lifted me back up. "You'll have to wait and see." He smiled at me, showing his straight top teeth.

The song ended and everyone cheered and hugged as the lights came on. This was really it, the end of all this. Heather ran over and threw her arm around my shoulder. She smelled like rum and Lily's perfume. "Can you believe it? We're almost outta here."

32

ugust 1996

As I SLID onto the seat in Will's truck, I realized he'd been on the ranch for almost two months and I'd never been in his vehicle. Whenever we needed to go to town we took Dad's or mine. And we didn't leave the ranch together often. In the week that had passed since I found the bus ticket, I'd been sneaking out to the cabin every night, spending every possible moment with Will, and then creeping back into the house before Dad and Lily got up.

Will drove a beat-up blue Chevy with a white stripe down each side. Dad had already helped him fix it twice to keep it running. Will said he planned to use a portion of the money he earned at the ranch to buy a newer one. The inside was clean. I was expecting it to be dusty and full of coffee cups, even though Will kept the cabin almost spotless. I waited in the passenger seat as Will talked to Dad in the yard. Over breakfast Will had asked me if I wanted a ride into town to meet Heather and Chrissy for the rodeo. A lie, but a good one. I'd nodded and kept my eyes away from Lily's and said thanks.

I wore brand new jeans that Heather had forced me to buy after I told her I'd asked Will to go to the rodeo. They were tighter than the ones I wore around the ranch, and tucked into my polished boots. I had traded my ball cap for a black cowboy hat.

Will opened the door and slid in beside me. I smiled at him. He still sent tingles through my body every time I saw him. Was this how a summer fling was supposed to feel?

"That dad of yours sure likes to talk trucks. He was worried she wouldn't make it into town and back." He patted the truck's dash and turned the key. He gave Dad a thumbs-up out the window when the engine turned over and caught. Dad waved and walked back into the barn.

"Yeah, he has a thing for trucks," I said. Will reached over and squeezed my knee. He'd polished his boots too and wore a clean button-up shirt.

As Will drove the dusty road to town, I spotted a small photo in the cupholder between us. "Who's this?" I asked, holding it up. It was crumpled at the edges, but I could see a little boy, perhaps three years old, holding a ratty teddy bear and grinning at the camera. The blue background had white and pink laser streaks across it.

Will looked sideways at me, his expression dark.

Who was the kid? Why did Will have a photo of him in his truck? I set the picture back in the cup holder and looked out the window, wracking my brain for a reason. Was it one of his brothers? Or Will himself? No, the photo looked too modern.

"Will?" I asked, as we passed through the one set of traffic lights that led into town.

"Yeah?" He kept his eyes on the road. My chest clenched, making it difficult to breathe. Maybe I didn't want to know.

"Nothing," I said. I leaned over and kissed him on the cheek. "I'm glad we're doing this."

WE MADE it to the grandstand as the steer wrestling started. Will found our seats and then left to get snacks. I looked around to see if I recognized anyone. The rodeo in Jessop brought in lots of out-of-towners. Chrissy and Heather had been avoiding the day portion of the rodeo since we turned eighteen. Well, sixteen for Chrissy, when she got her fake ID from her older sister. They would be at the Bull Ring later that night—a tent bar set up every year for the rodeo. Both townies, neither Heather nor Chrissy appreciated the rodeo like I did. Dad had stopped taking me when I was twelve, but I'd kept going with Radek. I loved the loud, dusty stadium; the quiet tension as the rider got his mount; the wild yells and fist pumps when a cowboy narrowed in on a winning ride; the barrel racers, their hair flying in the wind under their cowboy hats, their legs bouncing at the horses' sides as they kicked their way over the line.

Will dropped into the seat beside me with two cans of beer squeezed between the fingers of his right hand and two hotdogs balanced in the other. He handed me one of each. He'd run a thin line of ketchup along each of the hotdogs.

"I wasn't sure what you'd like," he said, when he noticed me looking.

"This is perfect," I said. I liked relish only, no ketchup. But ketchup-only might be better. Which reminded me of how different things were with Radek. Radek would know I only wanted relish. It was strange and wonderful to be spending time with a person who hadn't met me before I could walk, someone who didn't know every detail of my past and childhood, someone who knew only what I'd told him.

Will leaned forward, took a bite, and wiped his mouth with a napkin. "Now we're ready for a show," he said, after he finished chewing. "What'd I miss?"

"Jason Myers made 6.7 seconds. Not so bad."

"Not bad for a Canadian boy."

"Hey!" I elbowed him. "I don't see you out there. And besides, he's from Texas."

"You see this body? I'm not made for steer wrestlin'."

He was right. All the steer wrestlers were like Chucker: big, square, tall guys.

AFTER THE BULL riding results were read and the day's winner did his lap of the stadium, Will stood and pulled me from my seat.

"Let's get a jump on the crowd." He pushed me in front of him, his hand resting in the small of my back protectively.

I'd seen a few people I knew—regulars from the Red Lion, the odd person from high school, Heather's Uncle Burt, whose claim to fame was having not missed the rodeo in fifty-three years. I figured if anyone saw us there and told Radek, I'd tell him I didn't want to go alone. Radek still hadn't called, and neither had I. It was the longest we'd ever gone without talking. I wasn't technically doing anything wrong, was I? He had said he didn't want to talk about his stuff, so why did I have to tell him about mine? My throat felt thick. Would he think I'd be sowing my wild oats too? Never once had he asked about me and another guy.

"Hannah!" The deep voice had called across the crowd inside the stadium. I stepped away from Will's hand and tried to figure out who it was.

"Hannah! Over here." Chucker stood in line for the men's room. The only place I ever saw a line for the men's room longer than the line for the women's was at the rodeo. Or the Red Lion. He waved at Will and me.

"Hey, Chucker," I said, walking to stand in front of him. "You meeting up with Chrissy later?" Had he seen Will's hand on my back?

After the night at the Red Lion, Chucker had decided to stay in Jessop. He'd been working with Clarence at the Baileys' ranch and seeing Chrissy every chance he got. As far as she'd told me, he was just as good as she'd always imagined. And her parents approved, which was a first.

"You bet." He grinned and tipped his hat. "Hey, man." Chucker shook Will's hand. "I remember you from the Lion. You work at Hannah's place, right?"

Will nodded and released Chucker's hand.

"So, the Bull Ring?" Chucker said. The line moved and he stepped forward.

"Yeah. The Bull Ring." I smiled, stuffing my hands into my jeans pockets so he couldn't see them shaking.

Back in the truck, Will turned to face me before starting the engine. "You think he'll say something to Chrissy?"

I grimaced. "Probably. I'll tell her you drove me into town and no one else wanted to go to the rodeo." Why had I thought we'd be able to get away with going out in public? I couldn't do this to Radek. I had to tell him. Or did I? What were Will and I anyway? As far as I knew this was a summer fling with the rancher's daughter. Not something long-term. I swallowed hard. Saying goodbye to Will was not something I wanted to think about.

"I hate this," he said.

"Hate what?"

"This sneaking around. I just—" He shook his head and looked out the driver-side window, across the packed gravel parking lot. "I thought you'd made a decision . . . after the other night. I get not telling your dad and Lily because your dad would skin me alive, but when are you going to tell Radek?"

My mouth fell open. "I didn't think—" Will's eyes met mine,

sending my pulse soaring. "I thought this was only a summer fling for you."

"I'm not really the fling type."

"Well how am I supposed to know that?" Will didn't respond. I picked at a blister that had popped on my thumb after digging the irrigation ditch. The air in the small truck cabin was warm. Sweat tickled at my armpits under my T-shirt. I let out a long breath.

"It wasn't supposed to feel this way," I said, my voice low.

"Tell me about it," he said. He reached his hand across the truck and took mine. "So much for a summer fling." He grinned at me.

"Hey!" I pulled my hand away and smacked his arm. Will dodged me, laughing.

"What? Don't tell me you were thinking about this as anything more than that. I know that much about you. Good girl Hannah, slumming it with the ranch hand for the summer." His tone was teasing, but I knew there was more truth to it than he let on.

My face burned. He was right. That's what I'd wanted this to be. Sowing a few wild oats. Proving to Radek he wasn't the only one who could be with other people. Showing him and myself that I was more than just "Good girl Hannah," that I could be fun too.

"I—." My tongue caught in my mouth. I had no idea what to tell Will. I scrambled to pull the thoughts racing around my head together, to analyze, compartmentalize, solve. Telling Radek, really telling Radek how I felt about Will meant my life would never be the same, it would never work out the way I'd planned, the way we'd planned.

"It's okay," Will said. He put his arm around me and pulled me into his chest. Reflexively, my eyes scanned the parking lot, making sure no one we knew was nearby. It might be better if we stayed on the ranch. There we only had Dad and Lily to watch out for, and a lot more space. At least until I got up the nerve to tell Radek about it. Or until Dad sold the ranch. What the hell was I going to do then? I leaned into Will and breathed in the reassuring scent of him.

After a few moments, Will released me and picked up the picture in the cupholder. "If this is going to be more than a summer thing, there's something I need to tell you."

I sat up, pushing my hair back, out of my face. Was he going to tell me about the weed? That had been bothering me, but not enough to ask about it, and the coffee tin in the cabin seemed only to contain coffee now.

"This is my son."

I blinked hard, my entire body tensing. "Your son?"

"Yeah. Jackson."

I reeled back towards the passenger-side door, putting as much space between us as I could. His son? Who was the mother? Was he . . . Did he have a wife? A girlfriend back home? He'd said he didn't have a girlfriend. Had he been lying to me this whole time?

"You said you didn't have a girlfriend."

"I don't. I have a wife."

My eyes bulged, my face flushing red. "You lied to me!" I didn't care about the people in the parking lot anymore—let them listen.

"No, I said I didn't have a girlfriend." Will lowered his voice. "And I'm not with . . . her—my son's mother." He shifted on the seat.

"You're married."

"No. Yes. It's also complicated." Will smacked the steering wheel with the palm of his hand. "Fuck this is hard. I didn't expect this to happen."

What *had* he expected? A little summer fling with the rancher's daughter who wouldn't care that he had a wife back home? Something to entertain him until he moved on in the fall? But a son? And a wife? *I guess he didn't lie about not having a girlfriend*, I thought bitterly. I squared my jaw, gritting my teeth, my nostrils flaring as I breathed hard.

"Hey." Will caught my hand, holding it tightly in his. He brought his other hand to my flaming cheek. "It's not like that with her. We were together when we were kids, got pregnant by accident. We haven't been in love for a long time." He squeezed my hand. "I tried to get a divorce, but she won't sign the papers."

"But you left . . . Jackson?" The name felt thick on my tongue. There was a little version of Will out there, without his dad. I knew what it was like to be without a parent.

"Yes, but she wouldn't let me see him anyway. She's not well. She has issues."

I pulled my hand out of his, tipped my knees towards the truck door, feeling myself harden. Did she miss him? Did he support his son? Did she know about me? That must have been who he called the night he broke the glass.

"What's her name?" I whispered.

"Jolene."

We were quiet for what seemed like forever. I looked at the stadium, which was in desperate need of a reno. The red lettering on the *Rodeo* sign was faded and peeling so it looked like *Rode*. People moved through the fairgrounds like grazing cattle, clutching cones of cotton candy and plates of ribs. How many girls were out there, holding the sweaty hand of a guy they liked, hoping he would love them, hoping they'd figure out how it all worked?

"Hannah." Will tried to put his hand on my leg but I pushed it off. He threw his hands up. "Fine. This is exactly why I didn't want to tell you. But today made me realize I had to tell you because—" He stopped short and looked at me. I glanced sideways at him, my arms crossed and my face frozen. He shook his head again and then turned the keys in the ignition.

"Because what?" I finally asked. We were already on Main Street, heading towards home, I assumed.

"Because I'm falling for you. Or I guess I already have." He pressed his lips together into a lopsided smile. My chest squeezed tight. Hadn't I wanted him to say that all summer? I glanced at the picture of Jackson, now back in the cupholder. Will pulled the truck into the parking lot by the community centre.

"Where are you going?"

"*We* are going to the Bull Ring."

"We can't go there together."

"We can, and we will. We're going to have a few drinks and a dance or two, and then we're going to go back to the ranch. Together."

I tried to collect myself. How did he possibly have a child, a wife, or whatever she was? How did I not suspect anything? All along I'd been in this limbo with Radek, waiting for Radek but not *with* Radek. And Will had dealt with that. "This is complicated," I said.

"We'll figure it out."

"How?"

"We just will."

What kind of future could we have together though? Dad was selling the ranch. I had nowhere to go. I glanced sideways at Will. But maybe, together, we could figure it out. I let out the breath I'd been holding. My muscles hurt from pulling everything into myself. I relaxed my legs, letting the left one lean back against the middle console of the truck. Will glanced down at it. "I wish you'd told me," I said.

"Would it have changed anything?"

I thought of the nights we'd spent at the cabin by the creek, the looks we'd exchanged working on the ranch, the kisses we'd snuck, the tangible electricity that snapped between us. The warmth of his mouth over mine. Waking up beside him, breathing in his woodsy scent. "Probably not," I admitted.

217

Will looked at me for a moment and then took the keys out of the ignition. He walked around the front of the truck and opened my door, reaching his hand out towards me.

"What?"

"Just for tonight, let's forget about—" He caught himself before he said either of their names. "We'll just be you and me."

"This is very dangerous. You know that, right?" I said, but I took his extended hand and hopped out of the truck. The right thing to do would be to tell Radek about Will. To tell him I tried sowing a wild oat—*Avena fatua*— and it had turned into so much more. Something I wasn't in control of, something that had changed everything, like a seedling that had grown through a rock and cracked everything apart.

"I want to feel normal for a bit," he said. "And I want to dance with my girl."

My stomach flipped.

33

ugust 1993

THE DAYS after Radek left for university dragged on and on. The summer had been cool and rainy, and I threw myself into work on the ranch. Radek kept his promise and called every week with updates from training camp, and stories about his roommates, teammates, and coaches. He never once mentioned another girl. As the weeks rolled on, I figured the wild oats stuff had been a thing he'd said, not a thing he meant. We were acting like we were still together, weren't we?

The last Wednesday in August, after talking to Radek on the phone, I walked out to the cabin with a bottle of wine. Dad and Lily had gone to the Mortons' to play cards and I had nothing but time. I took a library book I'd been reading—about deciduous trees near the Rocky Mountains—and sat on the cabin porch, taking sips right from the bottle. I read until I had to squint to make out the words in the low light.

I picked up the bottle and tipped it to the side to see how

much was left. Not much. I slapped the book shut, went to the porch rail, and looked out over the rushing river. With all the rain it was flush and full, its sound my constant companion at the cabin. Years loomed ahead of me. What was I supposed to do? Wait until Radek got back? Nothing had been normal since he left. His voice was different on the phone. I missed the smell of his T-shirts, his goofy laugh, the way he could make me feel better about anything. But he'd left. What did he think I would do while he was away having fun at school? Just wait around for him?

I set the near-empty wine bottle on the porch and walked to the creek. My head was fuzzy, my mouth sour. I picked up a rock and threw it into the water. The sky was dark; not many stars were showing. What was the point of all this? I picked up another rock and threw it harder. Fuck Radek for leaving me here all alone. Another rock. Fuck me for not sending in any school applications. Fuck Dad and fuck Lily too. I threw rocks at the river until my arm ached, then I slumped to the creek bank, anger coursing through me. What was I supposed to do with myself, other than wait here and rot? I lay back on the muddy grass, not caring if I got wet, and looked up at the almost starless sky.

I wait for Radek to get back, I guess. The thought made me feel better for a moment. But then what? Chrissy knew what she wanted: a husband and babies. Heather seemed happy to live day to day. I wanted more—more than what everyone thought I wanted. I wanted to be more than "Radek's girlfriend" or Dad's ranch helper. But I hadn't told anyone; I'd coasted along without choosing—not choosing was easier than picking the wrong thing. Did I even want to stay on the ranch? Even considering leaving made my stomach heave. I rolled over and threw up red wine into the creek. When my stomach was empty I lay back on the grass, wiping tears from my eyes, depleted but calmer. I thought about Momma for the millionth time, her features blurry in my mind. What would she have told me to do?

As I drifted off to sleep, I imagined her. She walked across the field, her nightdress blowing in the wind. She kneeled beside me by the creek and brushed my hair off my face with cool fingers. She kissed my forehead, scolded me for drinking too much wine, especially by myself, near water I could roll into. She held my hand and told me everything would be okay. Told me that if I was a good girl everything would work out. She rocked me in her lap as I fell asleep, her long hair tickling my nose.

THE NEXT MORNING I found Lily standing at her bed folding laundry. She turned when I came into the room.

"Oh, hon," she said, plucking a leaf from my hair. "You look like you got run over by a truck. A big one."

"I drank your wine."

"I don't even like the stuff. Gives me headaches."

I laughed and rubbed my eyes. "Me too."

We sat together on the side of the bed. Lily took my hand and rested it in her lap. She rubbed her warm hand back and forth, waiting for me to speak. I laid my head on her shoulder.

"I don't know what to do," I said.

"Maybe you don't need to know yet."

"What do you mean?"

"When I don't know what to do I wait. I wait until something comes along or something happens and then I know exactly what to do. Not knowing means you're not ready to know yet."

34

ugust 1996

WE WALKED across town from the community centre parking lot. Parking spaces at the Bull Ring tent were virtually impossible to come by. Lots of people arrived early in the morning, as soon as the tent opened, and left their vehicles overnight. Every year the big tent was set up in the middle of the high school's parking lot, a few blocks from the stadium. It took up at least half of the lot and was flanked by a long line of porta potties that got grosser as the night went on. Will and I walked side by side but didn't touch. I tried to push our conversation out of my mind, but the weight that had been my guilt about Radek for the past few weeks was much heavier. And now I knew Will must have been feeling as much, if not more, guilt than I had. But when I caught his eye and he smiled, it all faded away.

. . .

"THERE," Will said, pointing to a table in the back left corner near one of the makeshift bars. "I can see Chucker."

I followed him, my gaze darting left and right. Heather jumped up from her seat beside Chrissy and threw her arms around me. Her face was a rosy red, and she'd tied her hair back in a ponytail, something she did only when she was drunk. "What took you so long?" she yelled. "It's Chucker's turn to buy."

Chucker and Chrissy sat close together. His arm wrapped protectively around her shoulders as she took her seat again. She looked tiny beside his huge frame, her smile wide.

"Will! I finally get to officially meet you, when you're not fighting a one-armed man." Heather's words were sloppy. Will laughed and shook her hand and then took the seat beside me. No one asked why we were together. Maybe Will was right—we could do what we wanted. His hand rested on my leg under the table, warm and firm. This time I didn't move. The round of shots Chucker had ordered arrived, and Will ordered another round of drinks for everyone before the server left.

I ended up with a bottle of Lily's favourite beer. Not my favourite, but the server had forgotten what we'd ordered and opted for a tray of assorted drinks. Will had scored a dark fizzy one. He caught me looking at it. "Want some?"

I took the plastic cup from him and sipped. Jack and Coke. As I passed it back I noticed Chrissy staring at me. She looked momentarily confused, and then she frowned. Johnny Cash came on the speaker system, and Chucker pulled Chrissy out of her seat and onto the dance floor in the middle of the tent. The wide smile returned to her face. Did she know? She couldn't have figured that out because we shared a drink, could she? Heather made her way down the table to sit beside a dark-haired cowboy with a scar between his eyebrows. I excused myself to use the porta potties. When I got back, Will and one of Chucker's other friends sat together, talking about bronc riding. I sipped my beer and watched my friends as the liquor loosened me. Will handed me another drink, a Jack and Coke of my own this time. Taking a deep breath, I tried to forget everything—that Will had a wife and son, that I needed to make a decision, that it was August and Dad was likely weeks away from putting the ranch on the market. I finished my drink in two gulps and set my cup on the table in front of me.

The song switched to an old, slow country song, and the guy Will had been talking with left the table.

"May I have this dance?" Will asked, a crooked half smile on his face. I hesitated. Heather and Chrissy were both on the dance floor. The tent was packed. What would one dance mean? Who would notice?

I let Will lead me to the floor. His hand was firm against my shoulder as he turned me around. He was a good dancer, too. I smiled at Heather when we whirled by, but she didn't notice—her eyes were fixed on that cowboy. I let my head come close to Will's shoulder. The lights dimmed as another slow song came on, and Will pulled me in a little closer, our bodies fitting together perfectly. I glanced around to see if anyone was looking, but everyone seemed focused on their dance partners, so I let myself relax into his arms.

"Wanna get out of here?" he said, his mouth by my ear.

I nodded. Chrissy and Heather danced with their partners on the other side of the floor. I left them alone and led Will out of the tent towards the line of cars waiting out front. Everyone who didn't drink became a cabbie during the rodeo. Even people from other towns.

"No Georgio?" he said. He took my hands, rubbing them between his as we waited in the short lineup.

"Oh he's here somewhere," I said. I glanced around.

Will pulled me into him, rubbing his hands up and down my back. I didn't bother looking around to see if anyone watched us. He brought his hand to my chin, tipped my face up, and kissed me. His mouth was soft and tasted of the sweetness of whiskey and pop.

"Your turn." A girl I didn't recognize tapped my shoulder and motioned towards a car. I blushed. At least I didn't know her.

"Thanks," Will said, smiling. He opened the door to the car and slid in after me.

WHEN WILL and I got back to Stillwater we checked for lights in the living room, and found it dark. He took my hand as we walked to the cabin in silence. Something had shifted in his mood. He was too quiet, too serious. When we got to the cabin he popped open two beers and handed me one. It was cool that night, so we sat inside on the sofa, side by side. I felt exposed, more naked than when we were actually naked—like now we knew too much about each other. We were sobering up, and everything was harsh and real. I tried to imagine what Jolene looked like. How old was she? Was she like me at all? What "issues" did she have?

"What are you thinking?" Will set his empty beer on the side table. We hadn't spoken since we sat down.

"I'm wondering about Jolene."

"I don't want to talk about her. Not right now."

I turned to face him, pulling my legs onto the sofa and under my body. "I can't stop thinking about it. I mean, do you miss her? Are you going back to her? Is she—" . . . *prettier than me?*

"Okay." Will stood and paced across the small room. "I guess I can't blame you for wanting to know. We got together in high school, like you and Radek." He looked at me as if to remind me I had someone else, too. "She wanted to get married right after school but I didn't. My parents were still hoping I'd go to law school like Anders, and Jolene and I always fought like crazy. I didn't want the rest of my life to be like that. We broke up for a while. She's got a lot of issues—gets depressed and angry a lot."

My shoulders lifted. Maybe he didn't love her.

"But we got back together for one night, after a lot of booze, and she got pregnant." He stalked to the door and looked out into the darkness. "Jackson came along and I had to do the right thing. I couldn't leave her with a kid." He walked back to the fridge and opened it, looked at the bottles of beer lined up there, and then shut it and opened a cupboard instead. He pulled out two glasses and a bottle of whiskey. "Want some?"

I nodded. Would he bring out the weed? I still hadn't mentioned it, and neither had he.

"We got married. And I tried to pretend everything was okay. But it wasn't okay. I loved being a dad—Jackson is amazing. But I didn't love her." He said the last part matter-of-factly. "It was eating me up inside, so I told her, and she lost it. She tried to get a restraining order so I couldn't see Jackson anymore. She left town and took Jackson to live with one of her aunts. I barely got to see him after his first birthday." He sat beside me again and handed me a glass of whiskey. His face was drawn, pale in the low light. "I tried to see him. I really did. But as he got older she told him so much bad stuff about me, mostly lies and a few truths."

I took a sip of the strong drink and pulled my legs out from under me, leaning back against the couch, not wanting to say anything that would stop Will from talking.

"The last time I saw him he was six. He told me Jolene had a new boyfriend, that he was his new dad." Will shook his head. "And that was it. I didn't go back again."

"How old is he now?"

"Ten." Will drained his glass in one chug. "I still call—that's who I was on the phone with the other night. But she never lets me talk to him."

I struggled for something to say. He'd tried, right? He'd tried to be there for his son. Was it really wrong he'd left? *Dad, bending down to tell me he was going away. Me, counting the number of days he had been gone until I lost track. His red truck, coming down the laneway at the Baileys', without the Barbie horse I'd wanted, but with Lily.*

I put my hand on top of Will's and squeezed. He stiffened this time, like I had that afternoon in the truck.

"I'm not a good person, Hannah. I'm not a good person for you. You deserve so much more than a guy like me." His voice was low, his eyes on our hands.

"No. No! Don't say that." I put my drink down and turned to face him, grabbing both of his hands. He hung his head, his shoulders limp and defeated. "You're a good person. You're my person." The words popped out of my mouth before I could stop them. I watched his face, half waiting for him to recoil, but instead he smiled at me and pulled me onto his lap, facing him. I thought about how Will must have felt when his son told him he had another dad. A pang for him ripped through my chest.

"We're in a predicament, aren't we," Will said.

I leaned my forehead on his shoulder. His hair ticked at my cheek. "Yeah. We are." I was no better than Will. What I was doing was wrong, too. So wrong. I was going to hurt Radek so much. We'd made a promise to each other we'd never imagined we wouldn't be able to keep. I lifted my face and let Will kiss me, let the world crumble around us. He pulled me tight to his body, my thighs around his waist. We took our time. We went to the bedroom, undressed fully, and got into bed. For long minutes, we lay there, looking at each other, running our hands over each other's bodies, breathing together.

A veil had been lifted between us. Where there used to be a barrier of secrets, it was now raw, naked, like soft, new skin touching soft, new skin.

"We'll figure it out," he said, for the second time that night.

∾

"WHAT WERE you doing at the rodeo with that ranch hand guy last night?" Chrissy asked as soon as I said hello. Her voice was hard, accusing. A part of me had been waiting for her call all day. I glanced at Lily and Dad on the sofa and tucked myself around the corner in the kitchen. Will had gone out to the barn to do the evening feed. "Chucker told me he saw you at the rodeo with him too. Hannah, what's going on?" Her voice softened at the last few words.

"I needed a ride into town," I said, realizing how lame it sounded as soon as it left my mouth.

"Please. Don't lie. I saw the way he looked at you, the way you looked at him. You drank out of his cup. You'd have to be an idiot not to see what's going on between you two. It's practically seeping out of your pores. Have you told R.W.?"

I sighed. I wasn't ready to be open about Will, but I was tired of hiding it. And I was tired from the night before, and from an early morning and a long day in the fields with Dad and Will. "So what if I do like him?"

She blew air out between her lips on the other end of the line. A deep voice spoke in the background.

"Where are you?" I asked.

"Home. Hold on." She muffled the phone and then came back on. "Now I'm in my room. Chucker is here for dinner."

"Good. And your parents like him?" I said, changing the subject.

It worked. Chrissy talked about Chucker and how her mom thought he looked like a younger, handsomer Arnold Schwarzenegger. "He's been *sleeping over*," she said, drawing out the last two words. "This is the real deal, Hannah."

I ignored the innuendo—that Will wasn't the 'real deal'—and forced myself to sound excited. "Chrissy! That's awesome!" I spoke too loudly, and Lily called out from the living room.

"What's awesome? Is that Chrissy?"

"Nothing!" I yelled back.

229

"Oh gosh," Chrissy said. "Don't tell Lily about the sleepovers!"

"Ha! No, I wouldn't do that." I hoped the lightness in her voice meant she'd forgiven me, at least for now, for whatever she thought was happening with Will.

"Look, what I wanted to say is be careful. R.W. is a great guy, Hannah. A *really* great guy. You don't even know this ranch hand, whatever his name is. R.W. will be back soon. I know it's been hard with him away for so long, but it's only two more years and then you'll get everything you always wanted, right?"

Everything I always wanted. And what was it I'd always wanted? I was tired of people telling me. I'd always assumed they were right, that I did want the ranch, that I wanted Radek and the quiet life that came with him, a safe life nothing like my mother's. I'd believed them when they said I didn't need to go to school, even though deep down I wanted to. I'd never told anyone how my hands had itched to tick off the biology courses I'd wanted to take in those university course books at school. Energy Flow in Biological Systems. Principles of Ecology. Plants and People.

"Hannah? You there?" Chrissy tapped the phone to check if the battery on her parents' fancy cordless had died.

"Yeah, I'm here. I heard you." I wanted to tell Chrissy that Radek wasn't who she thought he was, that he wasn't Mr. Perfect. When he'd left for school, I'd tried to explain our "break" to Chrissy, but she'd dismissed it with a wave of her hand. "He's just being a guy. He's not actually going to do anything," she'd said. What was the point? She'd already decided how my life should work out. I pinched my lips together.

"See you at Mere's next weekend?" Chrissy said. Mere's annual pig roast. I'd forgotten.

"Of course. See you then."

I WALKED through the dining room to the back door, moving quickly before Lily could quiz me about the phone call.

"Where're you going?" she asked.

"The barn." Even only a few days before, I would have tried harder to make up an excuse, but what was the use in pretending? If Chrissy was onto Will and me, then Lily knew. She looked at me over the back of the couch. She didn't smile but nodded. Dad's eyes were fixed on the baseball game on TV. I noticed he and Lily sat on opposite sides of the sofa, not touching. I hadn't heard them fight for a while, but things had been icy between them. Why wouldn't he just marry her?

ugust 1996

WILL and I sat on the porch facing each other, a worn metal stewing pot resting on the floorboards between our legs. We each had a metal mixing bowl full of pea pods—from Lily's garden—and a discard bowl.

"I'm better than you at this, too," Will said, his voice low. He smirked at me.

I kicked his leg and he pulled it back, rubbing his shin. I'd snuck out of the cabin early that morning and made it back upstairs to my bed before Lily and Dad got up. After the afternoon chores, Lily had asked if we would shuck the peas for her chicken potpies.

Will took a peapod from the bowl to his left, cracked the end, held it over the pot, ran his thumb along the insides to let the peas drop, and then released the empty pod into his discard bowl, on the other side of his chair. He hadn't cut his hair all summer and now it brushed the tops of his shoulders. The muscles of his thighs flexed under his jeans.

Will moved forward on his chair, bumping my bare knee with his jean-covered one.

"What are you grinning about?" he asked, dropping another empty pod into the almost-full bowl at his side. He was winning, dammit.

I shifted in my seat, not moving my knee. I thought of the early morning, Will's belly against mine, the quiet trickle of the creek outside the cabin, the owl's hoot that had made us both jump.

The porch door swung open and Will and I both sat up straight, moving our knees apart.

"You kids got those peas ready yet?" Dad asked. He had on his straw cowboy hat—the one he reserved for hot days—and was chewing on one of Lily's homemade pepperoni sticks.

"Almost." I gestured towards the pot between us.

Dad nodded and took the pepperoni stick out of his mouth. "Lily wanted me to say the chicken is done and all she's waiting on is you two." He leaned back against the porch railing and looked out towards the road. He looked almost happy, relaxed. I knew he shouldn't have been eating that pepperoni, but I didn't say anything. I wanted to enjoy his good mood.

"Whelp, I'm going to go check on those horses," Dad said.

"I can do it," Will said, rising to his feet.

"You help Hannah," Dad said. "Otherwise Lily might not finish those pies till midnight." Lily was making an army of pies, a few for dinner that night, the rest for the pig roast the next day.

Will and I watched as Dad walked across the yard to the barn, whistling.

"He's in a good mood," Will said, lowering himself back into his chair.

"Yeah." I frowned and cracked open another peapod. I hoped

he and Lily had sorted out whatever had them arguing so much the past few weeks.

Will glanced at the porch door behind him and then leaned forward, putting his elbows on his knees. I wanted to lean forward too. I imagined him grabbing the back of my head and kissing me, not caring if Lily or Dad saw. Someday. If I managed this right. If I told Radek without making him too mad. Maybe it wouldn't be so bad. Dad would eventually have to understand. I had no idea what we'd do, but a bloom of hope had grown since we'd told each other everything.

Will's faded T-shirt pulled tight across his chest. He was bigger than when he'd arrived. His collarbone was getting better. Maybe we could go to the States after the winter. He could rodeo again. I could apply to schools, get a degree. Become a scientist in a big city. Leaving Stillwater still turned my knees to jelly, but imaging Will might be with me when I left made it seem possible. I shifted until our knees touched again and smiled at Will. He put his hand on top of my bare knee and rubbed back and forth before moving it further up my thigh, a wicked grin on his face. "We should go to the cabin before dinner," Will said. "If you ever finish those peas." I laughed and then looked up as gravel crunched on the driveway.

I pulled my leg away, leaving Will's hand in midair. Mrs. Bailey's rusty old Ford farm truck rattled up the driveway and pulled to a stop on the grass beside the tractor shed.

"Shit."

"What?" Will squinted at the truck. "Who's that?"

"Fuck."

"Are you okay?"

I shook my head. Standing, I brushed my hands down my shorts. The truck door opened and Radek stepped out wearing dark jeans and a button-up shirt. It was way too hot for a button-up, but he'd done it up to the top button. He also wore a creamy white cowboy hat. He looked so . . . Texan. The only thing missing was a gun holster. But this wasn't a Texan. This was Radek. Radek who wore jogging pants and T-shirts. Radek my first everything. Radek who'd known me longer than almost everyone.

"Hey," Radek said. He walked towards us, a smile on his face. His gaze left me and landed on Will. The smile dropped, and he stopped a few paces from the porch. I looked anxiously between Radek and Will, my heart running wildly in my chest.

"Hey, Radek." I tried to force my face into a smile but produced only a pained grimace. I walked to the top porch step. "This is Will, our new ranch hand." I gestured towards Will and hated myself as the words came out. Just a ranch hand. I thought I saw Will wince, but he stepped around me and off the porch to shake Radek's hand.

"That's me, Will the ranch hand," he said, pumping Radek's hand a little too vigorously.

Sweat pooled under my arms, trickling down my sides under my shirt. This was not how I'd planned it. What was Radek doing here? He'd said he wouldn't be home until Thanksgiving at the earliest. What about his job at the gym? I needed more time to figure out how to tell him. But now he was here. Looming over Will. His body no longer lanky. Radek looked older, confident, mature. When had that happened?

The screen door creaked open and Lily stepped onto the porch. "Surprise!" she said, throwing her arms up and waving them around like she was at a rock concert.

I spun around. "You knew about this?" My voice creaked out. I shot daggers at Lily. She took a step back.

"Of course I knew. Why do you think I'm making chicken potpie, Radek's favourite?"

"Aren't you going to say hi?" Radek took his hands from where they rested on his massive silver belt buckle and opened his arms wide. He was him, but so not him.

Everyone watched, waiting to see what I'd do next. The

longer I waited the weirder it would get. Lily's mouth twitched into a frown so I forced a smile and stepped off the porch. I glanced sideways at Will before Radek's long arms wrapped around me and I breathed in the familiar-unfamiliar scent of him: his milky skin, the detergent his mom always used that he'd starting buying as soon as he left for school, and a new cologne. He squeezed me tightly and lifted me off the ground. "That's better," he said in my ear, so only I could hear.

Lily came down and hugged Radek too. "Look at you, all grown up," she said, holding him at arm's length. "I swear you shot up two feet this year."

Radek said something about his training regime and hard-boiled eggs but I didn't hear. My heart raced and my ears buzzed. I glanced up at Will, who was back on the porch. He had his arms crossed over his chest. He wouldn't meet my eyes.

"R.W. wanted to surprise you," Lily said. "He called us up and got your dad and me in on the plan." Her voice sounded chipper, but her raised eyebrow told me she was confused by my reaction.

I clenched my fists at my sides, my nails digging into my palms. How did Lily not know? How could she not have seen what was going on between Will and me?

"I'll go help Luke with the horses," Will said, walking towards the barn.

"Dinner is in an hour!" Lily called after him.

Will turned. He looked tired. No lopsided grin. "I forgot to tell you. I'm going into town with a few of the other ranch hands for dinner tonight." I could have sworn he enunciated "ranch hands." My face tingled; I was sure it was red and splotchy by now.

"Nice to meet you, man," Radek said. "See you at the roast tomorrow?"

Will gave a curt nod in Radek's direction. "See you," he said, his eyes on me.

Radek put his arm around my shoulder and squeezed. "Tell me what's been going on since I left. You're so hard to get on the phone lately." Had he tried to call me? I walked with Radek and Lily into the house, my shoulders tensed almost to my ears. *What have I done?*

WHEN DAD GOT BACK to the house he greeted Radek with a bear hug and then a handshake. They sat in the living room and talked about football and the weather in Texas while I helped Lily set the table for dinner. I followed her into the kitchen after the stove timer went off and watched as she pulled chicken potpies from the oven. The kitchen was stifling. I struggled to open the window.

"So," Lily said, her back to me as she cut one of the pies into slices. "If I didn't know better, I'd say you're more terrified than excited right now."

My eyes bulged, and I glanced behind me to make sure Dad and Radek were still talking. "Shhh!" I hissed. "I'm . . . surprised, that's all." I gave the window another push and it slid open, letting in the light afternoon breeze, and with it, some relief.

"When he surprised you by coming home that first Thanksgiving you seemed plenty happy to me."

I leaned back against the wall in front of the window, letting the air run across my sweaty neck. I remembered how I'd run out into the yard when I saw Radek's truck pull in. There'd been snow on the ground, and I'd gone out in my sock feet. "That was different."

Lily raised an eyebrow.

"You should have told me he was coming," I said.

"He wanted to surprise you. I'm missing something."

It felt ridiculous to hide it anymore. "You're missing Will," I whispered. I dropped my gaze to my bare feet, my face flushing.

"That?" She blew air out through her lips. "Oh honey, trust me, I've known you had a crush on that cowboy since the first day he walked onto this ranch." Lily waved the spatula around. "But that's all it is—a crush, right?" She drew out the last word. *Riiiiiight.*

Dad and Radek were standing up in the living room, making their way towards the dining room table and into earshot of our conversation.

I shook my head at Lily. My nose tingled. I took a deep breath. "No, not right."

This time Lily's eyes bulged. "Hannah—"

"Dinner about ready?" Dad asked. He came to stand beside Lily. "That pie smells damn good."

Radek leaned against the kitchen doorway and smiled at me. I noticed stubble on his cheeks. When we'd first kissed for real he'd barely needed to shave. I smiled back at him, and it made everything seem a little more normal.

We chatted as we ate dinner, Radek in Will's spot. The conversation flowed naturally, and for a moment I forgot anything had changed. Radek told us funny stories about his job at the gym, about fat men in the sauna, people stealing towels, women reading magazines and not breaking a sweat on the step machines. Lily shot me a few wary glances across the table, but eventually it seemed even she'd forgotten what we'd talked about in the kitchen.

Dad set his cutlery on his plate and cleared his throat. "I'm sure Hannah's told you we're selling the ranch."

Radek's eyes snapped up and met mine. My mouth went dry and I reached for my water glass, breaking eye contact. *Please don't say anything.* I held my breath, waiting for him to respond.

"That's too bad." Radek used the edge of his fork to break off a piece of the chicken pie. He slid it onto his fork and held it up before answering. "Hannah and I will be fine though." He smiled at me across the table and then popped the pie neatly into his mouth. *We'd be fine?* What was it he thought we'd do? I don't know what I'd expected. As I shovelled the last few pieces of my dinner into my mouth, tasting nothing, I realized I hadn't told him because I'd been worried about what he'd say. Worried losing the ranch would mean he wouldn't be able to see our future together clearly, that he'd start seeing a future with someone else instead. And yet he'd reacted as if Dad had told him he wanted to try planting canola instead of hay in the back field. I helped Lily clear the plates and bring out the blueberry crumble and a bucket of vanilla ice cream.

I sat up straight when I heard Will's truck start in the yard. I wished I could see his face as he got in and pulled away. That I could chase after him in my bare feet, beg him to stay so we could figure this out. I put down my fork and forced myself to swallow the crumble that had gone sour in my mouth.

"Hannah, you want to do that?"

Radek had asked me something.

"Hmm?"

"Of course she wants to," Lily said, saving me. "Hannah loves the canyon."

"Tuesday then, the day before I go back."

I nodded. "Sure. The canyon." I pushed my plate of half-eaten dessert away from me, appetite gone.

AFTER DINNER LILY shooed me out of the kitchen and onto the porch with Radek. We sat on the swing together, a foot of space between our thighs. Radek rested his arm across the back of the swing, around my shoulders but not touching.

"So were you surprised?" he asked.

"Yeah." I looked at my hands, clasped together in my lap. Could he tell I'd let someone else touch my body? Had he let someone else touch his? He must have at least kissed Fun Girl, or more than kissed. I wasn't sure if the thought of him touching someone else made me feel better or worse. "Are you wearing cologne?"

Radek laughed. "That's the first thing you ask me, after I take two flights with a three-hour layover to surprise you?"

"I guess I'm kind of in shock." I unclasped my hands and looked up at him. *I should tell him now and get it over with.* His deep brown eyes met mine. I'd looked into those eyes my whole life. We'd made a pact. Nothing else mattered. How could it, after all we'd been through together?

"Can you believe Dad's selling?"

"Yeah, I can. He had a heart attack. You can't run this place on your own."

I scrunched up my face. The last thing I wanted to think about was Dad being sick. "But what are we going to do?"

"Live at Mom's," Radek said, shrugging his shoulder like it was no big deal. How was this not a big deal? This was the only home I'd ever known.

"I missed you, Hannah." Radek lowered his arm to my shoulders and pulled me close to him. It felt familiar and good.

"I missed you too," I whispered. I let my head rest on his shoulder and listened to his breath go in and out of his chest. Home felt like home again.

ugust 1996

ASIDE FROM THE RODEO, THE BAILEYS' pig roast was my favourite event of the summer. All the neighbours came, and Mere even invited a few townies, including Heather and Chrissy.

Will drove me to the Baileys' after breakfast the morning of the roast. Neither of us said a word during the trip. I tried to talk when we got in, but Will had silenced me with a short shake of his head. "Not ready," he said. I chewed on my lip and looked out the window of the truck. The three-minute drive felt like three thousand minutes. We didn't move in to kiss each other when he parked, even though there was no one in the front window. I'd wanted to go out to the cabin the night before, but it felt wrong, with Radek's new cologne still clinging to my skin.

"Be back later with your dad and Lily," he said.

"Will—"

He shook his head sharply and looked straight ahead. "No. Don't."

I looked at his profile in the morning light. My hand itched to reach out and touch his face. I sighed and opened the truck door. I'd thought I'd decided what I was going to do before Radek got back, and then seeing him had crumbled every bit of figuring out I'd done.

I found Mere in the kitchen. Her usually perfect hair stuck out at all angles from her loose bun. "What can I do?" I asked, as she pulled me into a warm hug. I inhaled her vanilla scent and squeezed her back. It had been too long since I'd last seen her.

She pointed to three cabbages on a green cutting board. "Start chopping. The boys are over at the Mortons', picking up the pig." That was my least favourite part of the roast. It felt wrong to stand around while a pig that had been alive hours earlier turned on a spit. I'd learned long ago it was easier if I didn't look at its face. I chopped the cabbage and put it into a massive bowl then peeled carrots as Mere worked on the coleslaw sauce. Did Radek hope I'd learn to cook like his mom? Did he expect that when he got back from school I'd be doing this for him in whatever house we ended up in?

"Earth to Hannah." Clarence stood by the kitchen sink washing his hands. I hadn't even heard him come in.

"Oh hey," I said, blushing a little, as if he could see my thoughts.

"Daydreaming?" he asked.

I tried to laugh it off. "Guess so. How's the pig this year?"

"It's a big one." He reached for the dish towel to dry his hands.

"Oh thank goodness," Mere said. "I don't even remember how many people I've invited to this thing." She turned to me. "Are Chrissy and Heather coming?"

I nodded. "Chrissy is even bringing her new boyfriend."

"Wonderful!" Mere said. "I heard all about him from her mother at church."

. . .

244

Around noon I convinced Mere things were under control and shooed her upstairs to get ready. She'd hate it if guests arrived before she'd fixed her hair.

Clarence stood from where he'd been sitting to eat his breakfast at the kitchen table and picked up a pile of paper plates in one hand, a tower of cups in the other. "Grab those, will you?" he said, pointing to a package of paper bowls with his chin.

I picked up the bowls as directed and followed Clarence to the backyard. A tent had been set up with long tables for the food, and the pig was already rotating over a fire, its skin still pink. Mr. Morton waved from beside the pig as we walked by. "Where's Radek?" I asked Clarence, as we laid out the dishes on the table beside the boxes of plastic cutlery. Clarence shrugged.

"Said he had to go into town for something."

"Huh." What could he possibly need in town? Mere had shopped for weeks to get ready for the roast.

Chrissy, Heather, and Chucker appeared around the side of the house, lugging sleeping bags and a tent. "There you are!" Heather said. "Please tell me you know how to set up a tent."

As we struggled to fit the poles together and erect them into a semblance of shelter, more people trickled in. Most of the guests had brought tents, but a few close-by neighbours only dragged lawn chairs and coolers. Everyone brought food; the tables under the day tent filled with casseroles and salads, bags of chips and pans of home-baked goodies. Chrissy and Chucker were extra flirty with each other, teasing and sneaking kisses. I mimed puking at Heather as Chrissy and Chucker smooched for the third time while putting in the tent pegs. As soon as we'd finished I grabbed Heather and pulled her aside, near the back of the house.

"Radek's home."

"I know. Chrissy told me."

"How the hell did Chrissy know?"

Heather shrugged and dug around in the cooler she'd dragged

behind her for a drink. "Maybe Chucker talked to him? I don't know. Doesn't matter. What happened? Did you tell him?"

"No. Gosh no."

"I think you have to. Unless you've decided 120 percent you're done with . . . you know."

I swallowed hard. I would never see Will again. Or worse, I would, but I would never be able to touch him again, to catch him looking at me *like that*.

"I'm going to tell him."

Heather's eyes grew wide. "That it's over?"

Before I could answer, Mere emerged from the house behind us, her hair perfectly curled into place, pearls glimmering on her neck. Clarence followed with more foldable chairs.

"Did Clarence change his hair?" Heather asked me as they walked past.

"What? No, I don't know." I looked at her sideways. "Why are you asking about Clarence?"

She shrugged and smiled. "I saw him at the Bull Ring during the rodeo after you left and we talked a bit."

I tried to imagine what Clarence and Heather might have to talk about. She'd had a crush on him, like I had, when we were younger, but back then he was cool because he had a truck and we were still in junior high.

Across the lawn, Chrissy sat sideways on Chucker's lap in a lawn chair that looked like it could barely hold his weight, let alone both of theirs. His huge hand sat firmly on her butt.

"You know what she told me the other night? That Chucker is 'the one.'" Heather made finger quotes. "And that they walked by the real estate office the other day and looked at the pictures in the window. They're going to view that yellow house with the white pillars, across from the school."

"What? She hardly knows him!"

"It's what she always wanted, I guess."

"I think she's still mad at me about the Bull Ring." I'd called

Heather right after I talked to Chrissy to find out if she thought other people had noticed Will and I. She'd told me she'd been too drunk to notice herself, let alone anyone else in that "reeking cesspool of a tent."

"She'll get over it. Let's go help Clarence with those chairs."

As the afternoon wore on, I kept glancing around, wondering when Will, Dad, and Lily would arrive. I was thankful to be busy running back and forth, getting supplies for Mere, helping to direct people towards the snacks. Anything to keep me from being alone with Radek.

"Hey."

I jumped at the voice close behind me and almost dropped the bowl of coleslaw I was ferrying to the food tables for Mere. Will stood behind me, his face serious. He glanced around at the growing crowd. He held three of Dad and Lily's lawn chairs. I fought back the initial urge to hug him. Lily stood behind him with three Tupperware containers of chicken potpie. "There you are!" she said. "Here, take this would you, Chickadee." She passed the containers into my free arm then fanned her face with her hands. "That pig fire is hotter than the pits of hell." She took one of the lawn chairs from Will and walked off to find a place far from the fire to sit. I watched her navigate the lawn in her high heels and fitted yellow dress.

"Hi," I said to Will, careful not to look at him too long. This wasn't like the Bull Ring, where there'd been a huge crowd of drunk people. These were all people we knew, people who were still relatively sober, people who would be watching. Not to mention Radek was around somewhere. He'd been helping Clarence set up the horseshoe pit the last time I spotted him.

"Want any food?" Will asked.

"No, thanks." I set the bowl and the Tupperware down and we

stood side by side watching the poor pig turn on the spit, its pink skin turning a crispy, bubbly black.

"You didn't come last night."

Of course he's ready to talk now, with all these people here to watch. My eyes darted around, making sure no one was looking at us. I took Will's arm, pulling him a few steps away, behind the barn, where we'd be less likely to draw attention.

"I couldn't. I just . . . couldn't."

"Were you with him?" Will's voice was thick with anger. He set the lawn chairs on the ground beside the barn.

I grabbed at his hand but he pulled it away. "No! Of course not."

"I don't think it's an 'of course not,' Hannah."

I stepped back as a few kids came around the side of the barn, talking about Radek and football.

"Great. Even the kids think this guy's a hero," Will said, after they'd passed.

"Will, this is complicated. You said you understood complicated."

"I understand *my* complicated. This I don't understand. It seems pretty simple. You want to be with him or you want to be with me."

I shook my head. "But what does 'with you' mean? I don't even know if you're going to stay after the summer. Or if you want me to leave with you." I expected Will to get angry, but he looked surprised.

"I guess you're right."

I wanted more than anything to reach out to him. Why couldn't we be having this conversation somewhere else? I hoped no one had noticed I was missing. "Can we talk about this later, at the cabin?"

"I don't see what there is to talk about," he said. He turned and picked up the lawn chair and began to walk away, around the side of the barn. This time I grabbed his arm and pulled him back.

"I don't even know you!" I said, anger rising hot from my stomach. "For all I know, you're a drug dealer." I whispered the last two words. He narrowed his eyes at me and I let go of him.

"How did you find out about that?" he said, his voice quiet. My face burned as I remembered sneaking into the cabin, finding the coffee tin.

"I'm not a *drug dealer*, like some movie mobster," he said. "It's only weed."

"Shhh!" I hissed, doing another shoulder check for prying eyes. Everyone seemed distracted by the food and pig-on-a-spit.

His eyes met mine and held them. "I got it from a guy I met—a rancher. Before I came here. He grows the stuff in one of his fields." He took a deep breath. "I just sell it to the ranch guys, nothing risky." So that's why it hadn't mattered he wasn't getting paid much working for Dad. I reached my hand out again and then let it drop.

"Please don't go away." My voice sounded small, close to tears. Before I could say more, I spotted Chrissy across the yard, sitting in a chair beside Lily, glaring at me. I stepped back from Will. "I'll come tonight," I said, and walked back to the food tent, looking for something to clean up.

I was on edge all night waiting to run into Radek. It wasn't unusual for us not to spend time together at a party. He knew how to "work a room," as he called it. I caught sight of him now and then, making his way around the yard, visiting with everyone. I overheard people asking him the same questions, over and over again. "How'd the team do this year?" "When are you back for good?" "You hear about the high school team at playoffs?" I went into the house to use the bathroom and ran into Chrissy in the upstairs hall. She grabbed my shoulders.

"You've got to stop. It's not okay, Hannah." Her voice was hard, not understanding like it had been at the end of our last phone call.

I shook her off, feeling heat flush through my body. "I'm not doing anything."

"We both know that's a lie."

A cheer went up outside, and we went to the hall window and looked out at the yard. From above we could see how many people had gathered, a decent crowd. Mere would be happy. I strained to see what everyone was looking at, and then spotted Radek at the horseshoe pit. Apparently he'd done something good in the game.

"That's why you have to stop," Chrissy said, her voice quieter now. "Don't you want to be a good person? R.W. has been nothing but good to you. This is a bad thing you're doing to him. But if you stop now you can marry him and start a family. Like Chucker and I are." She smiled at me, her hand on her belly.

"We're on a break" I said meekly. I hadn't seen Radek since Christmas. Eight months. So much had changed in eight months, but even from the upstairs window I recognized the familiar slope of his shoulders, the confident handshakes and back claps he gave the guys who greeted him. I scanned the crowd for Will: he stood back from the fire, smoking a cigarette and looking out towards the mountains. I leaned against the window sill, heart hammering in my chest. How did he do that to me? Every. Single. Time.

Chrissy moved her hand from her belly to clasp my hand in hers. It was warm. Mine was cold. "Listen, there's something I have to tell you before we go back out. I already told Heather, but only because she guessed when I didn't take one of her gross drinks." She squeezed my hand. "I'm pregnant!"

"You're what!" I tried to count back. How long had she even been with Chucker?

"Yes! It's super new, I only found out a few days ago. Chucker is soooo excited. And . . ."

I put my hand to my head. Too much at once.

"And we're getting married!" She shot her left hand out, showing off a silver ring with a small diamond and two blue stones. "Chucker didn't want to wait, and he didn't want my parents thinking he was a bad guy. Of course it's really fast, but it feels right, you know?"

"I'm so happy for you," I said, and I meant it. I hugged her, squeezing her tight.

She looked at the ring on her finger as I pulled away. "I can't explain how I feel about him. It's just, like, when we're together, everything feels so easy and . . . right. You know?"

I did know.

I congratulated her again and promised we'd talk wedding plans soon.

"Go see your boyfriend!" she said. She smiled at me as she walked into the bathroom. Her face had changed so much it seemed like our conversation about Will hadn't even happened. I pulled at my hair. I wanted to ask her how she could call Radek my boyfriend when he was with Fun Girl. To tell her she knew nothing about who Will was or what makes a good person. To tell her to fuck off. But I didn't. I bit my cheek and walked downstairs.

At the sink in the kitchen, I splashed water on my face, then dried it with a dish towel. My reflection flashed in the small round mirror Mere kept tacked on the wall above the sink to check her makeup. My face was pale. Dark circles lined my eyes. How was I going to do this? What was I going to do? Maybe I could fake it for one week—Radek wouldn't be home for that long. Then he would go back to school and I'd have two whole years to figure things out before he came back for good. *What do you want? What do you want? What do* you *want, Hannah?* I shivered and shut off the kitchen light before going back outside.

ugust 1996

I APPROACHED the food tent and found Radek with Mere. She was filling a plate for him. As soon as she spotted me she set the plate down, clapped her hands, and held them at her chest. "There you are! We were looking for you." She smiled, her eyes moving between the two of us. "Well I'll leave you two alone. I need to refresh the salads anyway." Mere took two near-empty bowls from the table and strode back to the house.

I struggled for something to say, something old Hannah would have said, something that would make things feel normal.

"Nice pig this year," Radek said, breaking the silence for me. He picked up the plate his mother had prepared for him and shoved a piece of pork into his mouth. After all this time he wanted to talk about the pig? "Your dad and Lily look good."

"Mmhmm," I said. I opened one of the coolers at the edge of the tent and pulled out a beer. "Want one?"

"Since when do you drink beer?"

"I don't mind it. Want one?" I tried to keep my voice light, but he could tell something was off.

"I guess so," he said, his tone uncertain. He was wearing a shirt I'd never seen before, a plaid button-up with pearl buttons. A real Texan shirt. Who had picked that out? Mere usually sent him clothes, but this didn't look like something she would have chosen.

"Nice shirt." I leaned back against the table beside him. I tried to force my brain to not make comparisons, but they came flooding in. If Will and I were alone, we wouldn't be talking about the quality of the pig or how Dad and Lily looked, that's for sure. I looked down, avoiding Radek's eyes.

"Yeah, Bucky and I went shopping."

I tried to remember how Radek and I used to be when he was home, and then realized it had always been like this. Just, normal.

"Well should we go back out to the fire? Don't want anyone thinking we're up to no good in here." He laughed at his own joke. I picked up my beer and followed him. Guys clapped him on the shoulder as he passed, welcoming him back like he was a war hero. It was getting ridiculous. As soon as Mr. Morton pulled him aside I slipped away. I found Heather in a lawn chair outside the massive tent she was sharing with Chrissy and Chucker.

"Holy hell that looks awkward. Even from over here. Why is this so awkward?"

I sat in the chair beside her. "I guess for obvious reasons."

Heather kept her eyes on the fire as I scanned the crowd for Will.

"Did Chrissy tell you?"

"Yes. Crazy."

"Looks like I'll be the only one of us who isn't barefoot and pregnant in the next twelve months," Heather said bitterly. She took a swig from her red plastic cup.

"Oh come on!" I punched her lightly in the arm. "I'm in no

rush for any of that." She raised an eyebrow at me. "Not anymore at least. What's in there?" I pointed at the cup.

"Lemon gin and Fresca."

"Ew." I took it from her and drank anyway.

"Even though you're not in any rush, someone else might have other ideas."

"What do you mean?"

Heather nodded towards Radek, who had appeared at the edge of the food tent again, this time with Chucker and Chrissy in tow. "I mean, why do you think he left Austin to come back here and surprise you?"

She was right. "Do you think someone told him?"

Heather took another sip of her drink and grimaced. "You're right, this is gross. No, I don't know who would have. But maybe someone hinted at it. You'd have to be half stupid not to see what's going on between you and Will."

"Shhh!" I elbowed her and looked around us. "Have you seen him?"

"I saw him walking away across the field, smoking, being his broody self."

I let my head fall back on the chair. *Phew.* I'd see him at the cabin soon.

AFTER THE FIRE had been put out and everyone had retired to their tents, I helped Clarence, Radek, and Mere carry leftovers into the kitchen. As Radek and I passed each other in the mudroom he stuck his tongue out at me, like when we were kids.

"You're dumb," he said.

"You're dumber." I smiled back at him and my shoulders relaxed a little.

"You threw one hell of a party, Ma," Clarence said in the

kitchen, his words slurred. I only ever saw him tipsy once a year, at the pig roast.

"You may be an adult, Clarence, but you know better than to say that word in this house." But she smiled as she said it.

"Go to bed, Mom." Radek came up beside Mere and rubbed her shoulder. "We can take care of the rest. It's pretty much done anyway."

Mere hugged each of us and stood back. "It's so nice to have all of you in my kitchen again," she said. She blew us kisses and walked up the stairs.

Clarence took a handful of chips from a bowl and shoved them into an egg salad sandwich. "I'm putting myself to bed," he said, taking his plate with him up the stairs.

Radek came towards me and put his hands on my hips, just above the waist of my jeans. "You look different."

My face flushed. "Different how?" I could smell beer on his breath.

"I don't know. More grown-up or something."

"Well it has been awhile." My words came out in a whisper. I'd thought the same thing about him.

"Want to watch a movie?" Our code for sex.

"I better go home." I struggled for words. "It'd be so obvious if I stayed. Your mom would—"

"Since when do you care about that?" Radek stepped back and let his hands drop. He rubbed the back of his neck.

"It's just been a lot in one night, you know? Did you know Chrissy and Chucker got engaged?"

"She told me," he said. "And she's knocked up."

"Yes! So fast."

"It's not fast if they're in love."

I looked at him out of the corner of my eye. "Says Mr. Traditional."

"What do you mean by that?"

"I pretty much had to beg you to sleep with me when we were in high school."

Radek laughed, and the tension was broken. "Well you wouldn't have to beg me now. Come on, Han, it's been so long. And we made a pact. Whenever I'm back, we're back together." He reached for my waist again and I sidestepped away.

"You can't just waltz in with your new clothes and cologne and expect me to submit to your demands. Maybe I'm more traditional now." I put my hands in my pockets and tried to meet Radek's eyes, but my stomach felt like it held a lump of heavy dough. Who was I?

"Okay, okay. See you tomorrow then. You'll be here for breakfast?"

"Sure . . . yes." I went to the mudroom and took a wool sweater I'd left there off a hook.

"Let me drive you home."

"You've been drinking."

"So? It's not far."

"Far enough." I gave him a peck on the cheek and stepped out the back door.

At first I walked towards the field that would take me straight to the house, but as soon as I was out of sight, I took a sharp left and headed towards the cabin.

3 8

ugust 1996

I SAW the red ember of Will's cigarette glowing on the cabin porch before I saw him. All the cabin's lights were off. His eyes were on me as I walked up the steps and came to stand beside him.

"Can I have some of that?" I pointed at the glass on the porch rail. He passed it to me and I took a big swig, enjoying the burn of the alcohol on my throat. Maybe it would clean me, take me back to when I was good.

"Didn't think I'd see you tonight. You haven't seen your *boyfriend* in a long time." The way he said *boyfriend* reminded me of the day we'd met and he'd teased me about being the "future wife of a college man."

"I said I'd be here."

He took the empty glass from me and went into the cabin. I heard him moving around the dark kitchen, opening and closing cupboard doors, cracking ice out of its tray by the shallow light cast by the refrigerator. Will returned and handed me my own glass of whiskey on ice. I thanked him and sipped more slowly this time. We stood side by side, silent, looking out at the creek. I listened to his breath, the sound of ice cubes clinking against glass. Tension buzzed between us, sad and powerful at the same time. I wanted to turn to him, to hug him and feel like everything would be okay. To hear him say "we'll figure it out" again. I reached for the pack of cigarettes he'd placed on the rail and took one out, gesturing at him for his lighter. He raised an eyebrow but handed it to me.

I'd only had a few cigarettes in my life, the first one from a pack of Marlboros Heather and I found in Lily's sock drawer. After that one I'd spent the afternoon on the couch, puking into a bucket while Lily made fun of me. She pretended I had the flu when Dad got home, though.

I managed to light it and took a small inhale that dissolved into a coughing fit. I wanted the smoke to burn, to hurt. Will laughed at me and patted my back. "I thought proper ladies didn't smoke."

"I don't feel like a proper lady."

"Well I don't feel like a proper guy, so that makes two of us." He took a sip of his drink. "I understand if you want to be with him." He'd turned from the creek to face me, his eyes serious. I tried to take a drag but ended up in another coughing fit. Will took the cigarette from my hand and put it out in the coffee tin he was using as an ashtray. "I mean it," he said. "I'll step back. What you've had with him, it goes so far back. And I, of all people, get that."

My chest burned, and I heaved in a deep breath. Thoughts flowed through my head like sticks down a river. *I should let him go, I should do the right thing, Radek and I have what everyone wants, don't we?*

Will emptied his glass and set it on the porch ledge, and then sat beside it, his feet dangling a few inches above the porch floor-boards. "You're golden."

At first I thought he meant I looked golden in the light, but there was no light.

"What do you mean?"

"I mean . . . to me you're perfect, golden. I don't want to ruin you, to make you the kind of girl who . . ." He took a deep breath. "I don't want you to have regrets. I want you to get exactly what you want."

I moved to stand between his thighs, and he pulled me into his chest, holding me tight. I breathed deeply, taking in his smell, pushing my face into his chest.

"Can we—" Before I finished, he moved me aside and slipped off the porch rail. He stopped short before opening the cabin door, his eyes on his feet.

"Go home, Hannah." His voice was low.

My stomach lurched. "But—"

"Just go home."

I STORMED across the dark field, my hands balled into fists at my sides. He'd rejected me. Told me to go home like I was an annoying kid. I climbed Blueberry Hill until I was halfway up and then sat, looking out over the acres of land. Even in the dark I could make out the woods and mountains beyond. Soon all of this would belong to someone else.

I wanted someone to tell me what to do next. Who to choose, where to go. I tried to remember a time when I'd felt this lost, so unsure of what I wanted. What would life with Will be like, anyway? Dad might not sell with Will here to help. I could move out to the cabin. It was small but we could make it our own. No matter how mad Dad was he would still need help on the ranch, and I knew he liked Will. I pictured Will and me fixing up the place, buying a new fridge and sofa, dishes that weren't chipped. Spending every night in the twin bed, having coffee and breakfast together without a deadline for leaving. Going into town and not having to pretend we weren't together. But Radek would be home in two years and he would live next door. Radek sent my mind spinning in a whole different direction. How could my life not have Radek in it? I didn't know life without Radek. Radek and the ranch.

I stayed until the dew on the grass soaked the back of my jeans. I looked at the mountains, grey and surrounded by fog in the early morning light. Where had the orphaned bears gone? I hoped they'd found a new home, somewhere deep in the mountains.

THE HOUSE WAS quiet when I stepped in the back door. I let Mickey Two slip in, and found leftovers in the fridge for his breakfast since we'd be eating at the Baileys'. Part of the pig roast tradition was breakfast the next morning. A smaller crowd gathered and Mere used leftover ham and eggs and potatoes to create a brunch feast. The floor above me creaked. Dad came down the stairs first, grunting hello and taking a seat at the small table in the kitchen. I pulled out the kettle and coffee press.

"Nice to see R.W. back." He pressed his fingers into his greying eyebrows, rubbing back and forth. How much whiskey had he had at the pig roast? The throbbing at the base of my skull told me I'd had a little too much. And no sleep. But coffee would fix that.

"Yeah." I kept my back to him, pouring coffee grounds into the press, silently begging the water to boil faster. "It's been a while."

Dad lifted his head. "Why are you here anyway? Didn't you stay over at the Baileys'?"

Shit. I always stayed at the Baileys' after the pig roast, in the basement with Radek. I hadn't thought of how strange it would look for me to be at the house this early. Lily padded into the kitchen dressed in jeans with rips at the knees like girls my age wore, and a tight plaid orange top. "I came back to take you guys over," I said feebly, hoping Lily's entrance would distract Dad.

"We're not going to breakfast," Dad said. He refused to meet Lily's gaze.

"Water's boiling," Lily said, her voice low. Her right cheek was puffy and a little red. I opened my mouth to speak but she shook her head sharply, her dark eyes on mine. I poured the water over the grounds. He'd hit her in the face. He never, ever hit her. What had set him off? Anger rose from deep inside me and turned my face boiling hot.

I handed Lily and then Dad cups of coffee in the silent room. Dad took his and went out to the porch. I cornered Lily in the kitchen and forced her to show me her face. It was swollen, but the skin wasn't broken. The bruise had only begun to show, and she'd tried to cover it with makeup so I couldn't tell how bad it was.

"What happened?"

Lily looked like she was going to cry. Like she had been crying all night.

"He thought I was flirting with one of the Baileys' ranch hands." She kept her voice low so Dad couldn't hear her on the porch. "Or, the whiskey in his belly thought that." She dropped herself into a chair. "I wasn't. Not even a little bit."

"That was it?" Every few weeks Dad decided Lily was flirting with someone, usually one of the guys who worked at the Red Lion, or a regular customer. She always talked him down.

"No. I'd been drinking, too. And I brought up how Chrissy is getting married to a guy she just met, how she's going to . . ." Lily's voice broke as tears tipped out of her eyes. Chrissy was getting everything Lily had been waiting fifteen years for in a matter of months. I sat across from her and reached my hand over the table to hold hers.

"I'm so sorry, Lily. I'm so sorry," I said, hoping "sorry" would cover everything. Sorry he'd hit her, sorry he'd never given her what she wanted, sorry she was stuck here, with us, this messed-up triad.

"He just hit me, Hannah. He just wound up and hit me. Told me to stop blubbering like a teenage girl. That he'd never have another child, that he'd never marry again. And if I didn't know that by now I was a stupid—" She closed her mouth and let tears roll down her cheeks.

Blood pounded in my ears. "No."

"It's not your fault, Chickadee," she said, but her voice was flat.

I walked around the table and hugged Lily over the chair. Her shoulders heaved. After a few moments she sat up, took a deep breath, and wiped her face. Mascara had run down her cheeks, leaving long black trails below her eyes.

"Would you look at me," she said, her voice light again. "I'm a mess." She opened her mouth, about to say something, and then shut it again. "I'll go do myself up again. I bet we can still make it in time for breakfast if we can talk your dad into it." She stood and walked out of the kitchen.

I heard Will's footsteps on the porch, his greeting to Dad, Dad telling him there was coffee inside. Fury mixed with the sour coffee in my stomach. How could Lily just brush this off? How could we go on pretending these things weren't happening, pretending everything didn't happen? As Will opened the porch door, dipping his head to step in, I barrelled past him.

"Whoa, hey—" He tried to stop me, but I was on the porch and in front of Dad before he could catch me.

"You killed her!" I screamed at him, knowing even as I did it I'd lost control. I didn't care. Dad's mouth dropped open, but nothing came out. "I know you did it! You did it on purpose!" I choked on tears, trying to catch my breath. "You killed Momma and you're going to kill Lily, too! You killed her because she was cheating on you." I spat the last few words at him. The weight of the summer, the past few days, everything, fell onto my shoulders.

Dad put his head in his hands, rubbed his hair. I'd expected him to fight back, to yell. "I don't know," he said, his voice calm and even.

Will stood a few steps behind me on the porch, not moving.

"What do you mean you don't know?"

"I mean I don't know anything, Hannah. I don't know if she was having an affair. I don't know if she was leaving. I don't know if I killed her on purpose. I don't know." Where I'd expected him to be angry, he was only sad, and that hurt worse.

"Why did you hit Lily? Lily's not Momma."

Dad shook his head and looked out at the field. His cheeks looked hollow, his face older than it had been at the beginning of the summer. "That was an accident," he said.

I took the porch steps two at a time. Will followed me, matching his stride to mine. "Hannah, wait." I didn't stop. When we got to the barn door, he wrapped his hand around my wrist. "Wait, please."

I looked into his eyes and shook my head, tears pouring down my face. I shook my head and he let go of my arm. I opened the barn door and walked into the tack room, grabbing a bridle from the hooks on the wall. I fit it onto Honcho's face as Will watched. I didn't bother with a saddle. I pulled myself onto my horse's back and arranged the reins in my hand. Will opened the back barn door, and I could feel him watching us as we trotted across the yard. I kicked Honcho into a gallop as soon as we reached the back field.

ugust 1996

I RODE ALONG THE CREEK, past the cabin to a place I knew would be shallow enough to cross. The sun had come up hot in the sky, and I wished I'd brought a hat. I let Honcho drink and then urged him into a trot towards the edge of the woods. Under the cool shade of the trees we slowed to a walk as we weaved our way deeper into the forest. Dad only owned part of this wood. I knew from spending so much time in it as a kid that eventually Honcho and I would reach a post with an orange marker and a long-ago stretched out and broken fence wire. We could continue on from there. The land behind ours was owned by the Baileys. They were beside us and behind us, surrounding us.

I dismounted in a clearing and let Honcho graze as I lay back against a tree. My life had changed so much in two short months. Despite all that had happened, so good and so bad, I couldn't deny something inside me had shifted. I felt better—more alive—

than I had in years. Maybe ever. A thick grey blanket of fog had been lifted from my face. I could breathe again.

Honcho munched on the long green grass in the clearing, disturbing butterflies from their resting places. A brilliant blue butterfly landed on my arm and I watched it walk, its tiny feet tickling my skin. *Butterflies taste with their feet,* I remembered from school. I'd always loved this clearing. There was something magical about it. A memory of being in this place with Momma flooded back. She'd picked forget-me-nots—*Myosotis*—from the field and we'd sat with a blanket and eaten warm sandwiches wrapped in parchment paper. She stuck the flowers in one of our empty pop cans and said we were eating a meal fit for the Queen. I thought about the bus ticket again. Momma had been planning to leave, I was certain. Was that wrong or right? Wrong to give up on Dad, or right to follow her heart? But if Dad was hurting her, how could she have stayed? Why were there no easy answers?

When sun left the clearing and the air cooled, I mounted Honcho and headed back to the house. I wouldn't leave Lily. Not after all she'd done for Dad and me.

WHEN I GOT BACK, I found a peanut butter and jelly sandwich wrapped in wax paper in the refrigerator and a note from Lily saying she and Dad had gone to town for an early dinner. An apology dinner, I guessed. I took the sandwich out to the porch and chewed it slowly as Mickey Two begged at my feet. Will came across the yard from the barn, temporarily distracting Mickey, and asked to use the phone. I wanted to ask if he was calling Jolene, but just nodded. When he came back out to the porch, he sat beside me on the bench, leaving a generous space between us.

"I'm heading to the Red Lion tonight to meet the ranch hands from the Baileys' place. Not the Bailey boys." He added the last part quickly. "Are you okay?"

"I don't know." That was the most honest answer I had. I wanted to reach across the bench and take his hand, or go back to the cabin with him, but I could practically feel Radek's presence across the field. Will shifted on the bench, looking uncomfortable.

"I've gotta go. See you at breakfast tomorrow?"

My breath caught in my throat. I wouldn't be spending the night at the cabin?

As if he could read my mind, Will reached his hand across the bench and squeezed mine. "We'll take the horses out after chores tomorrow, ride the tree line and spend some time," he said.

His rough hand was warm and comforting on mine. "Okay." Why did it feel like he was getting ready to leave? Dad had agreed to keep him on until the first snow. I watched as he pulled his truck onto the dirt road, kicking up dust.

AFTER WILL LEFT, I went into the house and flipped through the channels on the TV. I let the droning of the TV fill my ears, willing my mind not to think. *Sleep, if I could only fall asleep I wouldn't be able to think.* I was jolted awake by the sound of tires on the gravel on the laneway and got up and looked out the window. Radek climbed out of Clarence's truck and walked to the porch. I stepped out to greet him.

"You didn't come to breakfast," he said, his voice monotone. He stood across from me, his hands in his pockets.

"No." I didn't have it in me to make up another lie. "Dad and Lily had a fight, and then Dad and I did too." I wanted him to ask me what it was about, to give me an excuse to tell him about her bruises, about how Dad had been drinking too much, about how he'd been sad rather than mad when I finally confronted him about Momma. I wanted to tell him all I had were questions, no answers.

"You missed a good one. Mom made blueberry pancakes along with everything else." Radek took his hands out of his pockets and hooked them on his belt, widening his stance.

I bit down on the tip of my thumb until it ached. I didn't let my eyes meet Radek's. "That sounds good." I paused, gnawing on my nail. "Your mom's pancakes are the best."

"Hannah, I'm getting the sense you don't want to see me."

I took my thumb out of my mouth. "It's not that, I'm—I'm confused."

"Is this about that ranch hand?"

I glanced up at him. "What?" My voice was high and sharp. What did he know about Will?

"That ranch hand, what's his name—Will? Chrissy told me you'd been spending time together."

Chrissy! After years of friendship, she meets a guy and becomes holier than anyone. How much had she told him? I dropped into one of the porch chairs. Radek sat on the railing across from me.

"Look, it's okay. It's not like I haven't hung out with other girls. We agreed not to talk about it." He shifted, crossing his feet at the ankles.

"Other girls?" I said, drawing out the *s*. "The only one you told me about was Fun Girl."

"Who?"

"Never mind." It was one thing to think it, but another thing to know.

"There were a few," he said, crossing his arms over his chest. "I didn't think you'd want to know—"

"So you've been lying, this whole time." My whole body went stiff, suddenly cold. All this time I'd been feeling so guilty about Will, and here Radek had been dating for years.

Radek uncrossed his feet and stood. He adjusted his ball cap and looked out across the yard, avoiding my eyes. "Not the whole time."

"Not the whole time?" My voice rose, and Mickey Two lifted his head from my foot. "Did you—" How could I ask him what I wanted to know when I'd done so much worse? "Did you sleep with any of them?" I pulled my legs up into my chest and Mickey set his head back on the porch boards with a sigh.

"We said we weren't going to talk about this. And it doesn't matter anyway. None of those girls were like you." Radek sat beside me. "We've got plans, Hannah. We've been planning for this our whole lives and we're so close. I'm almost done school."

I was planning for this. *Was.* "Dad's selling the ranch." Saying it out loud made it feel final.

"I know. You should have told me. Clarence wants to get more cattle. There'll be lots of work for me at home. We don't need it."

"Don't need it?" *What about me? What about what I needed?* I lowered my face to my knees and bit into the hardness of my knee cap, rocking a little.

"Hannah?"

I glanced sideways at him, my cheek on my knee.

"Don't you have anything to say?"

I didn't. I really didn't have a clue what to say. I only knew I didn't want to lie anymore. "I need time, Radek. Everything has changed. With Dad and Lily, the ranch. With—"*Will*, I thought but didn't say. "I've got some stuff I need to figure out." He knew so little about what was happening in my life. I knew so little about him. Did we even know each other at all anymore?

"We've got our whole lives ahead of us. Remember, we pinky swore."

The pinky swear. My stomach rolled. I stood and opened the porch door. "I've gotta go to bed."

"It's not even nine."

"I'm tired."

Radek puffed air out through his lips, his eyebrows high on

his forehead. "Fine." He pushed his hands into his thighs and stood from the bench. "Tuesday then. The canyon. I'll pick you up after lunch." His face looked wary.

"Okay." I leaned on the open porch door and watched as he pulled the truck back onto the road. I couldn't hide from him much longer.

DAD AND LILY came in a few hours later. I crawled out of bed and went down to see how their night had gone. Dad was drunk—humming songs with his arm wrapped around Lily's shoulders. Lily smiled at me, but her eyes didn't crinkle at the corners. She got Dad set up in his easy chair with a short whiskey and turned on a baseball game for him.

"Hannah," Dad said. "You're a good kid."

An apology of sorts? I nodded at Dad and followed Lily into the kitchen.

"You okay?" Lily asked me in the kitchen. I walked to the fridge and pulled out a half-empty jar of pickles. I fished one out with my fingers. "Is that your dinner?"

I smiled. "I'm lost without you."

Lily laughed and pulled out a chair at the table. I sat across from her with the pickle jar. Every few minutes we'd hear Dad either cheer or grumble from the other room.

"I guess dinner went well?" I nodded towards the living room.

"Yeah, we went to the Italian place."

"He brought out the big guns." The Italian restaurant in Jessop was the most expensive restaurant in town, and the best, too.

"He feels bad, Hannah. He didn't mean to do it."

I wanted to tell her to run away, to leave him like Momma might have been about to do. To leave him before he broke her heart even more. To leave and find someone who wanted to get married and have babies before it was too late. But it was so much more complicated than that.

"Lil!" Dad called. "These goddamned Blue Jays couldn't win a game if someone handed it to them in a bucket."

"Well, that's me, off to bed," Lily said, pressing herself up from the table. "Love you." She kissed me on the top of my head as she walked by.

≈

I WOKE from a dream where Lily was floating down the creek in her yellow dress, her hair spread around her, a smile on her face. My shirt was soaked in sweat, my heart racing. I lay still, trying to catch my breath, my mind tugging at little bits of the dream as they faded away.

Thwack.

I sat up straight and swung my legs to the ground in one movement. Something had hit the window. I pressed my face close to the glass and squinted to make out shapes in the darkness. Will stood below on the lawn, waving.

Had Lily and Dad heard the rock hit my window? I stood still for a moment, listening for movement in their room down the hall. After a few breaths I motioned to Will to wait, and stepped into the jeans I'd left on the floor. Then I pulled Will's sweatshirt over my ratty sleeping shirt and rammed my ball cap on my head.

Will met me on the porch, his face split in a wide, drunken grin.

"You're crazy. Lily and Dad could have heard that," I said, but I was smiling too.

"I thought you might need cheering up," he said loudly. "Nice sweatshirt."

I *shh*'d him and pulled him away from the house, towards the barn where we could speak normally.

We stopped in front of the barn, and Will pulled me close, pushed my hat back on my head, and kissed me, taking me by

273

surprise. Before I could question him, he took my hand and pulled me behind him. "Let's go."

As we neared the cabin, he dropped my hand and asked me to wait where I was, a few feet away. He jogged inside, lights turning on and off as he moved through the two rooms. He was back out in a few minutes, carrying a bottle and a blanket.

"Whiskey," he said, lifting the bottle so I could see the label.

"Where are we going?"

"You'll see." He took my hand again, and we walked side by side along the creek until we reached the aspen grove. I followed as he walked to the middle of a small copse. He pulled a candle from his back pocket and dug it into the dirt before laying the blanket out and pulling me down to sit beside him.

"This has been one hell of a summer," he said, handing me the bottle and then lighting the candle.

I took a sip and winced. "It sure has."

"I'll never forget it." His voice sounded sad, a bit far away.

"I don't know what to do." My lip quivered and I stopped talking. I didn't want to cry. I'd cried enough already for fifteen summers. I took a few deep breaths. "I'm just so stuck."

"What do you want to do?" Will set the bottle between us and turned away from me to light a cigarette. "Don't think about it. Say the first thing that comes to your mind."

"Go away somewhere else."

"And what else?"

"Go to school. Do experiments, learn about plants. That sounds so lame. I don't know." I sipped from the bottle again.

"And what about Radek?"

I shrugged. "I don't know. I truly don't know. We have so much history, but . . ."

"But?"

I glanced at Will and then down at my hands. "But, I don't feel the way I feel with you when I'm with him."

Will held the bottle by its neck in his free hand and poured whiskey into his throat. He swallowed, grimaced, and turned to look at me.

"I don't want you to fuck up your life because of me."

"What? How?"

"What do I have to offer you? I don't have a house, I rodeo—hell, I can't even do that right now." He glanced down at his collarbone.

"I don't care about that." I took the bottle from him and drank again.

"Then why haven't you told Radek about you and me?"

I wiped my mouth with the back of my hand. I thought of Radek's face, of how certain he was of our future together. I tried to imagine telling him everything we'd always planned for would never happen. I set the bottle beside me.

"It's not that simple."

He stubbed his half-finished cigarette out on a rock and took another drink. "Come here." He turned my face to his and looked at me. "It is that simple." He leaned forward and kissed me.

ugust 1996

THE HOUSE WAS quiet when I snuck in the next morning. I crept up to my room and lay in bed, looking up at the cracked ceiling for what seemed like forever until I heard Dad and Lily moving around in their bedroom. I listened as Lily banged pots in the kitchen, and waited for the scent of breakfast to make its way up the stairs.

"Hannah!" Dad called. "Food's up."

I pulled on jeans and Will's sweatshirt again and went to the table in bare feet. Will was already seated across from me. He smiled when he saw his sweater. Lily reached around us to pour coffee before taking her seat.

"So we'll head out to the west pasture today, clear out that brush before it gets too hot."

We'd be swatting bugs all day, the sun beating down on us. The rain had made the swarms of mosquitoes thicker than I'd ever seen them before. Great start to the week.

"Sounds good," Will said, digging into the cheesy scrambled eggs on his plate. I picked up a piece of bacon and noticed it was slightly burned. Lily never burned the bacon. I looked up at her. She stared out the window, her eyes a million miles away. It looked like she'd applied her foundation with a paint scraper, but I could still see the bruise blooming on her cheek.

"Hopefully Lil still has some of that bug spray she concocted," Dad said. When Lily didn't answer, Dad looked back down at his plate.

AFTER BREAKFAST I scraped leftovers into Mickey's bowl and then followed Dad and Will out to the barn to saddle the horses.

"Here," Will said, handing me Skoal's reins. He'd saddled my horse for me. I glanced at Dad to see if he'd noticed, but he'd gone into the tack room.

I smiled. "Thank you." I walked towards the back barn door and then stopped. "Hey, did you notice anything strange with Lily at breakfast?"

Will looked up from cinching the saddle girth. "She was really quiet."

Something wasn't right. As we rode to the west pasture, I thought about Lily's face looking out over the yard.

"Hey, Dad, I forgot the bug spray."

He turned in his saddle to look at me.

"I'm going to go back and get it before these mosquitoes carry us off." I swatted around my face for effect.

"Hurry up about it then," he said gruffly.

I nodded at Will and then turned Skoal towards the house.

I TIED the horse to the rail near the oak tree so he'd have shade and took the porch stairs two at a time. I didn't kick off my boots on the mat.

"Lily!" She wasn't on the main floor. I'd known she wouldn't be. My boots were loud on the stairs as I made my way to the bedroom. I leaned against the doorway. My chest tightened. Lily shoved clothes into a brown-and-tan leather suitcase that lay on the unmade bed. The window was open, and the lace curtains flapped in the cool, late-morning breeze. "You're not leaving are you?" I asked, even though I knew the answer.

Lily looked up at me, her eyes puffy. "Never you mind," she said, but her voice was soft. "Aren't you supposed to be clearing brush?"

"I forgot the bug spray." I stepped into the room, feeling uncomfortable in the house with my boots on. Lily didn't seem to notice. I pushed aside her clothes and sat on the end of the bed. I could smell smoke from the Red Lion in Lily's hair, even a few feet away from her. No matter how hard Lily tried, or what she washed her hair with, that smell never came all the way out. Dad would sometimes jokingly call Lily "Smoky" and say he'd never need to smoke more than once a day—all he had to do was smell Lily's hair. "Please don't go." My voice came out in a whisper.

Lily stopped packing and looked at me, and for a moment I thought she was going to start crying. Then she pulled down the top of the suitcase, leaned on it, and snapped it shut, struggling with the old clasps. It was the case Lily had brought with her from Calgary, so long ago.

What had she put in the case? Had she taken all her clothes? Her hair clips and jewellery? Her crosswords? The bag didn't look big enough to hold all of Lily's life. Maybe she'd be back. Maybe she was just going to give Dad a scare so he'd finally marry her.

Lily stood in front of me. "Don't tell your dad you saw me, okay?"

I picked at the rumpled bedspread, pulling at a loose thread in the yellowing lace cover, desperately trying to come up with the perfect thing to say to get her to stay. *I'll wear anything you want.*

I'll never leave you alone with Dad when he's been drinking. Let's do a crossword together. I knew none of these tricks would work though, because this wasn't about me, it was about Dad, and I couldn't change him. "Okay," I said finally, my eyes burning. "Where are you going?"

"I don't want you to have to keep that secret, Chickadee." She picked up her suitcase.

"But how will I know where you are?" I stood up, panic fluttering in my chest like trapped butterflies. "You can't just leave!"

"Oh, honey, I'll write to you, don't worry. I'm not leaving you." She reached her free arm out and pulled me into a hug.

Tires crunched on the gravel outside.

"That's my ride," Lily said, stepping back from me.

I nodded. "Write me—I'll come visit," I said, trying to pull myself together. Part of me felt proud of her for doing what I'd thought she never would.

I followed Lily as she lugged the suitcase down the hall. As I pulled the bedroom door shut, I looked back out the window. The wind had picked up again, and it whipped the lace curtains into the room. The sky outside shone electric blue, no clouds in sight.

I LET Dad go into the house by himself that evening. I wouldn't be able to lie about seeing Lily leave while watching him discover she was gone. He'd probably walk in the door, pull off his boots, and call out for her when he realized there were no dinner smells coming from the kitchen. Had she left him a note? I lingered in the barn, finding small chores to keep myself busy as Will repaired the latch on a stall door. Lily had lived with us since I was six. Almost a lifetime. I swallowed hard, refusing to cry again. When the sound of Will hammering on the stall stopped, I went to find him.

"Lily's gone."

Will looked up from the water bucket he rinsed. "Holy shit." He put the bucket down and came to stand in front of me, putting his hands on my upper arms. "Why didn't you say something today?"

I shrugged. "She asked me not to tell Dad."

"Where'd she go?"

"She wouldn't say, but I'm guessing back to Calgary? I don't know if she knows anywhere else. She doesn't have any family left but us." I bit my lip, scrunching up my face. It wasn't like Calgary was close. When would I see her again? Will pulled me into a hug.

"Your dad's going to lose it."

I nodded, my face in his chest. "That's why I'm out here."

"Let's go into town for dinner."

I pulled back and looked up at him, my eyebrows lifted.

"For burgers or something—takeout. We'll eat in the truck."

Like two fugitives. Always running, always hiding.

LATER THAT NIGHT I crept into the house. I'd left the cabin after a few drinks, hoping Dad would be in bed. I'd have to figure out how to cook breakfast the next morning. Mickey Two greeted me as I opened the door. "How'd you get in here?" I whispered in the dark. He moved towards Dad's easy chair in the dark room.

"Dad?"

As my eyes adjusted to the lack of light, I could see him sitting there in his old chair, staring straight ahead at the blank TV screen. He raised a half-full glass to his mouth. An almost-empty bottle sat on the table beside him.

"Are you okay?" I asked.

I walked around to face him. His eyes were blank. "Lily's gone. But I'm guessing you already know that."

I didn't bother trying to lie. "Yes."

"Can't say I'm surprised."

"Dad . . ." I wanted to make him feel better. Despite it all, he was my only family. He hadn't been the best dad, but he'd always tried. He'd tried to raise me right, to be a good person. To do good.

"No, Hannah. It's time I face up to who I am. What I've done." He set his empty glass on the table beside him. "That's my last drink."

The room looked bare without Lily's things strewn around—her latest book of crosswords, her glossy magazines, her warm, perfumey, smoky smell. She'd taken only one suitcase. There was no way she could have fit everything in it. Maybe she'd thrown everything else out.

I sat on the arm of the sofa and stared at the blank TV with Dad. He seemed relatively sober.

"I'm sorry," I said, and then felt stupid. Lily hadn't left because she was unhappy here. She'd left because of Dad.

He shook his head and finally looked at me. In the moonlight from the window I could see his face was tired, his eyes drooping and red. Maybe he'd been drinking more than I thought. Mickey Two let out a sigh and rolled onto his side on Dad's foot. I was about to get up and go upstairs when Dad spoke.

"I've made a lot of mistakes in my life, Hannah." He looked right into my eyes. "A lot of mistakes."

I froze. Did he mean Lily? Me? Momma? Or something else altogether?

"A lot of them are thanks to this," he said, holding up his empty glass. "But a lot of them were just me."

My mind raced. I wanted him to tell me about Momma, but I suspected he was talking about Lily.

"Well maybe it's not too late," I said feebly. "You could try to find her." She'd promised she'd write to tell me where she was. I couldn't tell him unless she wanted me to.

He shook his head and pushed himself up from the chair,

disturbing the dog. "No, it's too late. It's too late to fix any of it." He picked up the empty glass and looked at it before putting it back down again. "But it's not too late for fixing what I haven't broke yet."

He tousled my hair as he walked by on the way to the stairs, something he hadn't done for maybe ten years. That was as close to "I love you" as I'd ever get from Dad.

ugust 1996

TUESDAY CAME TOO QUICK. Radek steered Mere's Oldsmobile up the laneway. Dad and Will came out of the barn. Mickey Two weaved his way between their legs to meet Radek in the yard. Radek wore new blue jeans and a button-up shirt and suit jacket. Not exactly swimming clothes for the canyon.

"How are the sheep?" Dad asked Radek as they fell in step on their way to the porch, where I waited. Will followed.

"Great. Clarence has got everything under control, even without me." Radek stopped a few feet short of the porch steps.

I grabbed the bag I'd packed with my towel and two baloney and mustard sandwiches I'd patched together. Will's eyes met mine and I looked away. No one spoke.

"Well, let's get going," Radek said, reaching for my bag. He made a show of putting his hand on the small of my back as I walked down the last step. I glanced at Will; he was still watching me. My face flushed and I lengthened my stride so Radek's hand would drop from my back. "See you guys for dinner," I said over my shoulder.

"I can't believe Chrissy is trying to pull off a wedding in one week." Radek rested his elbow on the window well of the car. "I moved my flight to Sunday night so I can make it."

"If anyone can pull off a wedding in a week it's Chrissy and her family. Besides, they don't really have the luxury of time." I hadn't talked to Chrissy since the pig roast. I was still mad at her for telling Radek about Will. Heather had called early that morning from the diner to tell me all about Chrissy's wedding plans. Chrissy's parents hadn't taken the pregnancy news well. Her dad wanted her married before anyone else figured out his daughter was pregnant out of wedlock, even though he liked the father of her child. The wedding would be small, a quick visit to the church and then a party at the community centre.

I looked out the window as we crossed back roads to the canyon. The rain had made the grass green, and it brushed the sides of the car as we turned onto a narrow dirt road. Why was Radek acting so normal? Maybe Chrissy hadn't told him as much about Will as I thought she had.

"You're quiet," he said. "Is this because of Lily?"

News travelled fast. I guessed Dad must have called Mere. I didn't reply.

"She might come back, you never know."

"Maybe," I said, to stop the conversation. The house was so empty without Lily. Everything was too dark and too quiet. Nothing felt right.

The canyon was deserted, as it almost always was. We laid out our towels and sat with our feet dangling in the water. Radek pulled his pant legs up as far as his calves would allow to keep them from getting wet. He shrugged out of his coat and arranged it on the rock beside him.

I wiggled my toes in the cool water, wondering if I should bother to paint them for Chrissy's wedding. Lily would want me to. Was she in Calgary now? I could have been there too, if I'd applied for school there like Mr. Simpson had suggested. "I wish I'd gone to university," I said. "I should have sent in that application, even if it was to major in science."

"Maybe you can go to school later, after . . ." His voice lowered as his words drifted off.

"After what?"

"You know, after we have kids and stuff. You wouldn't want to be gone when our kids are young." He picked up a rock and threw it into the canyon. It landed with a hollow *plop* and I waited for the ripples to clear. Kids. He assumed I still wanted to follow the same old plan. Couldn't he tell so much had changed?

"You going to swim?" he asked, "or do you want to get out of here?" He fidgeted with his cuffs, unbuttoning and re-buttoning them for no apparent reason. Was he sweating? Served him right for wearing something so ridiculous to the canyon. Who was this guy? Where was the Radek I used to know, the guy who would have pushed me into the water instead of asking?

Yes. Yes, I did want to get out of there, out of the whole place. I stood and gathered my towel, shaking the dirt off it. We'd only been sitting a few minutes but it was so uncomfortable, so quiet. What had we talked about before he went away to school?

"Okay, let's go," Radek said. He brushed his hands together and rolled his pant legs down. I waited by the car as he donned his jacket and picked up his towel. *Who wears a jacket to the canyon?*

"Can you unlock the door?" I said. I pulled at the handle. "Why did you lock it anyway?" Radek came around and stuck the key into the door, opening it for me. He didn't say anything about my snippy tone, but he blocked my way into the car.

"Hannah, there's something I've been wanting to ask you." He pulled at his collar.

Was he . . .? No way. "Oh, no. Radek—" I clutched my hands together in front of my stomach and looked down at my bare feet, willing my heart to slow down. No. Not this. Radek bent down on one knee in the gravel. My chest hurt so bad I thought it might burst open. He held a blue velvet ring box open in his left hand. A gold ring with a small diamond glinted in the sun.

"Radek . . ." I brought my palms to my face, covering my eyes.

"I promised you I'd be back to marry you, and I'm keeping my promise. Hannah Tatum, will you marry me?"

I drew my hands down my face and pushed my fingers into the inside corners of my eyes. My head spun. *Breathe, in through your nose, out through your mouth. Breathe.* I thought of Will, back at the ranch, sitting on the porch with Dad, or at the cabin. Will and I had no plan, no past, no promises. But did we have a future?

"I got it in town, the day of the pig roast," Radek said. I let my hands drop to my sides. A raven circled the canyon, calling out as it passed. "Hannah? Say something." I looked down at Radek and his eyes met mine. It was all so right, but so wrong.

I closed the ring box in Radek's hand with a snap. "I'm so sorry, Radek."

"What? Is it the ring?" He got to his feet and stuffed the box back into his jacket pocket. "You wanted a different one? I showed Chrissy at the pig roast and she said it would be perfect."

Of course it wasn't the ring. *The bus ticket. Momma's hands folded under the quilt. The empty look in Harlon's eyes.* Clouds moved across the sky behind Radek's head. "It's not the ring, Radek. I can't marry you."

WE DROVE BACK to Stillwater in total silence. Every time I glanced over at Radek, his eyes were set straight ahead, on the dirt road, blinking hard. When he stopped the car in the laneway I reached into the back seat and pulled my bag into my lap.

"Radek, I'm so sorry."

He shook his head. "Don't. Don't say sorry like you feel bad for me."

I waited for him to say more, but he pressed his lips together and refused to look at me, so I pulled the door handle.

"Wait," he said. "Think about it for a few days. You'll have a year to plan the wedding. We can get married in June when I'm done the semester. This is what you always wanted."

Was. It was what I wanted. I gave him what I hoped was an apologetic look and stepped a leg outside the car. Radek reached across the seat to grab my arm.

"Just give it a few days. I've been gone so long and I know that hasn't been easy. Remember how good we are when we're together? You're my best friend, Han." He sounded like the Radek I knew again.

My throat constricted as I let myself sink back into the car. My voice came out in a whisper. "Okay."

After he left, I went straight upstairs to my room and shut the door, thankful Dad was out. I lay on my bed and pressed my face into my pillow and let out a moan. I'd wanted that moment so much, played it over in my mind, imagined what Radek would say, how a wedding ring would feel on my finger. What was I going to do?

"How am I supposed to know!" I screamed into the pillow. I sat up and pummelled the pillow with everything I had, smashing my fists into it until my wrists ached.

"So DID you talk about it after?" Heather asked. She'd finally phoned me back, after I'd tried her three times. She didn't want to pay for an answering machine.

"Not really, he just drove me home."

"What about the ring?"

"He kept it."

"Hmm." Heather crunched on something on the other end of the line. Likely Cheetos. "Sounds like he thinks you'll change your mind. Did you tell Will?"

"I haven't seen him." I thought about Will's eyes after I'd kissed him goodnight on the cabin porch the night before. They'd been so far away, it wouldn't have surprised me if clouds had flown across them.

"Well the wedding this weekend could be interesting."

I sighed. "It sure could. I've gotta go finish dinner. Dad and Will should be back soon."

I'd made spaghetti and defrosted meatballs I had found rammed in a back corner of the freezer. Dad came in a few minutes after I hung up.

"I think that horse is ready to go," he said. Whiskey. He'd come a long way with all the time Will and I had spent working him. A pang reverberated through my chest. That horse had grown on me.

I finished setting the table. Three plates. Three. I hadn't heard from Lily. And Dad hadn't mentioned her since that first night—I couldn't say I was surprised. He was clearly hurting, but what could he do? She hadn't left him a way to contact her either.

"Where's Will?" I asked.

"Hmm?" Dad looked up from the newspaper. He liked to read half of it in the morning and the rest before dinner. "Oh, he went out to the cabin for a bit. He said to eat without him."

I frowned. Will never missed dinner unless he had specific plans, and he hadn't mentioned anything.

I spooned pasta and sauce onto our plates. Dad was kind enough not to comment on the still-cold meatballs. At least they weren't frozen.

"Are you going to give Radek an actual answer?" Dad asked.

I dropped my fork with a clang.

"How do you know about that?" I asked, picking it up again.

"He asked me first, of course. I offered up your mother's ring, but he said he already had one."

Momma's ring. I didn't know Dad still had that.

"Does anyone else know?"

Dad took a sip of his water. "Only Will. I had to share the good news with someone."

"Shit." I pushed my chair back.

Dad's eyebrows shot up. "Forget something on the stove?"

I was out the door with my boots on before he could ask more.

I FOUND Will in the cabin. His duffle bag sat open on the chair in the living room. The few clothes he had spilled out of it.

"What are you doing?" I asked. He stepped out of the bedroom. The bed behind him was bare, the mattress yellowed and stained.

"Stripping the bed so you don't have to." He dropped the linens in a pile beside a garbage bag by the door.

My lungs constricted and I struggled to get a breath. "No."

"It's the right thing to do." Will took both of my hands and held them in front of me. I let them hang limply. "I saw the way he looked at you, Hannah. He still loves you. He wants to marry you, for fuck's sake."

"I didn't say yes."

"I can't go after another guy's girl." Will dropped my hands and pushed his clothes into the bag and zipped it shut. How was it possible that I'd watched two of the most important people in my life pack in one week? I crossed my arms across my chest.

"What about what I want?" Dark, thick anger rose from my belly, beating back the fear.

Will turned to face me. "I want you to be happy. I just don't know if I'm the guy to make you happy."

"Shouldn't I be the one worrying about whether or not I'm happy? And what will make me happy?" My voice rose.

"Hey, calm down."

"Don't tell me to calm down like I'm a child!" I stomped to the kitchen sink and picked up a glass he'd left on a towel to dry. He stayed quiet as I filled it with water. Lily had always told me to have a glass of water if I was angry, or crying. My hand shook as I lifted the glass to my mouth. I had to say something to make him stay.

"I made up my mind. I was going to tell you . . ." My voice trailed off. It was a lie and Will knew it. He shook his head and looked at the floor. "I didn't say yes!" I repeated.

"I can't be the reason you stay here," he said, his voice quiet.

"I don't even know if there will be a *here*. Dad's probably still going to sell. You and I can leave. We can go to the States, up to Calgary, wherever you want to go. We can work ranches together, buy our own. I have money saved—" My mind spiralled, trying to come up with the right words, the thing he wanted to hear, a new plan.

Will took two wide steps across the room and pulled me close to him. I set the glass on the counter beside me. He rested his forehead on mine. "Oh Hannah. I wish we could." His breath was warm on my face. I wanted him to kiss me, to tell me it would be okay. Instead he rubbed his nose against mine. I stepped back. Wrapped my arms around myself. Pulled into myself. Will opened the fridge and took out the few bits of food still in there—the ends of a loaf of bread, an apple, a moulding block of cheddar cheese—and put them in a garbage bag by the door.

"Aren't you scared of losing me?" I said.

He looked back at me. "Of course I am. But that doesn't mean I should stay. You need to make your own choices."

"So that's it?" I said. "You're going to run away, like you did from your wife?"

He staggered back like I'd hit him. "Fuck you." He spat the words out, his eyes boring into mine. "That was a fucking low blow."

I rushed towards him, knocking the glass over with my elbow as I moved. Water ran across the counter and dripped onto the linoleum. "Shit shit shit." I left the glass and tried to take Will's shoulder, tried to turn him to face me. Anything to take that look off his face. "I didn't mean that, I really didn't—"

He shook me off his arm. "Part of you did."

I dropped onto the couch and put my head in my hands. "No —I'm just so sacred. I can't lose you too." I sat up, running my hands through my tangled hair, pulling at my scalp. "I have no idea what to do. I thought I had everything figured out, and now nothing makes sense."

Will sat beside me, leaving space between our legs. I thought of all the nights we'd spent together, lying in the bed, our bodies twisted together, fitting perfectly.

"Some decisions are hard," he said, his voice distant, measured.

He knew all about hard decisions. Leaving Jolene, Jackson. I took a deep breath and pulled my hair into a ponytail and then let it drop onto my shoulders. I looked right at him, meeting his electric stare. "I tried to stop, you know?"

"Tried to stop what?"

"Falling in love with you. To be a good girl."

The corner of Will's mouth twitched. A few weeks ago I would have thought he was laughing at me, but now I knew better.

"Couldn't resist my charms."

"F you," I said, grinning at him.

"Not a true 'fuck you,' but I'll take it." He smiled back and leaned into the couch, crossing his ankle over his knee.

"Is it supposed to feel like this?" I asked. He tilted his head to the side and I continued. "Like once you leave I'll never be able to breathe again? Like I've been bucked off a horse and had the wind knocked out of me."

Will rubbed his hands across his face and sat forward, planting his feet on the floor. "I'm no expert, but it's never been like this for me before."

"Then maybe this is wrong, maybe we should try—"

Will took my hand and turned it over, circling his callused thumb on my palm. "Just because we feel like this, doesn't mean it's not right for me to leave. We don't have to be apart forever— just until you figure out what you want out of life. On your own."

I leaned my head against his shoulder. He was right. Still, why couldn't things be simple?

ugust 1996

IT FELT strange to pick out an outfit without Lily. If she were here, she and Dad would be coming to the wedding, too. Lily would be running around, adjusting her red lipstick and fussing with my hair. I'd asked Dad that morning if he wanted to come, but he'd only shaken his head. I heard the door slap shut downstairs as I wrangled my hair into a clip. I checked my reflection in the mirror. Not bad. Might even meet Lily's approval.

I FOUND Dad in the carbarn under his truck, wrenching away at something. "I'm off to the wedding," I said.

He pushed the platform he was lying on far enough out that I could see his face. "Give them my best."

He'd kept his promise so far—there was no whiskey in the cupboard. Maybe that was part of the reason he didn't want to come to the wedding. That and Lily.

"I will." I turned to walk to my truck.

"Hannah." Dad pushed himself the rest of the way out from under the truck and got to his feet, dusting off his shirt.

"Yes?" I'd been waiting for this, waiting for him to yell at me, to tell me I'd ruined my future and his by not saying yes to Radek. Dad shoved his hands into his jean pockets.

"I'm sorry it didn't work out," he said. "All of it."

My eyebrows rose involuntarily. I wasn't sure if I should thank him or leave before he said anything else.

"I'm proud of you for—" He cleared his throat. "For knowing yourself. Your mother would have been proud." His voice cracked, and he turned and put the wrench on his workbench and then dug around, searching for another tool. I stood in the doorway, too stunned to reply. "Go on now," he said, his eyes on the tools. "You don't want to be late."

I DROVE TO THE BAILEYS', feeling light enough I could have floated right out of the truck if I weren't buckled in. Mr. Morton's canola crops glowed yellow to my left, the clear blue sky stretching out beyond them. "*Brassica napus*," I said to myself, enjoying the hiss of the *s*'s on my tongue. This was the first summer he'd planted it, and I'd had to look the name up in the seed catalogue.

I smiled at Radek when he opened the passenger door and slid onto the bucket seat.

"What are you grinning about?" he said.

"Nothing in particular," I responded, channelling my best Lily attitude. We'd decided it would be better to arrive at the wedding together, so people didn't ask questions. I didn't want to explain, and I didn't want Radek to feel any worse than he already did. And I didn't want people talking about Radek and me on Chrissy's wedding day.

Radek kept his eyes straight ahead. I glanced sideways at him, at his face, so familiar. His skin wasn't browned like Dad's or

Will's or his brother's—he'd been in the city all summer. What would he look like in twenty years? Would we still be friends?

"Radek," I said.

"Don't." His eyes didn't move from the road in front of us.

"I have to say this." I gripped the steering wheel. We hadn't talked about the proposal since the canyon. We'd had one rushed phone call about the details of the wedding and that was it. He deserved to know why.

"No, you don't have to say it. It was bad enough with you and that ranch hand, but now he's gone and you still don't want to marry me."

I looked at him, my heart aching. His jaw was set hard, his neck bobbing as he swallowed.

"I . . . Why won't you let me explain?"

Radek threw his arms up. It was strange seeing him angry. "What's there to explain? You don't want to be with me. The end."

I wanted to reach out, to hold his hand, to make him laugh. To stick my tongue out at him and call him dumb. Anything to take the look of pain off his face, but I didn't think any of it would help.

"I'm so sorry," I whispered.

Radek set his mouth in a hard line. "Yeah, well, let's just try to get through today."

MOST OF THE seats were taken by the time we arrived. Blue bows had been hastily tied and attached to the ends of the pews. I spotted Heather waving from near the front, where she'd saved space for us. She gave me a questioning look when I sat on the wooden bench beside her, but I waved it away. Radek sat beside Clarence and they talked about last night's ball game. I scanned the crowd—at least fifty people, pretty great turnout for a wedding put together in a matter of a week.

"She looks amazing," Heather whispered as Chrissy glided

down the aisle. And she was right. Chrissy's dress had long, lacy sleeves and an epic train that dragged behind her. She smiled widely and looked relaxed, as though she'd been ready for this moment her whole life. Chucker had squeezed himself into a suit that looked two sizes too small for him, and stood sweating under the arch with the priest. The ceremony was short, and Heather and I stood and cheered along with the crowd as Mr. and Mrs. Charles Hartford walked back down the aisle. I caught Mere staring at me from the other side of the church. As our eyes met she looked away without smiling. So she knew. She'd forgive me, eventually. She had to. Heather and I followed Chrissy into the bathroom. Since they'd put the wedding together so quickly they hadn't bothered with a wedding party, but Heather and I had elected ourselves to take care of everything bridesmaids normally would. Chrissy and I still hadn't talked, but I didn't want to take anything away from her day by bringing it up. She'd been waiting for this her whole life. And after everything that had happened, it didn't seem as important anymore. The three of us crammed into the tiny space. I sat on the counter as Heather fussed with the dress, trying to bustle the train. We chatted about the ceremony and broke into giggles about Chucker's suit.

"It's his brother's," Chrissy said. "We didn't have time to get him one that fit properly. Poor guy."

"He's fine," Heather said, from behind the metres of train she was trying to hook to the back of Chrissy's dress. "Only he might want to undo his top button before he attempts any sort of fancy dance moves." She stood and clapped her hands together. "There, done. Move around and make sure it holds."

Chrissy shook her hips.

"This calls for a drink." Heather pulled a small silver flask from her purse. "Not for you," she said, pointing at Chrissy's belly.

I took a long swig and made a face. "Straight gin? Disgusting."

Heather shrugged. "In case the bar runs low later."

Chrissy moved in front of me. "I heard about Radek. And Lily. I'm so . . . I don't know what to say. I feel so bad that I'm getting married and here you are . . ."

I wanted to be mad at her, but I knew in her own way she'd been trying to help the situation, to save me from myself. "It's okay, it's all for the best," I said. And I meant it.

AFTER THE CEREMONY, we made our way to the community hall for dinner and dancing. Radek, Clarence, Heather, and I sat with three of Chrissy's cousins for dinner; we chatted about old times and the people at the wedding we hadn't seen since high school. Radek seemed to be acting normal, almost happy. After the main course had been served he put his hand on my knee and squeezed it and then smiled at me. "You look great," he said. I shifted a little to let his hand fall. Confusion spread across his face.

"I told you. I can't," I whispered. I kept my eyes on my plate.

"We all know you'll change your mind." His voice rose enough that the other people at our table glanced over. He'd been drinking more than usual. I glanced around and made eye contact with Heather. As if on cue, she clinked her glass and made a loud toast to the bride and groom. I held my glass up with everyone else, but spoke quietly to Radek beside me.

"I meant what I said."

"Bullshit," he said loudly. Heather bulged her eyes out at me and motioned towards the washrooms with her head.

"Let's not do this here," I half whispered to Radek.

"Why not? Everybody already knows." Radek swept his hand out to the room. "Everybody knows you left me for a *ranch hand*." He spit out the last two words like they were pieces of dirt in his mouth. I'd only seen Radek drunk a few times, but he'd always been a happy drunk. This was different.

"Okay." I pushed back my chair and placed my napkin beside my plate. "I don't *want* to marry you, Radek. Does that make it better? I don't want to." I thought the words would come out angry, but tears pricked at my eyes. I watched his face fall and then turned and walked towards the back of the hall with Heather right behind me.

IN THE BATHROOM I put my face under the tap and gulped cold water. Heather handed me a paper towel.

"That was intense. Holy shit." She pulled out her flask and passed it to me. I was glad for the sap-like burn of the gin this time.

"I feel like a terrible person," I said. "I can't believe I did that to him."

Heather shook her head. "He didn't really give you a choice. Come here." She pulled me into a hug that reminded me of Lily.

"I'm going to get out of here. Do you think Chrissy will mind?"

"I don't think she'll notice. Last I saw her she was holed up in a corner with her sister. I walked up and heard something about labour and disgusting fluids and I turned right back around."

I laughed. Thank goodness for Heather. She walked me back through the hall so I could collect my purse from the table. Everyone had moved to the dance floor. Radek stood at the bar, ordering shots for two girls I didn't recognize. He caught my eye and put his arm around the blonde one to his right.

Heather waited with me out in the parking lot until Georgio came by. "Call you tomorrow." She hugged me again. "You're still the most awkward hugger in the world," she said, releasing me. "I'm glad some things stay the same." She winked at me and went back into the hall.

I WALKED STRAIGHT to the cabin when I got home, a small part of me hoping Will hadn't really left. The grass that had shot up after the rain sliced at my bare legs. Maybe he'd moved his truck. Maybe he'd come back and parked somewhere else, to surprise me.

But when I got to the cabin it was dark. I stood on the porch and looked out across the creek towards the dark mountains looming in the distance. He was really gone. I hoped he'd be able to set things straight with Jolene, find a way to have a relationship with Jackson. That morning after breakfast he'd kissed me on the porch without even checking to see if Dad was looking, and he told me to call him as soon as I knew where I was going. "Don't forget me when you're a big-time scientist," he'd said. I ran my hand along the porch railing and tipped the coffee can to look inside. He'd even cleaned out the cigarette butts. I pictured his truck cutting across a map of the US, eating up miles, heading down, south, back to Nevada. Away from Stillwater. Away from me.

I opened the cabin door and stepped into the darkness. Everything was so quiet and still, like a thick blanket of dust had settled over it already. The kitchen light flickered and buzzed before turning on and exposing the emptiness. The cabin was clean, barren. He'd even wiped the fridge's shelves. What had I been expecting to find? A note? A memento? I thought of the time Radek left for Austin for tryouts. How he'd dropped off a grocery bag with one of his worn T-shirts in it, so I wouldn't have to miss the smell of him. At least I still had Will's sweatshirt.

I did a slow lap of the living room, running my hand across the back of the sofa. All those months, all that fuck-up-ed-ness. And for what?

I sat on the end of the bed and put my face in my hands. He'd gone back to make things right. He was going to be there for Jackson. He'd be there for the baseball games and Father's Day and graduation—all the things Momma had missed. As much as everything hurt, I knew he'd done what was right. I had to find my own way. I fell back on the bed. There was enough light from the kitchen that I could make out a shape on Will's pillow. Something paper-thin. I rolled over and picked it up, leaning to catch the moonlight from the window. An aspen leaf—*Populus tremuloides*. The edges had begun to curl in and turn amber. I felt something unfurl in my chest. I'd lost everything that mattered. Momma. Lily. Radek. Will. Dad as I thought I knew him. But I was still here, my heart running, my lungs pumping. I'd lost all but what was left. All but me.

I had done everything right with Radek, everything to keep him happy, and none of it had worked. With Will I'd done everything wrong, I'd treated him terribly, fought with him, never tried to keep him happy. And yet, he knew me better than anyone else ever had. He'd seen the real me, the part of me that wasn't a good girl, the girl who didn't need to spend all of her time trying to make everyone else happy. And he still loved me.

Being a good girl didn't mean only good things would happen to me. Not being a good girl hadn't ruined me. I couldn't change what had happened to Momma, but I could change what happened to me.

I put the leaf back on the bed and lay my hand over it, pressed my face into the bare pillow, and inhaled deeply, trying to pick up even the slightest scent of Will. I knew what I needed to do.

September 1996

I STOOD on the porch with my bag over my shoulder and looked around the yard. Mickey Two lay in the shade of the oak tree, panting. Today would likely be one of the last hot days of the year. A For Sale sign stood at the end of the laneway, close enough to the road for the few people who drove by to see.

I took a deep breath and walked into the carbarn. Dad sat on a stool turning a screwdriver in an engine part. I'd given up on trying to remember what they all were.

"So you're off?" Dad asked.

"Yeah." I ran my hand along the dusty workbench, over the tools and random parts. Dad had taken the news that I was leaving better than expected, but then again he'd surprised me more than once in the past few weeks. "I'll call when I get there." I'd been saying that a lot lately. I thought of my phone call with Heather the night before. She'd told me to drive safe, to call her when I arrived, and that she and Clarence were going out for drinks on Saturday night. I'd smiled into the receiver and sent Clarence a mental high five.

Did Dad know where I was really going? He hadn't asked for many details. "Are you going to be okay, Dad?" I asked. Not for the first time, I pictured him alone on the ranch. He'd be by himself all winter. Or at least until it sold. The doctor had given him the all clear for work, but I still worried. I guessed Clarence and Mere would come by. Heather had promised to look in on him, too.

"Me? Of course I will." He set the car part on the bench and came to stand with me. We looked out through the door towards the white clapboard house. "I always manage." We stood in silence for a few moments before he spoke again. "I'm thinking after the ranch sells, I might open a garage, give Marv a run for his money."

I turned to face him. "You mean like a business?" Why hadn't he done that years ago?

"Yeah. Like a business." Dad smiled at me. "You'd better get going if you want to make Calgary before dark."

"You won't sell all the horses, right?"

"No, not Honcho, not Buttercup, not Skoal or Red Gold. I'll keep them at the Baileys'." We'd sold Whiskey the week before, for almost three times what we'd paid for him. Dad had insisted I keep all the money. Between that and the money in my Crown Royal bag, I figured I'd be okay for a few weeks until I found a job. There was even enough to apply to university for the winter semester.

I'd almost called the whole thing off when I had to say goodbye to Honcho that morning. I'd rubbed my face in his tawny mane, breathing in his smell and telling him over and over I'd be back. And I would be back, but I didn't know when, or for how long. I thought of the aspen roots, living hundreds of years longer than the trees they supported. I might not be on the ranch anymore, but part of me always would.

"Well then," I said. I hugged Dad, both of us stiff and awkward.

"Drive safe," he said, leaning against the doorway as I walked across the yard.

Mickey Two glanced up from his spot under the tree as I pulled the truck door shut. "Bye buddy," I said. Dad would take Mickey with him when he left the ranch. He'd promised.

I took one last look at the yard. The porch where I'd spent so many nights with Dad and Lily, Radek, and, later, Will. The big white house in front of the mountains. The rebuilt henhouse with Momma's ghost. I backed the truck out and drove slowly down the lane, waving a hand out the window at Dad.

As I pulled onto the dirt road I glanced over at the envelope on the seat beside me. A letter peeked out of its flap. A letter that began with, "Chickadee! It's me!" Will had called that morning and I'd promised him I'd call from Lily's new place. He'd told me he'd gone home to his family's ranch, but not back to his wife. That he'd seen Jackson. That he missed me. That he was glad I was following my heart, and he hoped it eventually led me back to him.

The road spread out before me. Fields whizzed by and my hair whipped around my face. Sparse, wispy trees leaned over the backroad I'd chosen. I had no name for trees like this. Uncharted territory.

WANT MORE HANNAH AND WILL?

Subscribe to my email newsletter to receive a free bonus chapter from *All But What's Left*—something you can't get anywhere else!

Visit: CarrieMumford.com/ABWL-SignUp

Want to hear about new releases only? Follow me on BookBub: https://www.bookbub.com/authors/carrie-mumford

ABOUT THE AUTHOR

Carrie Mumford has lived on both the East and West coasts of Canada, and many places in between. She completed a degree in English literature, and went on to complete a master's in information studies. Carrie now lives in Calgary, Alberta, with her husband, three naughty cats, and one rambunctious dog. *All But What's Left* is her first novel.

For more about Carrie visit CarrieMumford.com.

ALSO BY CARRIE MUMFORD

Magpie: A Collection of Really Short Stories

Stories
by
Carrie
Mumford

Available wherever you buy ebooks!

LET ME KNOW WHAT YOU THINK

If you enjoyed the book, I would really appreciate it if you could take the time to leave a short review on the site where you purchased the book, or on Goodreads (or both!). Reviews help authors get the word about their books out to the world.

Thank you so much for reading!

ACKNOWLEDGMENTS

THANK YOU. . .

(BUCKLE UP, THERE ARE SO MANY PEOPLE TO THANK OH MY GOODNESS).

To Theanna Bischoff, teacher, mentor, friend: for being with this book from the beginning and seeing me through to the end.

To Tyler Hellard: for many, many, many hours spent writing at Swans, and your reality checks and continual support despite me writing a "cowboy romance."

To my ever-generous (and infinitely patient) early readers: Corrie Rabey, Courtney Forseth, Daphne Lobo, Eryn Shannon Kollecker, Isis Gutierrez, Jack Mumford, Jeff Mumford, Jill Lauren Thompson, Linda Mumford (hi Mom!), Rachelle Pinnow, Robin van Eck, Rona Reitsema, Tara Walmsley, and Tyler Hellard. Special thanks to Ray Reitsema, for his expertise on funerals and burial, and to Gene Mumford, for his hard-earned knowledge of ranch chores. Any inaccuracies are my own.

To Rona Reitsema and Eryn Shannon Kollecker: we began this writing journey together as strangers, but became writing sisters. I couldn't have done it without your encouragement and support.

To my brilliant editor, Rachel Small: none of this would be happening without your talent, support, friendship and straight talk! And the wine, don't forget the wine (see my comma use there? #nailedit).

To DAWP (aka Jill Lauren Thompson, Laurie Zottmann, Rachelle Pinnow, and Tyler Hellard): Sundays wouldn't the same without you and your (our) writerly angst (insert tomato emoji here).

To the businesses and associations and conferences that provided support, space to write, snacks, and the occasional adult beverage: Alexandra Writers' Centre Society (especially Robin van Eck!), Gravity Cafe (hi Andy and Caitlin!), Swans of Inglewood, and Port Townsend Writers' Conference.

Special thanks to: Maya Berger, proofreader extraordinaire; Jane Dixon Smith, cover designer of my dreams; Joanna Penn, queen of indie publishing; and Sarah Selecky, for the writing prompt that started it all.

And to Erik. For keeping me watered, fed, and (mostly) sane as I wrote this book. For listening to me talk about these beloved characters for so many years, for reading and giving me honest feedback (even if it risked marital strife), and for creating the space in our lives to make this happen. I will be on cat litter cleaning duty until further notice.